DEATH HEAD CROSSING

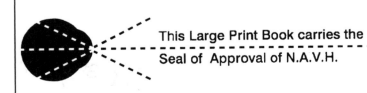

This Large Print Book carries the
Seal of Approval of N.A.V.H.

DEATH HEAD CROSSING

JAMES REASONER

WHEELER PUBLISHING
A part of Gale, Cengage Learning

GALE
CENGAGE Learning·

Detroit • New York • San Francisco • New Haven, Conn • Waterville, Maine • London

LIBRARY OF CONGRESS CATALOGING-IN-PUBLICATION DATA

Reasoner, James.
  Death Head Crossing / by James Reasoner.
     p. cm. — (Wheeler Publishing large print western)
  ISBN-13: 978-1-59722-693-6 (pbk. : alk. paper)
  ISBN-10: 1-59722-693-9 (pbk. : alk. paper)
  1. Large type books. I. Title.
  PS3568.E2685D43 2008
  813'.54—dc22   2007044703

Published in 2008 by arrangement with Pinnacle Books, an imprint of
Kensington Corp.

Printed in the United States of America
1 2 3 4 5 6 7 12 11 10 09 08

For Gary Goldstein, a hell of an editor.

PROLOGUE

Luther Berryhill was drunk. Pleasantly drunk. Happily drunk. Gloriously drunk!

He had a smart horse, and that was good. Luther had spent the evening celebrating; now his horse would take him home. He didn't have to worry about being so far gone that he couldn't see straight. That old four-legged bastard would take care of him and get him back to the ranch.

The night was as dark as a moonless night can be. The stars scattered some light over the plains, but not enough for anybody who didn't know where he was going. Luther swayed in the saddle and sang the praises of his mount as he rode. What a world it was! He didn't know who had invented whiskey, but he sure was grateful to the man, whoever he was.

Luther slumped forward and caught himself just before he toppled out of the saddle.

"Careful there, boy," he muttered to himself.

He knew damn well that he was going to get a good ass-chewing from the boss when he got back to the ranch. Young Mr. Benjamin Tillman didn't hold with his hands going into town and getting drunk. Luther didn't care what the little bastard thought, though, not when he was this happy. Not when he was this dizzy.

Thinking about Tillman put a solemn expression on Luther's face after a minute. Things sure hadn't been the same since the boy came out from the East to take over. He should have stayed where he was, back there in Philadelphia, where he could be a fancy sissy and not hurt nothing. Boy sure as hell wasn't cut out to run a ranch, nor to boss *real* men around and tell 'em they shouldn't drink whiskey, or cuss, or go visit the whores at Mama Lupe's.

Luther told himself to stop thinking about Tillman. He was just tormenting himself. Instead, he launched into song.

Tillman wouldn't fire him just for going off on a little toot, would he? The thought pushed into Luther's dazed brain and made him fall silent. Surely the boss couldn't be that mean. Hell, summer in this part of Texas always made a man thirsty, and he had to do something to quench that thirst.

Lost in worry about his job, Luther didn't notice the lights until several minutes after they first appeared.

Floating and dancing in the darkness, the lights twinkled in the hills in front of him. They were a merry sight as they winked and bobbed, and when Luther finally became aware of them, his eyes slowly widened and he pulled back on the horse's reins.

What the devil . . . ? Fireflies maybe? Luther frowned. He couldn't tell how far off the lights were, and so he couldn't make a guess as to their size. They didn't appear to be very big, though, and they surely didn't look threatening.

The horse saw them too, or maybe smelled them. He shifted his feet uneasily and started to back up.

"Hold on!" Luther hissed. "Nothin' to be scared of. Not like it's a damn snake or somethin'."

But the horse was acting like he had just spotted a rattler coiled in the path up ahead. Luther drew the bit tighter and held his mount still. The lights looked like they were coming closer now.

Luther thought about it and decided that these were ghost lights, like he had heard about over around Marfa. Nobody knew what those lights were, but they had never hurt anybody. Luther Berryhill wasn't afraid of some little bitty ol' lights.

He spurred the horse and urged him forward. When he hesitated, Luther raked the animal's flanks cruelly. The horse snorted and then reluctantly started toward the floating lights, nostrils distended in fear.

There was a smile on Luther's face. Maybe the little dancing motes of brightness were angels, he thought. Angels from heaven, come down to bestow some blessing on Luther Berryhill's head . . . Demons. That was more like it.

Luther cried out in sudden panic as a big hand grabbed him around the middle and jerked him backward in the saddle. He grabbed for the pommel to hold himself upright, but his grasping fingers slipped off the worn leather. He slid from the saddle and fell heavily. Dust puffed up around him.

Luther rolled from side to side as he tried to free himself. Vaguely, he realized that it wasn't a hand that had hold of him, but rather a couple of ropes. Still, they seemed to have dropped out of thin air. And they were too tight for him to tug free of them, almost too tight for him to breath.

He had lost his hat when he fell off the horse. Night breezes riffled his thinning hair. Luther struggled with the ropes as his horse galloped back past him and took off for parts unknown. "You damn jackass!" Luther screamed after him. "Come back here!"

A man on foot was a dead man. Luther knew that old saying and he knew the truth of it.

He was watching the retreating shadow that was the horse when something, some instinct, warned him. He jerked his head around. Shapes loomed around him, blotting out the stars. Luther couldn't tell what they were, only that he felt more scared than he ever had in forty-one years of hardscrabble living.

"Wh-who the hell are you?" he quavered. He wished it wasn't so dark tonight; then he could at least tell if these menacing shadows were men or animals or . . . something else.

There was no answer. No sound except the keening of the night wind.

Luther stopped fighting the ropes. He wet his lips and tried to remember a prayer.

"Vengeance is mine," a deep, sonorous voice intoned.

Light exploded in Luther's face.

The light was brighter and hotter than the sun, and as quickly as it came, it was gone.

So was Luther Berryhill's life.

Face blasted away, he sprawled on the sand, felt nothing, knew nothing. He wouldn't have to worry about that ass-chewing by Mr. Tillman. Shapes moved around him in the gloom, then faded away in the night. Far away, the sound of the runaway horse's hooves could still be heard for a few minutes; then it was gone too.

Luther never should have gone into Death Head Crossing for that drink. . . .

CHAPTER 1

The old man was going to keep screaming until Jackson rode down there and put a stop to it.

Three of them, and they had the old man staked out in the sun in the bottom of a dry wash. Only one of the men was working on him now. The other two were sitting in what little shade the banks of the wash afforded and sipping from a bottle they passed back and forth. The mid-afternoon sun glittered off the knife in the third man's hand as he bent over the helpless victim.

Jackson sat motionless on his horse atop a ridge a hundred yards away. They hadn't seen him yet, and he doubted that they would stop what they were doing even if they knew he was there. The shrieks of agony were what had drawn him. A town lay a few miles away, and that had been his destination until the old man's cries had sidetracked him.

Jackson had no way of knowing how long the old man had been undergoing torture, but even from this distance he could see the blood that flecked the long white hair and beard. The old man had been stripped so that the sun could get at him better, his clothes carelessly tossed aside, and now his three captors were probably taking turns with their blades. They would work their way down the leathery body, making cut after shallow cut until all the wounds added up to one terrifying, soul-numbing pain. They had learned the trick from seeing the victims of Apache raids, Jackson supposed. It wasn't any nicer when being done by white men, though.

Jackson sat his saddle easily, a man in dusty whipcord pants and a work shirt whose sleeves were rolled up over tanned forearms. His hat had seen better days, but pulled low over his forehead, its slightly rolled brim shaded a lean face that was mostly flat planes and angles. Carelessly trimmed dark hair fell on his neck. His boots and his saddle were scuffed and worn, but the leather of the holster he wore on his right hip was supple, well oiled, well cared for.

Just like the gun that rode in the holster.

His belly was growling and grumbling. He

had been looking forward to a hot meal in town after several days on the trail and several nights' worth of cold camps. But as the old man let out another wail, Jackson sighed and knew that his meal was going to be postponed. His face was still and enigmatic, but showing deep in his light blue eyes was the knowledge that he couldn't ride away from this.

He kicked the horse into an easy walk. No point in galloping up. The old man was probably too far gone to save. All Jackson could do was lessen his suffering. But if he came tearing down into the wash, the three men might just start shooting and wait until later to find out what he wanted. Instead, he rode slowly, his shoulders slumping like those of a man who's been in the saddle for a long time. That was true enough.

Several minutes passed while he covered the distance between the ridge and the wash. They knew he was coming now. He slitted his eyes and glanced out from under the brim of his hat. The one using the knife had stopped, and had even flung the blade aside. Its point dug into the sandy ground and the knife stood upright, hilt quivering slightly. The other two men joined the third one, and they made an uneven line in front of the old man as Jackson's horse stepped carefully down a path into the wash. He reined in about thirty feet from them.

Jackson put a smile on his sun-blistered lips but didn't say anything. His eyes swept over the scene.

The three men were typical hardcases. They wore range clothes and each of them carried a gun. Their horses, tied to a mesquite growing out of the bank a few feet away, looked tired and hard-ridden. Two of the men were bearded and older; the other was a youngster, already gone bad.

Jackson had seen hundreds like them. They could work as ranch hands when they had to, but they preferred easier wages than forty a month and found. They fancied themselves desperadoes, and even though they were almost nothing compared to some who rode the outlaw trail, they could kill you just as dead. Jackson knew them for what they were with only a brief look; then his gaze moved on to their victim.

Surprise made a muscle in his cheek twitch. The old man was an Indio, and it took a lot to make someone like him scream like a woman. They must have been at him for a long time. There were cuts all over him, and Jackson knew now that they had already finished one go-round and were starting another.

None of the three had spoken, and even the old man had fallen silent. His head rolled to one side, but his bloody chest kept rising and falling in a jerky rhythm. Quiet spread out and settled down over the wash.

"Must be one stubborn old man," Jackson said.

"Must be," one of the men agreed. "What's it to you?"

Jackson shook his head. "Nothing. Just heard the yelling and wondered what was going on."

"You've seen it." The invitation to keep moving was plain in the man's voice.

"True enough." Jackson was still smiling. His hands were resting on the pommel of his saddle, a long way from the butt of his gun. A Winchester was shoved into a saddle boot, but at least a couple of seconds would be needed to get it out, so it was no threat. All in all, Jackson didn't look too dangerous, especially facing three men.

"There a town around here?" he went on. He knew the answer to that question already.

The youngest of the three jerked a thumb over his shoulder. "Over yonder about four miles. They got good whiskey and bad women, friend. Why don't you go sample 'em?"

"Might do that," Jackson nodded. "Soon's you tell me why you're killing that old man and taking so long about it."

One of them spat. "You ain't related to the old bastard, are you?"

"Not likely."

"Then get out of here and stop frettin' about it. It's none of your damn business, friend."

"You're right about that. It's none of my business." Jackson held up his left hand in a deprecating gesture.

The old man turned his head and opened his eyes, blinking away the blood until he could see. From his position on the bottom of the wash, all he could make against the glare of the sun were the silhouettes of his captors. But he had heard Jackson's voice and knew that someone else was there.

"Help me, Señor," he gasped, the words obviously painful in his parched throat. "Please . . . you must help me."

"Was I you, I wouldn't listen to him, friend. That'd be a good way to get hold of more trouble than you can handle."

The young one turned and launched a kick that thudded against the old man's scrawny ribs. "Keep your mouth shut, you old buzzard, less'n you want to tell us where to find that treasure you got hid."

18

Jackson saw the other two wince. The boy had a big mouth, and he had just told Jackson what he wanted to know.

"Treasure, eh?" Jackson said, his smile slowly widening. "That's mighty interesting."

"Dammit, Hector!" one of the older men exploded. "If that old man was as talkative as you, we'd've been out of this sun a long time ago." He cut his eyes back to Jackson. "This still ain't none of your affair, mister. Just ride on and there won't be no trouble."

Jackson shook his head. "I think I'll take a hand in this, just to see how it plays."

"Then you're a fool."

Jackson's hand was still a long way from his gun. The other three men, though, were poised to draw. "Maybe you're right," he said.

He saw their fingers dip toward gun butts, and his shoulder moved. The .45 slipped smoothly into his hand, the draw so quick they never saw it. He squeezed the trigger once, twice, three times.

It was over in an instant. Gun blasts boomed against the banks of the wash and went rocketing away into the hot, still air. Jackson's first bullet caught one of the older men in the chest and slammed him backward. The second one made a mess of a bearded throat. The third one ripped through the youngster's lungs as he turned and clawed at his pistol.

Jackson holstered his gun and looked down at the three sprawled bodies. His horse had stood still during the battle, jerking only slightly as the gun exploded. The animal was used to noises like that.

None of them had gotten off a shot. The boy had cleared leather, but he was the only one. Jackson swung down from his horse and prodded all three with a booted toe. Nothing.

He turned to the old man and knelt beside him. Reaching behind him, Jackson slipped a knife from a sheath behind his holster and cut the thongs binding the tortured man.

"Gracias, señor," the Indio whispered. "They were bad men. They wanted to . . . to rob me."

"I know," Jackson said. He hunkered back on his heels. "Your treasure. Where is it?"

Something like reproach showed in the old man's eyes. "Señor," he said.

"I don't want to steal it from you, old man. I just want to see that it gets where you want it to go."

The Indio nodded in understanding, then spasms shook him. When he had controlled the pain, he said, "I think I can trust you, amigo. You do not lie to me and tell me that I will be fine. Yes. I trust you." He paused to gather more of his waning strength. After a moment, he went on. "I have a . . . a grand-daughter. You must take the treasure to her. Tell her . . . tell her that her grandfather loved her."

He lifted a bloody hand and clutched at Jackson's arm. A film settled over his eyes, and Jackson realized that the old man could no longer see him. "I have a cabin . . . in the hills, by a creek not far from here. Look there . . . under the floor. I am a foolish old man."

The fingers on Jackson's arm clenched tighter.

"An old man . . . full of too much mes-cal . . . talking too much in a cantina . . . foolish, foolish old man . . ."

He sighed, and the sigh became a death rattle. The old eyes kept staring sightlessly into the high sky. The fingers fell away from Jackson's arm.

Jackson stood up, took off his hat, wiped sweat from his forehead with his shirt sleeve. Another delay. But then, he wasn't really in a hurry. It wouldn't take him long to find the old man's cabin. The town could wait a few more hours. Once he had the treasure, whatever it was, surely someone could tell him where to find the granddaughter.

He didn't have a shovel. The bodies would have to stay where they were for now. Jackson turned away and walked toward his horse. A tiny sound warned him.

He spun, the pistol leaping into his hand once more, and saw the youngest of the trio struggling to lift his fallen gun. The boy wasn't dead after all. He had somehow found the strength to get his hand on the gun butt, but now the pistol was too heavy for him. The barrel shook, then tilted down and buried itself in the sand as the boy dropped the weapon.

He looked up at Jackson, the fiery pain inside him distending his eyes, and gasped, "Who . . . who the hell are you?"

Jackson smiled. "That's right," he said. "I'm Hell."

But he was talking to a dead man, a man who had died with confusion etched on his pain-wracked face.

CHAPTER 2

Jackson rode into the town of Death Head Crossing a little before dusk, a burlap bag slung over the saddle in front of him.

The day hadn't gone anything like what he would have expected when he broke camp that morning. He was a little tired. It had taken him an hour to find the old man's cabin, then another hour to rip up the floorboards and dig down into the ground underneath the building.

He had found the treasure, though.

Jackson looked down at the bag hanging on his saddle. Now all he had to do was find the old man's granddaughter and pass on the legacy.

His horse moved at a slow walk, which gave Jackson a chance to study the town. Its wide main street was well-packed dirt, lined on both sides with false-fronted frame structures. Some of the houses on the outskirts were adobe, but the business buildings were constructed of wide planks milled from lumber brought in from the hills. A narrow creek drifted along just to the west of town. Oaks and cottonwoods had sprung up along it, adding a touch of green to an otherwise flat and fairly colorless landscape around Death Head Crossing. Jackson seemed to remember hearing a story about how the community got its name. An early pioneer, passing through the area on his way to another dream somewhere else, had seen a grisly reminder of the nearness of death on the banks of the creek. A longhorn, wild most likely, had died there for some unknown reason, and scavengers had left nothing but a scattering of bones. The bleached skull, with its long sweep of horns, was prominent among them. The pioneer had told of seeing the longhorn's skull, and the place had gradually been dubbed Death Head Crossing. The name had stuck, and Jackson wondered what the citizens thought of living in a town with such a name.

Evidently, the name hadn't scared off too many people. Main Street was busy. Several men who looked like cowhands rode here and there, and carriages carrying townspeople rolled along, iron wheels cutting tracks in the dust. There was plenty of foot traffic too. Business was booming. The mercantile stores clustered at the near end of town were full of customers coming and going. Parked next to the sidewalks were farmers' wagons being loaded with supplies.

Jackson saw a bank, telegraph office, newspaper office, and sheriff's office and jail clustered near the center of town. At the far end of the street were the saloons and bawdy houses. Some of the citizens probably didn't like them being there, but Jackson had never run across a town without them. In this case, though, they were carefully separated from the part of town most frequently visited by the upright, God-fearing inhabitants.

He passed a whitewashed church surrounded by scrubby trees. Jackson pulled back on the reins and brought the horse to a stop. He swung down out of the saddle, looped the reins loosely over a bush, and walked to the doorway of the church.

The double doors were partially open, and Jackson pushed through them into the shaded interior. Inside, the church was cool compared to the late afternoon outside. Jackson's footsteps echoed hollowly as he walked down the aisle toward the raised pulpit at the front.

It had been a long time since he had been

in a church, a long time since he had wanted to be in a church. He called, "Anybody home?"

"Up here," a voice said, floating down from above.

A smile played around the corners of Jackson's mouth. With an answer like that, the logical assumption was —

He heard someone clambering down a ladder, and a moment later, a tall man in a broadcloth suit emerged from a small room at the rear of the church. "Excuse me, I was up in the steeple repairing the bell ropes," he said with a smile. "Can I help —" His eyes fell on Jackson then, and he broke off before finishing his sentence. The smile stayed on his face, but his eyes became hard and suspicious.

"What's the matter, preacher?" Jackson asked.

The minister's gaze moved over Jackson, took in the easy, alert stance, the way his right hand stayed within a few inches of his gun butt, the low, tied-down holster. "Everyone is welcome in the Lord's house," he said after a moment. The rest of his thoughts went unspoken.

"That's good. But I didn't come for praying or preaching. I want some information."

"I'll be glad to help you if I can, my friend."

"Do you know an old Indio, lives about five or six miles north of here in a run-down shack? Lived there, I should say."

The meaning of Jackson's statement wasn't lost on the minister. "That sounds like old Julio," he replied. "Has something happened to him?"

Jackson ignored that question for the moment and went on. "He's got a granddaughter. Do you know her, or know where I can find her?"

"Of course. Everyone around here knows Philomena. She works as a cook and a waitress over at the boardinghouse."

"She'll be there now?"

The preacher was obviously puzzled by the questions. "She should be," he said. "I insist you tell me what's happened to her grandfather."

"His body's in a wash up to the north," Jackson said, not sugarcoating the news. "Three men were working him over. Their bodies are there too."

The preacher had caught his breath at the news of old Julio's death. Now he blanched at the implications of what Jackson had told him.

"Merciful God," he breathed. "You killed them?"

"Seemed fitting, after what they'd done to the old man and all. But I figured somebody might want to bury 'em anyway." Jackson gave a brusque nod and started toward the door. "Thanks for the information about the girl."

The minister caught his arm as he passed. Jackson stopped and stood still, not looking at him, and after a long moment, the preacher dropped his hand from Jackson's arm. "Just a minute," he said. "Who are you? What business have you got with Philomena?"

"Name's Hell Jackson. And my business with Philomena is between her and me." The words came flat and cold from him.

He stalked out of the church without a backward look.

Reverend Martin Driscoll followed him to the door and watched him walk away, leading his horse. There was something about this man. . . . Driscoll had been in the West long enough to know a gunman when he saw one, but this Hell Jackson — what an unholy name! — this Jackson seemed even more dangerous than most.

Jackson had no trouble finding the boardinghouse. It was late enough in the day for the mouthwatering aromas of supper to be drifting out into the street from the open door of the two-story clapboard building. He tied his horse at the rail outside, held his hat in his left hand, and walked in.

To the right of the entrance foyer was a parlor, to the left the large dining room that all boardinghouses boasted. Several of the boarders were gathered around a long table, serving themselves from big plates of food in the center. As Jackson stood in the foyer and watched, two serving girls brought in more platters and deposited them on the table.

A heavy, middle-aged woman in a print dress appeared at his side. "Help you, sir?" she asked, but her tone was dubious. Jackson knew he didn't look like the boardinghouse's usual type of patron.

"I'm looking for a girl called Philomena," he said.

"Why?" the woman snapped back at him. "My girls are good girls, young ladies every one."

"I don't doubt it, ma'am. I just want to talk to Philomena. I have a message for her from her grandfather."

The woman snorted. "What sort of trouble is old Julio in now? Doesn't he think that girl has anything better to do than take care of him?"

"I don't know, ma'am." Jackson kept his voice soft. "If you'll just tell me which of the girls is Philomena . . . ?"

"Oh, all right." The woman raised her voice. "Philomena! Come here, girl."

One of the serving girls put a platter of potatoes on the table and then came toward the foyer with a worried expression on her pretty face. She kept her dark eyes on the floor, afraid to look up at Jackson. She was young, no more than eighteen or nineteen, with the loveliness of youth.

"Philomena, this man wants to talk to you," the woman told her. "Says he's got some sort of message from your grandfather." She folded her arms across her bountiful bosom and waited, evidently intending to hear whatever Jackson had to say.

He took Philomena's arm and said, "Maybe we'd better go into the parlor, Philomena. My name's Jackson."

He led the girl into the parlor, paying no attention to the disapproval on the woman's face. This was her place and she would be within her rights to order him out, but somehow he didn't think she would.

Jackson sat the girl down in an armchair with a lace antimacassar. She nervously twisted her hands in the white apron she wore over her long red skirt and still wouldn't look at him. He put his hat on a little table beside the chair and knelt in front of her, feeling more than a trifle foolish.

"I'm afraid I've got some bad news for you, Philomena," he said. "Your grandfather is dead."

Her breathing increased, the full young breasts rising and falling more quickly, but that was the only outward sign of her shock at the news.

"The men who were responsible for his death, they're dead now too," Jackson went on. "I got to your grandfather and talked to him before he died. He told me about you."

Philomena muttered something under her breath, and it took Jackson a second to realize that she was saying a prayer.

"He was thinking of you at the last, Philomena," he went on, trying to soften it as much as possible for her. "He told me about his treasure. He told me to get it and bring it to you."

Finally, she looked up at him. "You have his treasure?" she asked in a whisper, her words softly accented.

"It's outside, on my horse."

She didn't seem surprised that he would leave it unattended. That meant she probably knew what it was, Jackson thought. Still, she was touched by what he had done. *"Gracias,"* she said, looking away from him again. She got to her feet, went to the foyer, and spoke in rapid Spanish to the owner of the boardinghouse, who had stood there throughout the conversation, tapping her foot impatiently. Jackson stood up, plucked his hat from the table. He would give Philomena the burlap bag; then he could get on with his own life.

She came to him and stood before him. "Señor Jackson," she said, "will you please come with me to my house?"

The request surprised him. "I can just give you the stuff," he began.

"No. Please, come with me. I wish to thank you . . . for what you did for my grandfather."

Well, if she was going to put it like that, Jackson didn't see any way he could refuse.

"I will feed you," Philomena went on. Her eyes glanced back at her employer for an instant. "Better than what you would get here," she said, so low that the woman couldn't hear her.

Jackson tried not to grin at the comment. Still wearing her apron, Philomena went to the door, and Jackson followed her.

Outside, Jackson fell into step beside the

girl after untying his horse. The sun was gone now, though it still spread a fan of light in the sky, and the breeze that swept through the town carried a hint of coolness that was refreshing after the heat of the day. Philomena was silent as she walked, and Jackson didn't intrude on that silence.

She led him to an adobe hut at the edge of town, beyond the saloons. It was dark inside, but within moments, she had a candle lit, its glow spreading softly.

There was a table in the center of the room with several chairs around it. "Please, sit," Philomena said. "I will prepare your meal."

Jackson did as she told him. As she moved around the hut, he watched her in the candlelight. There was an easy grace about her, her muscles working fluidly and smoothly. She kept the grief she must be feeling off her face, and Jackson had to remind himself of it as her nearness and her beauty began to affect him. It had been a while since he had talked to a woman for any length of time. Being constantly on the move meant that a man missed some of life's pleasures.

She shared the meal with him, and he had to admit that it was probably better than what he would have gotten at the boardinghouse. He hadn't eaten all day except for some jerky in the saddle, and the tortillas and beans and corn mush were very good, especially washed down with some wine she had in a jug. She offered him another jug, this one filled with mescal, but Jackson said no to that. This wasn't the time for hard liquor.

When the meal was finished, Jackson decided he couldn't put it off any longer. He went out to his horse and brought back the bag. When he put it down on the table next to the remains of their supper, a faint clinking and rattling came from it.

"I'm sure sorry about your grandfather, Philomena," he said.

"He was a boastful old man," she replied with a rueful smile. "And a terrible liar besides. More trouble than he was worth. Still, he was my grandfather, and I mourn his death."

Jackson untied the knot he had put in the neck of the bag. "Wish I had more of an inheritance to pass on to you." He reached inside and took out an object. It was a small statue made of clay, a study of Madonna and Child. Very crudely formed and painted, it was obviously worthless. Another small sculpture, this one of the Crucifixion, followed. There were rosary beads, pendants, miniatures in gilt frames that had turned green with age . . . all the paraphernalia of ritual that an old Indio who had gotten religion might have collected, plus other items that were equally worthless.

"My grandfather's treasure," Philomena whispered as she sat at the table and looked at the array spread before her.

"Must've meant a lot to him," Jackson said. "Maybe that'll mean something to you." He settled his hat on his head. "My thanks for the meal." He turned away.

Philomena caught him before he reached the door. She took hold of his forearm with both hands. Her fingers were warm and strong.

"Please . . . do not go."

Jackson looked down at her and tried to read her face. There was grief in her eyes, but at the same time, the death of her grandfather hadn't been unexpected to her. He saw gratitude as well. She was grateful, and probably surprised, that a stranger would go out of his way to bring her a bag of worthless trinkets just because a dying old man had asked him to. And there was something else, something besides grief and gratitude. . . .

"That old hen at the boardinghouse knows I'm here," he said. "And the preacher has probably figured out as much, since he's the one who told me where to find you. Thanks again for supper, but we'd better leave it at that."

She shook her head. "I do not care."

"I do."

Jackson settled his hat on his head and turned away from her. Leaving that hut wasn't the easiest thing he had ever done, but after the things he had seen and done this day, it wasn't the hardest either.

Full night had fallen now, the stars overhead standing out brightly against the dark backdrop. Lanterns were lit in all the saloons, and as Jackson walked back down the packed dirt of the street, he heard the tinkle of music floating out of the buildings. A faint smile touched his grim lips as boisterous laughter drowned out the music for a few seconds. Now those were inviting sounds, and he intended to answer *that* invitation.

As he stepped up onto the plank sidewalk that ran in front of the saloons, a shadowy figure moved out of an alley a few feet away. Instantly, Jackson was ready. There was no tension about him, only an alert patience. To anyone who lived by the gun, that stance would speak volumes.

Jackson kept his hand where it was, close

to the butt of his pistol, as Reverend Driscoll said, "Good evening, Mr. Jackson. I trust you located Philomena without any trouble."

"That's right. My business with her is over."

"Then you'll be leaving our town soon."

In the gloom of the sidewalk, Driscoll couldn't see the flicker of anger in Jackson's eyes. Leaving Death Head Crossing was exactly what he had intended to do once he got a drink in his belly and a night's sleep. But now, out of sheer cussedness maybe, he changed his mind.

"No," he said. "I believe I'll be around for a while." He smiled at Driscoll. "I'm starting to like it here."

CHAPTER 3

"Excuse me, sir. I'm looking for a gunslinger."

The young man who tapped on Jackson's arm and made that request looked out of place. He was dressed for a drawing room in some New York City mansion, not a dusty, smelly saloon in a town like Death Head Crossing. Jackson turned slightly, rested one arm on the scarred surface of the bar.

"Is that so?" he asked. "And who might you be?"

"My name is Everett Sidney Howard," the young man replied. "I'm from the *Universe.*"

Jackson's eyes took in the black derby hat, the gray suit, the silk shirt with frills at collar and cuffs, the ascot with the glittery stickpin, and the brightly polished, uncomfortable-looking shoes. "Not the same one I'm from," he said.

"No, you don't understand. I'm a reporter

for the New York *Universe.* I'm looking for a man named Jackson. I was told that he's a famous gunman."

Jackson let his lips curve in a slight smile. "Don't believe everything you're told, boy. Haven't you heard about Westerners and their tall tales?"

"But I had it on good authority —"

"I'm Jackson," he cut in, lifting the shot glass of whiskey to his lips. "What do you want?"

The young man's earnest face lit up. He couldn't have been more than twenty-three, with honest, open features and carrot-colored hair under the hat. He smiled at Jackson and said, "I'd like to interview you, sir."

Jackson drained the whiskey, placed the glass back on the bar, and sighed. "What the devil for?"

"I'm sure our readers would like to know all about the life of a famous gunslinger such as yourself —"

"All the famous gunslingers are dead," Jackson said. "They didn't get famous until somebody put a bullet in them. Not interested, son."

"But, Mr. Jackson —"

"Not interested," Jackson repeated. He turned away from the bar and started slowly toward the batwing doors that led out onto the plank sidewalk.

Everett Sidney Howard took a deep breath and followed him. The byplay between the two of them had drawn the attention of nearly everyone in the saloon. The only one not watching them was the piano player, a thin, doughy-faced man in white shirt, checked vest, and sleeve gaiters. He kept playing in a sort of trance. Piano players saw it all, and sooner or later they stopped giving notice to any of it. But the bartender, bald and burly in a smudged apron, was watching. He knew Jackson, or at least had heard stories about him, and he didn't want any trouble starting here. There was nothing more difficult to get up off a hardwood floor than bloodstains.

There were half-a-dozen other people in the long, narrow room, two cowhands leaning against the bar and four townsmen grouped around one of the card tables. The hands paused in their drinking and the townies in their play to watch the dude from back East chase after Jackson. They were looking forward to being entertained by the results. On the railed balcony that ran in front of the second-floor rooms, a woman in a trailing, loosely belted robe wandered out of one of the rooms and looked down at the proceedings. It was too early in the day for much trade, and she was bored.

Jackson was almost to the batwings when two men appeared there and pushed them open. The men stepped into the saloon and stopped, blocking the doorway.

Jackson came to a halt, and behind him so did the young newspaper reporter. Without taking his eyes off the newcomers, Jackson asked, "Friends of yours, Everett?"

Everett shook his head. "No, sir," he said to Jackson's back.

"Good." Jackson smiled peacefully at the men standing in front of him. "You gents want something?"

"Yeah," the one on the right said. He was medium height and had the narrow, pinched face of a weasel. "We want a murderin' son of a bitch named Jackson."

"That's right," the other one added. He was shorter and stockier than the first man, with colorless hair under his Stetson. A scar on his cheek drew his mouth into a permanent leering smile. "Murderin' sumbitch," he chuckled.

"Well . . . my name's Jackson. Never killed nobody unless they drew on me first, though. Or tried to anyway."

"You're the one we want," the first man said. "Killed some friends of ours, you did.

Ambushed 'em and then tortured an old man who was with 'em until he died. You deny that, Jackson?"

Jackson nodded his head. "I surely do. It was your friends who were killing the old man. They didn't like it when I told 'em to stop."

One of the townsmen motioned to the piano player and finally got his attention. The tinkling strains fell silent, and the room was suddenly very quiet.

"Mr. Jackson," Everett said into the silence, "is there going to be a gunfight?"

"Looks like it, Everett. Looks like it."

"Lyin' bastard!" the leering man snarled. He grabbed for his gun.

Jackson's hand moved in a blur, but not toward the butt of his own gun. His long fingers clamped around the leering man's wrist and jerked. The man let out a surprised yelp as he was pulled over in front of his companion. His line of fire blocked, the other man cursed and tried to angle a shot toward Jackson.

Pausing just long enough to lift a booted foot into the leering man's groin, Jackson shoved him backward as hard as he could. The legs of both men tangled up as they stumbled backward. They hit the batwings and knocked them open; then a boot heel caught on one of the planks outside. The men fell heavily, and several townspeople walking nearby jumped for cover as Jackson appeared in the doorway, pistol held casually in his hand.

Jackson drew the hammer back, and the click cut through the string of profanity that was flowing from the two men. They stared up at the barrel for a long moment. Then both of them dropped their guns to the sidewalk.

Stepping out onto the walk, Jackson kicked the weapons into the dust of the street. "I don't think I'm going to kill you boys," he said. "Don't make me regret that decision later, all right?"

Under the gun, the two men scrambled to their feet and turned away shamefaced. They went into the street to pick up their guns, but they made no move toward Jackson. Instead, they holstered the pistols, strode angrily to two horses that were hitched at the rail, and swung into the saddles. With a last glance of fury and embarrassment, they spurred away from the saloon. Not until they had vanished into the dust cloud that their horses caused did Jackson slide his Colt back into its holster.

"Very impressive," Everett Sidney Howard said from the saloon's entrance. "And you said you weren't a gunslinger. I would like to know, though, why you didn't kill them."

"Stupidity," Jackson answered. He was watching the dust settle back onto the parched street. "I should have. Because one day one of those bastards will try to put a rifle bullet in me. They strike me as the type that might miss, though." Jackson brushed past Everett and entered the saloon again. The piano player went back to the ivories as Jackson signaled the bartender for another drink.

Everett stepped up to the bar beside him. "Why did you ask me if I knew them, if they were friends of mine?"

Jackson glanced over at him, an unreadable expression on his lean face. "Because if you were working with them and trying to divert my attention, I did plan to kill *you.*"

"Oh." Everett swallowed and stood silently for a moment, then lifted a hand to the bartender. "I believe I'd like a drink too, please."

Jackson sipped his whiskey and said, "Still want to interview me?"

Everett picked up the shot glass the bartender placed in front of him, drank the amber contents, and paled visibly. A shudder ran through him. "More than ever," he answered when he was able to speak again.

"You seem to be a fascinating man, Mr. Jackson."

Jackson nodded. "All right. You can ask me your questions. Ain't promising that I'll answer all of them, though."

"Fair enough."

They left the bar and walked side by side toward the door. As they emerged onto the sidewalk, Reverend Driscoll walked quickly toward them.

"Ah, Mr. Howard," the newcomer said to Everett, "I see you found him." He turned to Jackson. "I told this young gentleman where you would most likely be, Mr. Jackson. Frequenting a saloon."

"And good afternoon to you too, Reverend," Jackson said.

Everett was more polite to Driscoll. "Thank you for your help, Reverend. I didn't have any trouble finding Mr. Jackson."

"Yes, but you almost found more than you wanted, didn't you? I heard that there was some trouble."

Jackson smiled without humor. "Not much trouble. No dead bodies for you to pray over, Reverend." He turned on his heel and stalked away down the sidewalk.

Everett looked at Jackson's retreating back, glanced at the preacher, and said,

"Thanks again, sir." Then he hurried after Jackson. "Reverend Driscoll doesn't seem to like you," he said when he caught up.

"He makes judgments quickly," Jackson returned. "I've been here less than a week. I suspect it's my name he doesn't care for."

"Your name? What's wrong with Jackson?"

"Hell."

Everett frowned. "What?"

"That's my name. Hell Jackson."

"Oh." As in the bar a few minutes earlier, after being told casually that he would have been killed if he had been working with the two hardcases, Everett was at a momentary loss for words. He wondered if he dared to ask the question that was uppermost in his mind. *Well,* he told himself, *I am a newspaperman. It's my job to ask tough questions.*

"That's an unusual name," he said, taking the plunge. "Do you mind if I ask how you got it?"

"My old man," Jackson answered without looking at him. "My mother died when I was born. My father figured I was putting him through hell, so he might as well call me that."

The words were calm and quiet, but an iciness touched them. Everett glanced at Jackson, saw no sign of any emotion.

Even a reporter knows there are times to

leave something alone, and Everett suspected this was one of those times. He decided to change the subject.

"Those men in the saloon . . . they said something about some friends of theirs that you're supposed to . . . supposed to have —"

"Killed," Jackson said, supplying the word for him. "That much is true. But they were drawing on me, and like I said, they tortured an old man until he was nearly dead by the time I got there."

"What happened to him?"

"Died a few minutes later. My mistake once I got to town was telling a few folks about it so's they could go out and get the bodies, give them a decent burial. Word must've got back to those other fellows."

"Do you know what it was all about? Why they were torturing him, I mean?" Everett's voice showed that he accepted Jackson's version of the story.

Jackson stopped and looked over at the younger man. "I know," he said. "If I tell you, you planning to write about it?"

Everett took a deep breath and gathered his courage in the face of this scrutiny by the hard-featured man. "If it's a good story," he said, and hoped that his voice didn't shake.

After an eternity, Jackson shrugged. "You're the reporter," he said. "Come on. I want to introduce you to somebody."

CHAPTER 4

"Philomena, this is Mr. Everett Sidney Howard. You know what a reporter is?"

One of the loveliest girls that Everett had ever seen shook her head and smiled sweetly.

"He writes stories for a newspaper," Jackson went on. "He wants to know about your grandfather."

The smile threatened to leave Philomena's face. "Whatever you wish," she said in such a quiet voice that Everett could barely make out the words.

Jackson waved a hand at the rough table in the center of the room. "Have a seat, Everett," he said, "and I'll tell you a story."

They were in the one-room adobe hut on the outskirts of Death Head Crossing, a hut rudely furnished but scrupulously clean. As Jackson and Everett sat down on opposite sides of the table, Philomena went to the area of the room that served as kitchen and pantry and took a clay jug from a basket. She brought it to the table and set it between them.

Jackson pulled the cork, took a swig, and pushed the jug over to Everett. There was a glint of amusement in his blue eyes as the young man lifted the jug with some trepidation and put it to his lips. As he swallowed, his eyes grew large, and he returned the jug to the tabletop with a thump.

"Mescal," Jackson explained. "Got a little kick to it."

Everett jerked his head in a nod. "I'd say so," he gasped. The liquid seemed to have started fires all the way from his throat to his stomach. On top of the whiskey he had downed earlier in the saloon, the effect was potent.

"Probably should've warned you," Jackson drawled.

"No . . . no, it's fine." Everett blinked away the tears that threatened to overflow his eyes and run down his cheeks.

Jackson took his hat off and scaled it onto the bunk in the corner of the room. He drank from the jug once more, then wiped the back of his hand across his mouth.

"Philomena's the granddaughter of the old man I found being tortured," he began. "Before he died, he . . . gave me a mission, you might say. He told me about her and sent me to her."

Everett's eyes went to the girl, and again he was struck by her beauty. Her hair, parted simply in the center of her head, was long and fine and as dark as midnight, hanging nearly to her waist. The long-lashed eyes that looked shyly back at him were nearly as dark, and they were set off by skin the color of honey. She wore a plain white linen blouse, cut low in the neck to reveal the swell of young breasts. A small crucifix dangled from a plain gold chain in the soft hollow of her throat. A long red skirt, decorated with ornate embroidery, fell in sweeping folds to her bare feet. Perhaps she was just a simple peasant girl, Everett thought, but there was an earthy appeal to her that was stronger than anything the pale society ladies of New York could conjure up.

He pulled his attention back to Jackson. There was a hint of possessiveness in the gunman's manner, and the last thing Everett wanted was to make him jealous . . . or angry.

"Seems the old man had talked too much in a cantina and mentioned a treasure he had hidden," Jackson was saying. "These three fellas overheard him and trailed him out of there. They jumped him, took him out to a dry wash a few miles from here, and started working him over, trying to make him tell them where the treasure was."

Everett had to glance at the girl again. Philomena was listening to the story with a look of sadness on her face, and he was sure it was hard for her to hear about the death of her grandfather like this. "I suppose . . . you could tell me about this later," he suggested to Jackson.

"No," Philomena said, as if sensing that it was her feelings he was concerned about. "I grieve for my grandfather, but I glory in the death of his murderers." She looked up as she spoke, and ancient savagery danced in her dark eyes.

"I took care of those three bastards," Jackson went on, "and then before the old man died, he told me where to find his treasure. Told me to get it and bring it to Philomena."

"Did you?" Everett asked, caught up now in the story.

Jackson gestured to a shelf on the wall. It was cluttered with all sorts of knickknacks, most of them cheap religious ornaments. "Treasure," Jackson said.

Everett stared at the collection. "But that's —"

"Junk? Not to the old man."

Everett looked at the girl. "I'm sorry, Philomena, I didn't mean —"

She reached out and gestured for him to stop. "It is all right, Mr. Howard. Those things meant much to my grandfather. Enough for him to die rather than reveal their hiding place. Different things are important to different people. But at the same time I know they have no real value."

"Think that'll make a good story for your paper, Everett?" Jackson asked.

Everett took a deep breath, his mind racing. He sensed that the question wasn't as simple as it seemed. After a moment, he said, "It would make a wonderful human interest story, and I'm sure the readers of the *Universe* would enjoy it. But I don't think I'll include it in my dispatches."

"Why not?"

"I've no desire to intrude on anyone's privacy. The death of Philomena's grandfather should be remembered with dignity, not as just another story to be filed."

And just how much of that noble statement was true? Everett asked himself. He himself wasn't sure of the answer. Was he trying to do the right thing, or was he angling for some other objective? The look in Jackson's eyes told him that the gunman was considering the same questions.

"So you brought the treasure to Philomena," Everett went on. "I just want to make sure I've got everything clear, for my own understanding."

"That's right. The stuff was buried under the old man's shack. Once I had it, finding her was easy. Your friend Reverend Driscoll knew where she lived."

"He's not my friend," Everett protested, knowing the coolness that Jackson felt toward the preacher. "I've found that the local minister usually knows everything that's going on in a town."

"Comes from being a damn busybody," Jackson snorted. He nipped at the jug again. The mescal seemed to be having no effect on him. "You said you had some other questions to ask?"

"Yes." Everett reached into his coat and took out a sheaf of paper and a pencil. He looked inquiringly at Jackson, got a nod in answer. Pencil poised over the paper, he asked, "What's it like to be a famous gunslinger?"

"I told you, all the famous ones are dead. And I don't consider myself a gunslinger either."

"What do you consider yourself?"

Jackson considered before answering. "A

man who doesn't want any trouble."

"Rather contradictory, wouldn't you say, considering your reputation?"

"Sometimes causing a little bit of trouble can prevent a lot of it later on."

"Tell me about your life," Everett prodded. "The places you've been and the things you've done."

Jackson smiled. "Out here, that might be considered a rude question, my young friend, the kind that can lead to all sorts of problems."

Everett was afraid he had overstepped himself. Quickly, he started to apologize, but Jackson stopped him with a negligent wave of his hand. "Forget it. I don't mind telling you about some things. I was in the army during the War Between the States. First time I got to travel much. Then I drifted out here to the West. Was a deputy a few places, even sheriff a time or two. Went back to work for the army as a civilian scout for a while. Some called me a bounty hunter after that because I collected a few rewards, but that was all accidental. I never went out looking for hardcases, but I crossed paths with a few. Can work cattle or horses, and I've spent time as a ranch hand."

"You do hire your gun out, though, don't you?"

Jackson inclined his head and shrugged. "As a guide or a bodyguard, yes. You can't hire me to go shoot somebody just because you and the other fella have some sort of argument going."

Everett's pencil moved rapidly over the paper as he made notes for the story he would send back to New York. "How many men have you killed?" he asked without looking up.

"I don't keep count."

"Really? I thought you probably cut notches on your gun handle or something."

Jackson leaned forward, face intent. "Nope. And if I find out that you called me something like a Dashing Daredevil of the Plains or some other dime-novel shit, you and me are gonna have another little talk, Everett."

"Yes, sir," Everett replied, not meeting Jackson's eyes.

Jackson relaxed again. "You've been asking the questions," he went on. "Mind if I ask you a few?"

Everett shook his head. He was puzzled by the request, wondering what Jackson might want to know about him.

"What's somebody like you doing out here in the first place?" Jackson asked. "Somehow, you don't strike me as the type a paper would send to the frontier."

Everett brightened up considerably. "That's easy to answer," he said. "There's a book — you probably haven't heard of it — called *Roughing It* by Mark Twain."

"I've read it," Jackson put in.

Everett tried not to let the surprise he felt show on his face. "Well, my editor really liked that book," he went on. "He liked the idea of letting the people back East know what it's really like out here in the West. So he looked around for somebody to send and —"

"Decided to send an innocent abroad," Jackson finished for him. For the first time, a full-fledged grin stretched across his face.

Embarrassed, Everett looked down at the table again. Even Philomena was smiling at him. He nodded slowly. "I'm afraid you're right," he admitted. "So far, I've been sending back some good stories, though."

He didn't say anything about all the hopes and aspirations that had made the trip West with him. Everett Sidney Howard's father had been a newspaper reporter, and his father before him. Everett had heard people talk about having ink in their veins instead of blood, and as he grew into manhood, he knew the truth of that statement. Reporting was all he knew, all he wanted, all he could ever hope to do.

But not writing about some party given by a society matron whose idea of high drama was an evening at the theater, seeing and being seen by her cronies.

Everett wanted more than that. He wanted to find the stories that would move people to anger or outrage or tears. He wanted to cover all the laughter and tragedy that made up life.

And this Western journey was a good place to start. He had decided from the first that he was going to find one of the "fast guns" who so fascinated the readers and find out what such a man was really like. A tall, flinty-eyed man with a quick laugh and a quicker draw; a wanderer living constantly on the edge of death; a man who had seen and done it all —

A man like Hell Jackson.

This was going to make — Everett's lips curved in a wry smile at the thought — one hell of a story.

Now, if only Jackson would agree to Everett's proposal. More than anything else, he wanted to accompany this man on his travels. Everett was sure that he would encounter everything he needed to know about the West in company with Jackson. All he had to do was convince the gunman that he wouldn't be in the way. . . .

A shout from outside interrupted the thoughts that were racing through Everett's head. All three of the people around the table looked up, and Jackson came to his feet in one smooth, efficient motion. He stepped to the door and pushed it open.

"Looks like they're bringing a body into town," he said after a moment.

Everett and Philomena joined him, Everett raising himself up on his toes to peer over the older man's shoulder.

Several cowhands were riding down the main street of Death Head Crossing. One of them led another horse, and draped over its back was a limp figure. At the head of the procession was a young man in a suit, looking uncomfortable in the saddle of a magnificent stallion. The group drew a lot of attention as it made its slow way down the street, and by the time the riders drew up in front of the sheriff's office, there was quite a crowd on the sidewalks.

Jackson picked up his hat from the bunk and walked down to join the gathering. He didn't hurry. His interest was a casual one. Everett followed along behind him.

The riders dismounted, and two of them unlashed the burden from the horse they had been leading. They carried the corpse into the sheriff's office while a shocked murmur went through the crowd. Someone spoke a name — "Luther Berryhill! I know his horse!" — and the speculation started.

Everett stopped in his tracks when he saw the damage that had been done to the dead man's face. His stomach lurched suddenly. He had never seen a dead man before, let alone one that looked like somebody had set off a dynamite blast right in his face.

Jackson caught the arm of a man standing at the edge of the crowd. "Who is it?" he asked, nodding toward the doorway where the riders and their ghastly load had disappeared.

"Luther Berryhill, they say," the townie answered. "He's a hand out at Tillman's Winged T spread. Should say he was." The man grimaced. "Never saw the like of that, by God."

"Speaking of God," Jackson countered, tight-lipped.

Reverend Driscoll was pushing his way through the press of people. When he reached the door, he went into the sheriff's office and shut the door behind him.

"I should be in there," Everett said nervously, as if he were afraid someone would agree with him. "I'm a newspaperman, after all. And there's a story here."

60

"That's right, Everett," Jackson told him. "You go right ahead. Just bull right on in there."

Everett swallowed. "Of course, I'm not sure my press credentials would carry much weight with a local law officer."

Philomena had appeared beside them. "It is this town," she said with a sigh. "My grandfather came here to drink when he should have stayed in the hills, and now he is dead. This man, this Berryhill, he came here to drink as well, and now *he* is dead." She shrugged. "Some places are evil. This town, it is cursed."

Jackson smiled again. "There's your story, Everett," he said with a chuckle. "The Curse of Death Head Crossing."

CHAPTER 5

Everett gathered up his courage as he stood there looking at the closed door of the sheriff's office. Quite a few of the townspeople who had been attracted by the commotion still stood on the boardwalk in front of the building. Drawing a deep breath, Everett started trying to push his way through the crowd.

He wasn't having much luck at it until suddenly the press of people in front of him parted. A glance over his shoulder told him why they were stepping aside. Jackson had moved up right behind him. The citizens of Death Head Crossing were getting out of the gunslinger's way, not his.

If that was what it took to get the story, then so be it, Everett told himself.

He reached the door and opened it. The corpse had been stretched out on the floor of the sheriff's office by the men who had carried it in. The cowboys who had brought the body to town stood to one side looking grim while the sheriff knelt beside the mortal remains of Luther Berryhill. Reverend Driscoll was beside the desk, eyes closed and lips moving slightly. Everett figured he was praying.

With a sigh, the sheriff pushed himself to his feet. He was a tall, barrel-chested man, still powerful despite the fact that his face was weathered by the years and his hair and mustache were white. "Never saw anything like that," he muttered. "Hope I never do again." He looked up at Everett and asked, "Who are you, mister?"

"Everett Sidney Howard, from the New York *Universe*."

"Oh, yeah, that reporter fella from back East. I heard about you bein' in town. We ain't met yet, but I'm Sheriff Ward Brennan." The lawman's eyes flicked toward Jackson and narrowed with dislike. "I reckon I know who you are," he added.

Jackson didn't say anything. He was accustomed to star-packers not being too happy that he was in their towns.

Everett swallowed hard, gestured toward the mutilated corpse, and asked, "Is this man really Luther Berryhill, as people outside were saying?"

One of the cowhands spoke up. "It's Lute,

all right. Ain't no doubt about that."

"His horse came back to the Winged T with an empty saddle," one of the other men put in. "When we saw that, we knew something must've happened to him, so we went lookin'."

"Found his body a while ago," the first man said, resuming the story. "We carried it back to the ranch house first, and Mr. Tillman told us to bring him right on into town."

Brennan nodded. "You done the right thing, boys."

"You're certain about his identity?" Everett said.

"Why the hell wouldn't they be?" Brennan asked with a frown.

"Well . . ." Everett felt uncomfortable under the lawman's scrutiny, but he pressed on. "With the face, uh, damaged the way it is, I just wondered how anybody could be sure. . . ."

The cowboy who had done most of the talking said, "Those are Lute's clothes. He was wearin' 'em when he rode into town yesterday evenin'."

Jackson said, "Somebody else's corpse could've been dressed in Berryhill's clothes."

The same thought had been going through

Everett's mind. He wanted to give Jackson a look of gratitude, but he refrained.

"Look at his left hand," the cowhand said. "See that missin' little finger? Luther lost it when he wasn't quite careful enough takin' a dally around his saddle horn one day. Rope caught it and popped it right off when that steer's weight hit it. And there's a scar there on his chest where he got stabbed during a brawl when he was drunk. He was mighty lucky that didn't kill him right there." The cowboy shook his head. "But his luck sure ran out. Yeah, that's Luther, all right, no doubt about it."

Everett was satisfied with the identification now. He said, "Does anyone have any idea what happened to him?"

"I'll ask the questions," Sheriff Brennan snapped. He looked at the hands from the Winged T and went on. "What the hell happened to him?"

"Looks like somebody set off a stick of dynamite in his face," one of the men suggested. The same thought had occurred to Everett outside when he first saw the corpse.

Jackson shook his head and said, "No, even one stick of dynamite would have blown his head clean off his shoulders. Something else did that."

"You sound like a man who's seen things

like that," Brennan commented in an unfriendly tone.

"I've seen a lot of things," Jackson answered. "Some good, some bad."

Brennan glared at him for a second, then looked down at the corpse again. "Maybe a shotgun blast." He glanced at Jackson again. "Unless you want to point out some reason it couldn't have been that either."

Jackson just shrugged.

Reverend Driscoll said, "Isn't the fate of this man's immortal soul more important than the means of his death? I've been praying for him. I think you should all join me."

"No offense, Reverend," Brennan said, "but whichever way Luther went when he died, up or down, he's already been there for ten or twelve hours by this time, so I don't reckon prayin' for him's gonna do him much good either way."

Driscoll's mouth thinned in disapproval, but he didn't say anything else.

Brennan faced Everett and Jackson again and went on. "What business of yours is Berryhill's death?"

"I'm a reporter," Everett said, "and I think my readers will be interested in this story."

"Why would folks back in New York City be interested in anything that happens way out here in Texas?" Brennan looked and sounded genuinely puzzled.

"People back East are always interested in [w]hat's happening on the frontier," Jackson [said] in a tone of wry amusement. "That's [why t]hose damn dime novels are so popu-

[doo]r of the sheriff's office opened [. . . m]an who came in was in his thir- [. . .] his relatively unlined face [. . .] carried himself, but his [. . . t]hinned down to almost [. . . s]hirt he wore under a [. . . da]rk stains on it, and [. . .]rs. That was all [. . .] what profession

[. . . ple]asant tone.
"

ve
this

[. . .]atch I
[. . .]hed in
print in

[. . .]m looked
[. . .]t can you

[. . .] take a look
[. . .]uch as I do.
[. . .]ce blown off
[. . . dri]nkin' last night
[. . .]d Saloon myself
[. . .]rounds — and
[. . . m]ighty bad trouble
[. . . th]e Winged T."
[. . .]am asked.
[. . . th]e cowhands, who all
[. . . fro]m the ranch was with
[. . .]d.

Berry- hand

68

"Everett Sidney Ho[...]

Graham nodded

name. "The distingu[...] the Fourth Estate fr[...] about you being in to[...] don't you stop by th[...] we can discuss the p[...]

"Thank you. I'll do[...]

"In the meantime[...] beaten me to the pu[...] unfortunate man's d[...]

"Not at all," Everet[...] file will take some ti[...] New York. You'll have[...] your local paper long[...]

"That's true, I sup[...] at Sheriff Brennan a[...] tell me about this, Wa[...]

Brennan grunted. [...] for yourself and kno[...] Luther Berryhill got[...] somehow. He was in to[...] — I saw him in tow[...] while I was makin' m[...] evidently ran into some n[...] on his way back out to t[...]

"He was alone?" Grah[...] Brennan looked at th[...] shrugged. "Nobody fr[...] him," one of them sa[...]

"I'll ask around town and see if anybody noticed him ridin' out, and whether or not anybody was with him if they did," Brennan said. "And I guess I'd better ride out and take a look at the place his body was found. You boys notice anything strange about it when you went lookin' for him?"

Head shakes from the men. "There were quite a few hoofprints around," one of them said, "but hell, it was right close to the main trail, so there was nothin' unusual about that."

"All right." Brennan blew out his breath in an exasperated sigh, fluttering his drooping mustache a little. "Thanks for bringin' him in. He got any kinfolks around here, do you know?"

"I don't think so. He was from Georgia or somewhere, came out here after the war like so many others. But Mr. Tillman said to tell you that he'd pay for the buryin'."

"I'll tell Cecil Greenwood." Brennan glanced at Driscoll. "Reckon we'll have the funeral in your church, Reverend?"

"Of course," Driscoll answered without hesitation. "I don't approve of drinking and carousing, but everyone deserves to be laid to rest properly, no matter what sort of scoundrel they were."

"I'm sure Berryhill would be glad to hear

that," the sheriff replied.

Remembering what Philomena had mentioned outside, Everett said, "Sheriff, this isn't the first tragic death in the area recently. It's been suggested that Death Head Crossing is . . . cursed somehow." Brennan started to glare again, so Everett rushed on. "What do you have to say to that?"

"I say it's the biggest bunch o' bull droppings I ever heard!" Brennan replied, his voice rising almost to a roar. "There's no such thing as a curse."

Reverend Driscoll said, "I'd have to disagree with you about that, Sheriff. Curses are mentioned numerous times in the Scriptures. What about Job and all the unfortunate things that befell him?"

"That's different," Brennan insisted. "Them was Old Testament times, and anyway, God was just testin' Job."

"Perhaps He's testing our community now. Perhaps Death Head Crossing has been judged and been found evil, and this is just the first manifestation of that judgment."

"Berryhill's not the first to die," Jackson said. "Don't forget that old Indio, Philomena's grandfather."

Driscoll almost sneered. "That old heathen was tortured to death by outlaws. It's not the same thing and you know it." He pointed to Luther Berryhill's ruined face. "The Lord works in mysterious ways."

Jackson took hold of Everett's arm. "Come on," he said. "Let's get out of here. I never did like the smell of self-righteousness."

CHAPTER 6

"Pompous jackass," Jackson muttered as he and Everett walked toward Philomena's shack. "Old Julio was no heathen. You could tell that by the things he considered his treasure."

Everett nodded. "Yes, there were several religious artifacts among them. Clearly that wasn't enough for the reverend."

"I'm not sure anybody could be pious enough to suit the reverend," Jackson said. He shook his head. "No point in worrying about that now, I reckon. What do you think about what happened to Berryhill?"

"I . . . I don't know what to make of it. I never saw anything quite like it."

"I never did either," Jackson admitted. "I think when the sheriff rides out to take a look at the place where Berryhill was found, I might trail him. Wouldn't mind doing a little poking around myself."

"Why would you do that?"

"Well, you want the story, don't you?" Jackson asked with a grin.

"Yes, but —"

"Let's just say I've taken a liking to you, Everett. I don't have anywhere else to be or anything else to do right now, so giving you a hand will pass the time."

Everett's eyes widened in excitement. "Does this mean you agree to what I suggested earlier? You'll let me . . . what do they say out here? Partner up with you for a while and write about it?"

"For now. We'll see how it goes."

"Thank you, Mr. Jackson. I promise you won't regret it."

"Best not to make promises you might not be able to keep," Jackson advised. "Now, we're going to have to get you a horse."

"You mean . . . I'll have to ride?"

"Only way to get around where I'll be going, I expect."

Everett didn't look too pleased by that prospect. Jackson wondered if he'd ever even been on a horse back there in New York. They had a big park in the middle of the city where folks sometimes went riding, or at least so Jackson had read in *Harper's Weekly,* but that didn't mean Everett had ever done such a thing.

Philomena was waiting for them at the

shack. "What happened?" she asked. "Did you find out anything about that poor man with the destroyed face?"

"Not much," Jackson told her. "He was a ranch hand, rode for a spread called the Winged T. Know anything about it?"

"A man named Tillman owns it," she replied. She looked at Everett and added, "He came from somewhere in the East, like you, Señor Howard."

"Has he been out here long?"

Philomena shook her head. "A year or so, I think. The man who owned the Winged T before must have been related to him. His name was Rufus Tillman. But then he died, and Señor Benjamin Tillman came out to take over the ranch."

"Berryhill worked on the ranch while Rufus Tillman was still alive?" Jackson asked.

"I do not know," Philomena said with a shrug. "I think so, but I am not sure."

A wagon rolled past outside. Jackson saw it through the open door and read the legend painted on its sideboards: GREEN-WOOD'S UNDERTAKING PARLOR. He recalled Brennan mentioning someone named Cecil Greenwood, who was obviously the undertaker here in Death Head Crossing. A blanket-covered shape lay in the back of the wagon, all that was left of the luckless cowhand Luther Berryhill.

A few minutes later the group of Winged T hands rode past. Sheriff Brennan was with them. They were going to show the lawman where they had found Berryhill's body, Jackson figured. He said, "Come on, Everett. There's a livery stable right down the street. We can rent a mount for you there."

"All right," Everett said. "If you think that's best."

"You can stay here with Philomena if you want."

Jackson saw the way Everett glanced at the young woman and knew that he was sorely tempted. Any young man would be. But Everett's devotion to the duties of his profession won out, and with a sigh he said, "No, I'll come with you, Mr. Jackson."

"You can call me Hell if you want," he said as they left the shack and started toward the livery stable.

"I'm not sure I'd be comfortable doing that. Is it all right if I just continue to call you Mr. Jackson?"

"Whatever you want, Everett."

When they told the bandy-legged hostler at the livery stable they needed a horse for Everett, the old man brought out a mean-eyed dun that Jackson spotted right off as trouble. He knew what the old-timer was up to. He wanted to see the young Eastern dude get bucked off and thrown right on his ass. Under other circumstances, Jackson might have gotten a chuckle out of that sight himself. But they didn't have time for it now, so he pointed to another horse in the corral behind the livery barn and said, "That roan right there."

"You've got a fine eye for horseflesh, son," the old-timer said in a high-pitched voice. "Your friend'll be needin' a saddle too, I reckon?"

"That's right."

Ten minutes later, the roan Jackson had picked out for Everett was saddled and ready to ride. "Left foot in the stirrup first," Jackson instructed. "Hang onto the reins and grab the saddle horn good and tight. Now step up and swing your right leg over."

Everett did as he was told and settled into the saddle. The roan shifted a little underneath him, prompting him to clutch the saddle horn even tighter. Jackson had thought the horse looked like a pretty steady animal, the sort that Everett would need, and it settled down quickly.

"Ever ridden before?" Jackson asked as he climbed onto his dun.

"No. Never in my life. What else do I need

to know?"

"Well, the main thing," Jackson said, "is that if we have to ride very far, your balls'll probably hurt like hell in the morning. Still want to go?"

Everett looked a little panicky, but he managed to nod.

"Follow me then," Jackson said. "Just bump your heels against his sides. He'll come along."

They rode out of the settlement, heading in the same direction as Sheriff Brennan and the hands from the Winged T. Jackson gave Everett some tips as they went along, warning him not to jerk the reins or lean too far to one side. It was plain to see that Everett was scared of the horse, but the only way he would ever get over that was by riding and getting used to being in the saddle.

"The sheriff and those other men are a long way ahead of us," Everett pointed out as they jogged along. "Will we be able to follow them?"

Jackson pointed lazily toward the trail. "They left fresh tracks. Not only that, but I can still see a little of the dust that their horses' hooves kicked up."

"You said you were a scout for the army. I suppose you must be pretty good at tracking people."

"Done my share," Jackson said. "Most of 'em didn't want to be followed, so I had to worry about being drygulched too. Don't think that'll be a problem today. Not with the sheriff up ahead of us like that."

But he couldn't rule it out entirely, he reminded himself. Out of long-standing habit, he kept a close eye on their surroundings, watching especially for the telltale glint of sunlight reflecting from a rifle barrel.

Nothing happened, though, except that they rode across some fine-looking rangeland. To most people the terrain probably looked sparse, arid, and rocky, but Jackson's experienced eyes noted the pockets of green on the hillsides that marked lush pastures and the sparkle of water where clear creeks flowed. Hardy breeds of both men and cattle were required to make a go of it in country like this, but the rewards would be great for those willing to put in the necessary effort.

The trail curved around some large boulders and then dipped across a broad valley. As they rounded an outcropping of rock, Jackson reined in and said, "Slow down, Everett." He had spotted something ahead of them.

Not surprisingly, Everett hauled back on

the reins too hard, hurting the roan's mouth and making the horse jump around a little as it came to a stop. Everett let out a frightened yell. Jackson reached over and grasped his arm to steady him.

"Hold onto the reins! Firm, but not too hard. Don't jerk 'em."

With Jackson's help, the young Easterner brought the skittish roan under control. "Sorry," Everett panted. "I guess I'm not much of a horseman."

"You'll be fine, you just need some practice."

"Why did we stop?"

Jackson leveled an arm. "Look yonder across the valley, about five hundred yards."

Squinting, Everett looked where Jackson was pointing. "I don't see anything."

"The sheriff and those other hombres have stopped, and Brennan's looking around."

"Oh," Everett said. "Oh, yes, I see them now. You must have really good eyes, Mr. Jackson."

Jackson reached into his saddlebags and brought out a pair of field glasses that had once belonged to a Confederate officer. He lifted the glasses and peered through them for a minute, then grunted and handed them to Everett.

"They don't seem to be finding anything."

"No, they're just sort of milling around," Everett agreed. His voice quickened. "Now the sheriff is getting back on his horse."

Jackson took the glasses back and stowed them away. "Let's get off the trail," he said.

He led the way into the rocks, putting the largest of the boulders between them and the trail. A few minutes later, they heard the hoofbeats of a single horse as Sheriff Brennan rode past on his way back to Death Head Crossing.

"The rest of 'em went on to the Winged T," Jackson guessed. "We'll give them a few minutes and then go have a look around the spot."

While they waited, Everett took his derby hat off and pulled a handkerchief from his pocket. As he mopped sweat from his face, he asked, "Why are you really doing this, Mr. Jackson? It's not just to help me out, is it?"

Jackson hooked a leg around his saddle horn to ease his muscles. After a few seconds of silence, he said, "Let's just say that I'm curious. The first thing I came across when I rode into this part of the country was an old man being tortured to death. I got the feeling right then and there that something was mighty wrong around here. There's a certain smell in the air . . . the scent of evil, I guess you could call it if you wanted to be dramatic about it. But it got my hackles up, and the way that cowboy was killed just made it worse."

"You don't think the two deaths are connected, do you?"

Jackson shook his head. "Not directly, no. I know why Julio died, and the men responsible for it are buzzard bait now. But I've still got the stink of brimstone in my nose, and I don't like it."

"With a name like yours —" Everett began.

Then he fell silent as Jackson looked at him and said, "It's been long enough. Let's go."

CHAPTER 7

While watching through the field glasses, Jackson had paid particular attention to the spot where Sheriff Brennan was tramping around, about fifty yards off the main trail, so he was able to locate it without much trouble.

"Berryhill was headed back to the ranch after a night of drinking in town," Jackson said, thinking as much to himself as he was talking to Everett. "As full of whiskey as he was, the horse probably knew the way home about as well as he did. But when he came along here, he must have seen something, because he left the trail."

"Maybe he passed out and the horse just wandered off the trail," Everett suggested.

Jackson shook his head. "No, if Berryhill had gone to sleep or even passed out in the saddle, the horse would have stayed on the trail and gone straight back to the Winged T. Berryhill rode over here on purpose."

Jackson looked around, his keen eyes searching for anything out of the ordinary. A low range of hills rose about half a mile away. He wondered if Berryhill had seen something in that direction. It was unlikely, since it had been the middle of the night, but *something* had drawn the man off the trail.

As the cowboys who had brought the body in had said, there were quite a few hoof-prints scattered around the area. However, it was impossible to tell if those tracks had been made the night before or sometime in the past. The weather hadn't been particularly windy, and there hadn't been any rain in several weeks. Tracks might last a long time under those conditions.

"Shouldn't there be some blood?" Everett asked.

Jackson turned his head to look at him but didn't say anything.

"I mean, the man's face was gone," Everett went on. "There was nothing left but bone. With such a horrible injury, there must have been quite a bit of blood."

Jackson nodded. "So we'd be able to see some of it on the ground, is that what you're saying?"

"Well, yes. I don't pretend to be an expert

on such matters, but that seems logical to me."

"Not if he wasn't killed here," Jackson pointed out. "Maybe he was killed somewhere else and his body was just left here."

Everett looked crestfallen. "I suppose that's possible."

Jackson pointed at something on the ground. "Look at those marks, the narrow ones that twist around some."

Everett studied the markings for a moment, then said, "They look like they were made by snakes crawling through the dirt. There are snakes in this part of the country, aren't there?"

"Plenty of them, mostly diamondback rattlers and sidewinders. You don't want to run into any of them if you can help it. But those marks weren't made by snakes. They were made by ropes."

"Ropes?" Everett repeated.

Jackson nodded. "Somebody lassoed something, then cut it loose and pulled the ropes back in. I'm betting it was Berryhill they dabbed their loops on."

"You can tell that just by looking at some marks on the ground?"

"It's what you'd call an educated guess."

"So," Everett said, "someone roped Mr. Berryhill . . ."

"Dragged him out of the saddle," Jackson continued, "and then blew his face off somehow without leaving a drop of blood on the ground."

"That's . . . amazing. Unbelievable even."

Jackson just shrugged. He knew what he saw, whether he understood the how and why of it or not.

"Let's ride on out to the Winged T," he said. "I want to have a talk with the fella who owns it. Tillman, I believe Philomena said his name was."

They returned to the trail and turned away from the direction that led back to Death Head Crossing. Everett was beginning to handle his horse a little better now, but his nervousness was still apparent.

"You don't believe Berryhill was killed somewhere else, do you, Mr. Jackson?" he asked as they rode.

"Not really. I just brought that up as a possibility. Those rope marks in the dirt make me believe somebody jumped him right back there, though."

"We have to ask ourselves who would have wanted him dead. From all we've heard about him, he was just a cowboy, without any real enemies."

"Everybody has enemies," Jackson said. "The friendliest man in the world has rubbed somebody the wrong way, some-time, somewhere."

"Enough so that someone would kill him for it?" Everett sounded skeptical.

Jackson shrugged. "You never can tell what'll prod a man into killing. It may not seem like much to everybody else, but not to him. Problem is, I think there were several men involved in Berryhill's death. That makes it trickier. A bigger group of men needs a bigger reason to kill."

They continued talking about it as they rode toward the Winged T, but didn't reach any conclusions. Several miles farther on, they topped a hill and saw the ranch head-quarters in a little valley that spread out before them. The valley was well watered by a creek that meandered through it. The main house sat on a knoll beside the creek. It was a sprawling, two-story log structure surrounded by trees. Several outbuildings clustered nearby, including a long building that was probably the bunkhouse, a smoke-house and cookshack, a blacksmith shop, and a couple of large barns with a complex of corrals around them. Judging by its headquarters, the Winged T was no little greasy-sack outfit. It was a large, profitable ranch.

A couple of dogs came running and bark-

ing to greet the two riders. The canine commotion attracted some attention. Several
men emerged from the bunkhouse, and two
more came from one of the barns. They
gathered together in front of the main house
as Jackson and Everett rode up and reined
in.

Jackson recognized some of the men as
the ones who had brought Luther Berryhill's body into town. The one who had
done most of the talking there stepped
forward and gave them a curt nod. He was
a stringy, middle-sized man with a gray
mustache. "Something I can do for you
gents?" he asked. "I'm Ned Dawson, the
ramrod here."

"We came to see Benjamin Tillman," Jackson said.

"If you got business involvin' the Winged
T, you talk to me," Dawson rasped. "I told
you, I'm the ramrod. I run the operation."

Jackson wasn't phased by the man's hostile
attitude. Sitting easily in the saddle, he said,
"We still want to talk to Tillman."

The door of the main house opened and a
man stepped out onto the long porch that
ran across the building's entire front. "What
is it, Ned?" he asked. "Who are these men?"

The newcomer wore boots, jeans, and a
work shirt, but he didn't look like he ever

did any actual work in them. He was a little below medium height and had wavy brown hair that was starting to recede despite the fact that he wasn't more than thirty years old.

Jackson turned his horse toward the porch and said, "Are you Benjamin Tillman?"

"That's right," the man said, a puzzled frown on his unlined face. "Who are you, sir?"

Before Jackson could answer, Ned Dawson said, "He's a gunslinger, Boss. Name of Jackson. The fella with him is some sort o' newspaperman from back East. We saw 'em in town, in Sheriff Brennan's office. They was takin' a mighty big interest in what happened to poor Lute Berryhill."

Benjamin Tillman seemed more intrigued by Dawson's mention of Everett's profession than by anything else the ranch foreman had told him. He looked at Everett and said, "Are you really a journalist? For what paper?"

"The New York *Universe*," Everett replied.

"I'm familiar with it. A fine paper. My family owns an interest in the Philadelphia *Chronicle.* I take it you're from New York?"

"That's right."

"I've visited there many times. Come in, come in. It'll be nice to sit down and chat with someone from a more civilized part of the country."

As Everett dismounted carefully, Tillman moved to the top of the porch steps and extended his hand.

"We haven't been properly introduced. I'm Benjamin Tillman."

"Everett Sidney Howard," Everett said as he came up the steps and gripped Tillman's hand. "And this is my friend Mr. Jackson." He didn't give Jackson's first name.

Jackson smiled faintly at Ned Dawson as he dismounted. Dawson had tried to keep him and Everett from talking to Tillman, but that effort had failed. Jackson wondered briefly if Dawson had just been trying to shield his boss from being bothered by strangers . . . or if there might be some other reason the foreman didn't want them talking to Tillman.

"Come inside," Tillman said again. "It's getting late in the afternoon. You'll stay for supper, won't you, Mr. Howard? And you too, of course, Mr. Jackson."

"We'll see," Jackson said. As he stepped up onto the porch, he glanced over his shoulder and saw that the group of cowboys in front of the house was breaking up, with most of them heading back to the barns or the bunkhouse.

All but Dawson, that is. The ramrod still stood there, eyes narrowed in suspicion and thumbs hooked in his gun belt.

Tillman took them into a large room furnished with heavy, comfortable furniture. Thick, woven Indian rugs lay on the floor, and stuffed heads of deer, antelope, and mountain lions adorned the wall. A massive fireplace took up most of one side of the room.

Tillman gestured toward the animal heads and said, "I apologize for that barbaric display, gentlemen. My cousin Rufus was quite the hunter, and he liked to have the heads of his prey mounted, I suppose so that he could brag about them to visitors. Rufus was quite the braggart too, I suspect, even though I never actually knew him."

"You never met him?" Jackson asked.

"Not in person, no. His communications with the family back in Philadelphia were all by letter."

A wave of Jackson's hand took in not only their immediate surroundings but also the rest of the ranch. "Why did he leave all this to you then?"

"I was his closest relative. We were actually second cousins, but the rest of the family was even more removed from him. He was a lifelong bachelor, and I gather he

90

didn't have any close friends out here." Tillman moved to a sideboard that held a decanter and several glasses. "Some lemonade before dinner, gentlemen?"

"No, thanks," Jackson replied before Everett had a chance to say anything. "I'm not sure we'll be staying for dinner either. We just rode out here to ask you some questions."

Tillman turned back toward his visitors, curious but also a little annoyed. "What sort of questions?" he asked in a crisper, less friendly tone of voice.

"About Luther Berryhill and what happened to him."

"He was killed in some grotesque fashion, that's all I know. And while I regret any man's death, of course," Tillman added, "I have to say that whatever happened to Mr. Berryhill, he probably had it coming!"

Chapter 8

Jackson was going about this all wrong, Everett thought. The man was used to asking questions in a blunt fashion and expecting answers. Even though Everett was young and hadn't been in the newspaper business for all that long, he already knew how to interview people and find out what he needed to know from them.

"I'd like a glass of lemonade, Mr. Tillman," he said quickly. "After the long, dusty ride out here, I could use something to drink."

"Of course." Tillman seemed a little mollified as he poured lemonade into a glass and brought it over to Everett.

"Thank you." Everett sipped the cool, tart beverage and went on. "It must have been quite an adjustment for you, living back East and then coming out here to the frontier."

Tillman smiled. "You could even call it a

shock." He waved toward one of the heavy armchairs. "Please, have a seat, Mr. Howard."

Everett sat down, and without being invited to do so, Jackson sank onto one of the divans. Jackson looked like he was willing to step back and let Everett handle things for the moment, so Everett went on. "Tell me about it."

"About coming West, you mean?"

"That's right. Surely just because you inherited this ranch, you didn't have to come out here and run it yourself. From what I understand, many Eastern investors own ranches, but they employ managers to actually run them."

Tillman sat down in another armchair, leaned forward, and clasped his hands together between his knees as he said, "Yes, and I suppose I could have done that too. I think poor Ned would have been happier with that arrangement. He tries not to show it, but I'm afraid he resents my interference with the day-to-day affairs of the Winged T."

"You don't have any experience running a ranch," Jackson pointed out.

"No, but how is anyone supposed to learn without jumping right in and getting your hands dirty, so to speak?" Tillman leaned back and waved off Jackson's comment. "Anyway, I needed a change of scenery. I'd been in school for a while, and when that didn't work out, I decided it might be best to get out of Philadelphia."

"You were attending one of the universities there?" Everett asked.

"I was a seminary student," Tillman replied. "I know it's unusual for someone from a wealthy family to enter the ministry, but that's what I felt called to do."

Everett made an effort not to arch his eyebrows in surprise. It was indeed unusual to find a wealthy preacher. Most men who followed that calling were more humble sorts. But there was nothing to prevent it, he supposed.

Tillman continued. "When I realized that I had made a mistake, I looked around for something else to do, and about that time I received word from Cousin Rufus's attorney that he had passed away and left me this ranch. It seemed like a perfect opportunity to make the change in my life that I was looking for. Unfortunately, it hasn't worked out all that well."

"Why not?"

"Well, just look around you," Tillman said with a faint laugh. "The lack of amenities, the isolation, the absolutely barren cultural atmosphere, the crudeness and vulgarity of the people who live here . . . At times I wish I had never left Philadelphia."

Everett surprised himself by thinking that the people who had to deal with Benjamin Tillman probably felt the same way about him. They probably wished he was still back in Philadelphia too.

"What did you mean about Berryhill getting what was coming to him?" Jackson asked.

Tillman lifted a finger. "You see, that's exactly what I'm talking about. Luther Berryhill was a drunkard and a whoremonger. He was always riding off to Death Head Crossing — and that's a terrible name for a town, isn't it? — to guzzle rotgut whiskey in the saloons and degrade himself with the painted women who frequent such places. If he hadn't been prone to doing such things . . . well, he'd still be alive, wouldn't he?"

Everett couldn't argue that point, but he wasn't sure he agreed that Berryhill's habits had actually been responsible for his death.

"Do you know anyone who had a grudge against him? Anyone who might have followed him to town or ambushed him on the way back?"

"Why are you asking all these questions

about Mr. Berryhill?" Tillman wanted to know. "No offense, Mr. Howard, but what business is it of yours how and why he died?" But before Everett could answer, Tillman went on. "Ah, now I understand! You want to write about what happened for your newspaper."

"I hate to say it," Everett admitted, "but the bizarre manner of Berryhill's death would be of interest to my readers."

Tillman's mouth tightened in disapproval. "I daresay you're right. Common people have an insatiable appetite for sensation."

"Seems like you'd want to know what happened too," Jackson drawled. "Berryhill rode for you, after all. Or doesn't loyalty count for anything where you come from?"

"Of course it does," Tillman snapped. "I plan to pay for Mr. Berryhill's funeral and see to it that he's buried properly. But I just don't know anything about what happened to him, and to tell you the truth, I don't really care."

He might have said more, but at that moment a footstep sounded on the stairs leading up to the ranch house's second floor, and the three men turned their heads as a woman's voice said, "Benjamin, you didn't tell me we had company."

She came down the stairs gracefully, a

smile on her pretty, slightly rounded face. She had long, light brown hair, the same shade as Tillman's but straight instead of wavy. Everett thought she was about twenty years old.

All three men stood up as she reached the bottom of the stairs and came toward them. Jackson and Everett took off their hats. Tillman moved to take the young woman's arm and said, "Gentlemen, allow me to present my cousin Deborah, also one of the Philadelphia Tillmans. She's come out here to visit with me this summer. Deborah, this is Mr. Everett Sidney Howard of the New York *Universe* and his friend and associate, Mr. Jackson."

Deborah Tillman smiled at them. "Hello, gentlemen. I'm very pleased to meet you."

"The pleasure and honor is ours, Miss Tillman," Everett said. He hoped he wasn't being impolite and staring. But Deborah was only a few years younger than he was, and she was very pretty.

Jackson just nodded and said, "Ma'am."

"Don't let me interrupt," Deborah said. "Please go on with your conversation."

"It was nothing important," Tillman said. "We were just discussing Mr. Berryhill's unfortunate death."

Deborah's smile disappeared. "Yes, that

was terrible. I didn't see the poor man's body, you understand. Benjamin wouldn't allow that. He always tries to protect me from anything that might disturb me. But I heard the men talking about it, and I'm sure it was simply awful."

"It certainly was," Everett agreed.

"You saw him, Mr. Howard?"

"Unfortunately, yes. It was a sight I won't forget any time soon."

Tillman's arm was still linked with Deborah's. She disengaged from him gently and said, "I was just on my way to speak to Hiram about supper. Shall I tell him we'll be having two guests?"

Jackson shook his head before Everett could reply. "No, ma'am, Mr. Howard and I have to be getting back to town. But we appreciate the offer."

"Oh, that's a shame." She looked and sounded genuinely disappointed, which made Everett's pulse jump a little. He hoped that while he was in these parts, there would be another opportunity for him to sit down to dinner with Deborah Tillman.

She nodded and went on. "Please come back to see us any time, gentlemen." Then she left the room through another door. Everett watched her go and hoped he wasn't being too obvious about it.

When he turned back to Tillman, he said, "Your cousin is charming."

"Yes, she certainly is. I'm glad she came to visit."

"How is she taking to the West?"

Tillman chuckled. "Better than me, to tell you the truth. She goes riding nearly every day. I'm not comfortable on horseback myself. I prefer a good buggy."

Everett didn't care much for riding either, but the prospect of it had suddenly become more appealing. He could imagine taking a ride through the hills and running into Deborah. It would be quite pleasant to ride alongside her and talk. He thought she would be a charming conversationalist.

Jackson settled his hat on his head and said, "Let's go."

"You don't have any more questions for me?" Tillman said.

"You've told us everything you know about Berryhill's death, haven't you?"

Tillman nodded. "Of course. I'm sorry it happened, but I'm not surprised. The man's immorality was bound to catch up to him sooner or later."

Jackson didn't say anything. Everett put his hat on and shook hands with Tillman again. "Thank you for your hospitality. And say good-bye to your cousin for me, if you would."

"Certainly. A gentleman such as yourself is welcome on the Winged T any time, Mr. Howard."

Everett noticed that Tillman didn't extend the same invitation to Jackson.

They left the house and reclaimed their horses from the hitching post where they had left them earlier. Nothing was said as they mounted up and rode off, heading away from the ranch house and back toward Death Head Crossing. Everett waited until they were well out of earshot of the house before asking, "What did you think of Benjamin Tillman, Mr. Jackson?"

"Thought he was a pompous, arrogant, holier-than-thou little son of a bitch," Jackson answered. "Most of the time I felt like giving him a swift kick in the ass."

"He was rather full of himself, wasn't he? And yet, he claimed to have studied for the ministry."

Jackson scraped a thumbnail along his jaw and frowned in thought. "Yeah, that struck me as a mite strange too. And he didn't seem all that bothered by Berryhill getting killed."

Everett looked over at his companion and said, "You don't think he had anything to do with Berryhill's death, do you?"

"Seems like a mighty far-fetched idea. I don't reckon we can rule it out, but I'd be more inclined to think that somebody who actually knew what he was doing was responsible for that. Tillman's head is so far up his rear end, I can't see him being able to pull off any kind of killing."

"Unless, of course, that was exactly the sort of impression he was trying to give."

Jackson laughed. "I'm starting to like the way you think, Everett. Nice and suspicious. Come on, let's get back to town and have some supper."

CHAPTER 9

Luther Berryhill's funeral was held the next day at the Baptist church in Death Head Crossing, the Reverend Martin Driscoll presiding. The coffin made by Cecil Greenwood had already been nailed shut. Given the condition of Berryhill's body, there was nothing the undertaker could do to make it presentable for public viewing.

The crowd in attendance at the funeral wasn't a large one. Sheriff Brennan was there along with a few townspeople. Benjamin Tillman and his cousin Deborah, dressed in their Eastern finest, came into town in a buggy, accompanied by Ned Dawson and several of the Winged T hands. The editor of the local newspaper, Malcolm Graham, showed up, unobtrusively taking notes on a pad of paper.

Jackson and Everett were in attendance too, seated on one of the church's rear pews.

Everett had been able to get a room in the

same boardinghouse where Jackson was staying. At breakfast that morning — which had been served by Philomena — they hadn't had a chance to talk about what had happened the day before. The other boarders had been there around the big table, and Jackson didn't want to discuss it. But now, as Reverend Driscoll played the pipe organ before the service got under way, Jackson leaned over toward Everett and said, "Looks like everybody who had much to do with Berryhill is here."

"What do you mean by that?" Everett asked. His derby was perched on his knee.

"Could be whoever killed him is in this room."

Everett's eyes widened as he looked around the church. "You really think so?" he asked in a half whisper.

Jackson nodded toward one of the townsmen sitting a couple of pews in front of them. "That's Jasper Whitten, the owner of the Big Bend Saloon. The girls with him all work there. I don't imagine Driscoll's too happy about having them in his church. But from what I've heard, that was Berryhill's favorite place to drink and gamble when he came to town. Chances are if he got in trouble with anybody in Death Head Crossing, it happened while he was in the Big Bend."

"Nothing's been mentioned about him getting into an argument with anyone on the night he was killed," Everett pointed out.

"Maybe the trouble happened sometime earlier. Folks have been known to hold a grudge for a long time before ever doing anything about it."

Everett nodded slowly, knowing that Jackson was right about that.

"Then there's the Tillmans, and Dawson and the other fellas who ride for the Winged T," Jackson continued.

"You can't seriously think that Benjamin Tillman had anything to do with what happened," Everett said. "We already talked about that yesterday afternoon on the way back to town. And as for the possibility that Miss Tillman could be involved, why, that's just ludicrous!"

"Maybe. But Dawson and the rest of that crew are a pretty salty bunch."

"Luther Berryhill was one of them. He was their friend."

"Friends have been known to have a falling-out."

Everett's expression made it clear he thought Jackson was grasping at straws.

Jackson saw it as trying to consider all the possibilities.

Driscoll brought the hymn to a close and got up from the pipe organ. Carrying his Bible, he walked over to the pulpit, in front of which sat the pine box containing the mortal remains of Luther Berryhill. He motioned for the mourners to stand and said, "Let us pray."

Jackson wasn't surprised that Driscoll was long-winded about it. The prayer was interminable, and so was the sermon that followed it. Unlike some funerals, nobody cried at this one, but there was plenty of foot-shifting and squirming around on the pews before Driscoll was finished. The sense of relief in the church was palpable when the minister finally launched into his closing prayer.

As soon as the service was over, Jackson and Everett were the first ones out the door. They stood under the tree that shaded the church's entrance, Everett with his back ramrod straight, Jackson leaning a shoulder casually against the trunk. They watched the mourners come out, followed by stout Cecil Greenwood and three equally stout younger men who looked like his sons. They carried the coffin and placed it in the back of the undertaker's wagon. The cemetery was behind the church, only a short distance, but too far to carry an occupied coffin in this heat.

Ned Dawson strolled over into the shade where Jackson and Everett waited. His fingers were already busy with the makin's, rolling a quirly. He licked the paper, sealed it, and lipped the cigarette. Around it, he asked, "What are you two doin' here? You didn't even know Lute."

"Just figured we'd pay our respects to the deceased," Jackson said. "A fella can't have too many folks at his send-off, now can he?"

"Reckon not," Dawson said. He fished a lucifer from his pocket, snapped it into life with his thumbnail, and set fire to the gasper. As he ground out the match under his boot, he went on. "But some might say it's a little nosy to attend the funeral of a gent you didn't even know."

Jackson ignored that and asked, "Where's the rest of your crew? The Winged T has to have a lot more hands than the ones who rode in today."

"Of course there's more of us," Dawson snapped. "But you don't think we'd go off and leave the spread deserted, do you? Most of the boys are out on the range where they're supposed to be, ridin' the boundary lines and keepin' the boss from gettin'

106

robbed blind."

"Been losing some stock, have you?" Jackson's question sounded like idle curiosity, but actually he was very interested in the answer.

Dawson shrugged. "Some. It ain't that unusual. Drifters pass through and lift a few head on their way out of this part of the country. And the border ain't that far away either. We get some *bandidos* comin' across every now and then, not to mention a few bands of Bronco Apaches who're still holed up in the mountains in Mexico."

"Sounds like you might have trouble from time to time, all right."

"Damn right we do. And this whole business with Lute gettin' killed don't help matters." Dawson puffed on his cigarette and shook his head. "The boys who saw him have talked about what he looked like with his face gone. Word's got around. Nobody can figure it out, but it sure makes a man uneasy to think about it." He glanced at Everett. "You're awful quiet today, boy."

"I don't like funerals," Everett said. "They remind me of my own mortality."

Dawson grunted. "How old are you, twenty-three, twenty-four, something like that?"

"I'm twenty-four," Everett said.

"You got a ways to go yet before you have to worry about your own funeral. Hell, wait until you get to be fifty, like me." Dawson took another drag on the quirly, then dropped the butt and ground it out like he had the match. "I got to go to the buryin'." He stalked off.

Jackson and Everett walked after him, toward the cemetery where the mourners were congregating around the open grave that had been dug that morning. "He's wrong, you know," Everett said.

"Wrong about what?" Jackson asked.

"Not having to worry about death. No one knows when it's going to come calling for them. I would think that out here on the frontier, where daily life is more dangerous, that the uncertainty would be even worse."

A grim smile tugged at the corners of Jackson's mouth. "You're a smart young fella, Everett," he said. "I reckon that's one reason I like you."

When the graveside service — thankfully shorter than the funeral inside the church — was over and the sound of shovels biting into dirt and showering the clods down on the coffin lid filled the air, Benjamin Tillman came over to Jackson and Everett and shook hands with both of them.

"A sad day," he said, solemnly shaking his head. "A very sad day."

"Most funerals are," Jackson said.

"Well, we'll just have to put this behind us now and move on with our lives. We can't bring poor Luther back."

"And you've got other troubles to worry about, don't you?"

Tillman frowned. "What do you mean by that, Mr. Jackson?"

"I've heard talk around town that you've been having a problem with rustlers."

Tillman looked surprised. He said, "I'm sure it's nothing out of the ordinary. All ranches lose some cattle, don't they?"

"Sometimes. Whether or not it's a problem depends on how often and how many head you're losing."

"We'll take care of it," Tillman said. He didn't seem to want to discuss the subject. "Excuse me, I have to get back to my cousin. I'm sure she's ready to leave."

"Say hello to her for me," Everett put in.

Tillman smiled for a second and nodded before he turned and walked toward the buggy. Deborah had already gotten into the vehicle, assisted by one of the ranch hands.

"It bothered him that we knew the Winged T is losing stock," Jackson mused.

"Is that why you didn't tell him that it

was Mr. Dawson who mentioned it?"

Jackson nodded. "Yeah. Dawson's not very friendly, but there wasn't any point in getting him in trouble with his boss. I get the feeling that Tillman is a proud man. Maybe too proud. He doesn't want to admit that running a ranch like the Winged T may be more than he can handle." Jackson straightened from his casual pose. "There's the sheriff. Let's have a word with him."

They moved to intercept Ward Brennan as he walked toward the main part of the settlement. Everett took the lead this time, asking, "Have you discovered any new information pertaining to the death of Luther Berryhill, Sheriff?"

"You mean have I found out who killed the poor bastard, and how?" Brennan grunted. "Hell, no. I don't know any more'n I did yesterday."

"Have you investigated the possibility that he may have had trouble with someone while he was in town the night before last?"

"He didn't get into any kind of ruckus, if that's what you're talkin' about. He drank some in the Big Bend, played a little poker, joked around with one of the gals, but didn't take her upstairs. He didn't have enough money for that. That's why he got in the card game, hopin' to win enough to buy himself a good time. Didn't work out that way, though. He lost what little *dinero* he had left."

"Did he get angry about it, or threaten anyone?"

Brennan shook his head. "Nope. Berryhill was a good-natured cuss. Everybody who knew him agrees on that. Even when he got cleaned out, he just laughed about it."

"So, you see, you *have* discovered something, Sheriff," Everett said. "You've established one more reason that *didn't* cause Mr. Berryhill's death."

Brennan tugged at his mustache. "Yeah, I reckon you could look at it that way," he admitted. "But what good does that do?"

"You've narrowed the field of suspects. Eventually, that should make it easier to discover who the real culprit is."

"Maybe." Brennan didn't sound convinced. "But that still leaves another question. . . . How the hell do you do something like that to a man's face anyway?"

"Figure out that part," Jackson said, "and the answer is liable to lead you straight to the killer."

CHAPTER 10

Matt Harcourt rode easily through the night, unbothered by the darkness. He knew where he was going.

And he knew what would be waiting for him when he got there, too.

Or rather, *who* would be waiting for him.

He had first seen Lucy Vance six months earlier, at one of the dances held occasionally in Death Head Crossing. He'd looked across the floor and there she was, laughing and spinning around the floor in the arms of a lucky partner. His eyes were drawn irresistibly to her dark hair and her sparkling eyes and her slender, graceful figure in the blue gingham dress. She was without a doubt the prettiest girl he had ever seen, and he had known right then and there that he had to have her.

The only problem with that resolve was the fact that she was already married.

Harcourt had ridden back to the Winged

T that night with the rest of the hands who had come to town for the dance, and as his horse plodded through the night he was torn by two contrasting emotions, desire for Lucy and hatred for Fowler Vance, her husband.

Vance was a rancher, but not much of one. He had a little spread east of the Winged T, in a part of the range where the graze wasn't as good and the water was limited. Not surprisingly, his cows seldom brought as much from the cattle buyers as those of his neighbors, but Vance scratched along and made ends meet somehow. He'd even saved up enough money for a trip to San Antonio a while back.

When he returned to Death Head Crossing on the stage, he had Lucy with him. They had met and married in San Antonio. There was some speculation around town that she had been a soiled dove and had married Fowler Vance to escape from that life, but nobody knew for sure, and since she was sweet and friendly and definitely nice to look at, folks accepted her pretty quickly.

Then Matt Harcourt had laid eyes on her at that dance, and everything had changed.

But not right away. Harcourt managed to get one dance with her that night, and he introduced himself as they swung around to the strains of a waltz, hating his awkwardness as he stumbled over his words, wishing he could be as nimble-tongued as some fellas were. Lucy was polite and smiled at him, but then, she was polite and smiled at all the eager cowboys who managed to snag dances with her that night. Her feet must have ached some before the festivities were over. She was the most popular girl there, bar none.

Harcourt was a little surprised, a week later, when he ran into her again in town and she remembered who he was. They were both in the general mercantile, picking up supplies. Old Hiram, the Winged T cook, had sent Harcourt on that errand, and as soon as he saw Lucy in the aisles of Bender's Emporium, he could have kissed the old-timer on top of his bald, ugly head for putting him in position to talk to the gal again. Lucy smiled at him and said, "Oh, hello, Matt. It's good to see you again," and if Harcourt hadn't been lost before, he sure was then.

He helped her load her purchases in the back of the buckboard she had driven into town, then was bold enough to say, "If you want, I'll ride out to your place with you and unload those things for you."

"Oh, no, Fowler can do that," she replied.

His heart sank at the reminder that she already had a husband. Even though Fowler Vance wasn't much, he owned a ranch. He wasn't some scruffy cowpoke who had never earned better than forty a month and found. Lucy was a smart girl. She wasn't going to abandon her husband for *him.*

But then she'd said, "If you'll come by tomorrow evening, though, I'll fix supper for you, to repay you for your help today."

He had accepted, even though it meant he'd probably have to sit down at the supper table with her husband too. He was at the point where he would put up with just about anything in order to spend more time around her. He just hoped he didn't look too eager as he said, "Sure, I can do that. Much obliged, Miz Vance."

"Please," she'd said with a laugh that tugged at his heartstrings. "Call me Lucy."

Looking back on it now, he knew he shouldn't have been surprised when he rode up to the little ranch house the next evening and found her there alone. Fowler Vance was miles away, combing some breaks on the northern reaches of his range with the two Mexicans who worked for him. One of the vaqueros had spotted some strays up that way, and the men were going after them. They would be gone until the next day.

Lucy had never looked more beautiful than she did that night, in the soft lamplight. She'd had supper ready for Harcourt, and the food was delicious, but he barely tasted it. As he ate, he kept staring at the soft curve of her cheeks and the way the dark wings of hair brushed over them, and the smooth expanse of skin at her throat, and on down lower to the shadowy valley at the top of her breasts.

He might be a damned fool, he told himself later, but he wasn't stupid. He knew what Lucy had in mind. And husband or no husband, once she had led him into the bedroom and untied the belt around her waist and shrugged out of the dress she wore so that the fabric slid down whisperingly over her bare shoulders, there was no way he was riding off and leaving her there. No way in hell.

So in one way it started at the dance, and in another it started when they ran into each other in the store, and in yet another it began that night in her bed, the bed she usually shared with Fowler Vance.

Harcourt had been back since then, of course. He'd been back a whole heap of nights, every time Vance was gone and Lucy could get word to him. From the top of a hill on Winged T range, he could see the Vance place. When Lucy hung a particular bright yellow tablecloth on the clothesline behind the ranch house, that meant it would be safe for Harcourt to ride over that night. He rode up to the top of that hill every chance he could to check, and this morning the yellow tablecloth had been flapping in the breeze.

After that, his impatience to be with her had made the day's work seem even longer, harder, and more tedious than ever. But the sun finally went down, and as soon as Harcourt had cleaned up a mite, he saddled one of the horses from his string and started toward the Vance place. Nobody asked him where he was going. Ned Dawson was a hard man, a real taskmaster when it came to the chores on the Winged T, but he didn't care what the boys did on their own time. That attitude was common among all the hands.

He topped the hill where he rode to look for their signal. Now that night had fallen over the landscape, he couldn't see the ranch house itself, but he spotted the soft yellow glow of lamplight in one of its windows. A couple of miles beyond the house loomed the dark bulk of a long, rugged ridge. As Harcourt started down the hill, he thought he caught a glimpse of something on that ridge. Another light, he thought. Maybe several of them. But they had winked in the darkness for a second or two and then were gone, and their appearance had been so fleeting he wasn't even sure if he had really seen anything or just imagined them.

He forgot all about that as he neared the house. Lucy must have heard his horse, because the front door swung open as he reined to a stop in front of the building. The lamp in that room was out, but one burned further back in the house, in the bedroom. It cast enough light so that he could see her standing there, nude, silhouetted beautifully against the glow. His breath caught in his throat and his heart began to pound like a trip-hammer in his chest. She was the most beautiful woman he had ever laid eyes on, and she held out her arms to welcome him into her embrace.

In the next half hour, he didn't think once about the fact that she was married, and judging by the way she cried out and clutched at him, neither did she.

In the time he had left to live, Matt Harcourt couldn't have said what alerted him that something was wrong. It was an instinct as much as anything else. But something caused him to lift his head off the pillow and reach for the gun on the chair beside the bed. No matter how drunk with desire he was for Lucy Vance, he always paused to coil his shell belt around the holstered Colt and place it on the chair where he could get it in a hurry if he needed to.

It was just common sense, after all, when you were sleeping with another man's wife.

Lucy stirred sleepily beside him. "What is it?" she asked in a voice dulled with satisfaction.

"I thought I heard something."

"Don't worry about Fowler, honey. He won't be back from Fort Stockton until tomorrow."

"Don't you ever worry that he might suspect something and try to cross you up?"

"Fowler? Suspect something?" She laughed softly. "Matt, darlin', that man doesn't have any idea what goes on between us. He doesn't even know what I'm thinking most of the time. Hell, he thinks I actually love him."

An unpleasant twitching went along Harcourt's spine at the coldness in Lucy's voice. He forgot about whatever had disturbed him and said, "You didn't love him even when you married him?"

"Good Lord, no. I just wanted to be somewhere else, and Fowler was somebody to take me. Don't get me wrong. He's not a bad sort, I suppose, and he honestly cares for me. But he can't do for me what you do, honey."

Harcourt sat up and raked his fingers through his tangled hair. For the first time, he felt sort of bad about what he was doing with her. She'd said that Vance wasn't a bad sort, and Harcourt knew that to be true. Sort of dull, yeah, but he was a decent hombre. Maybe I ought to give her up, he thought. It would be the right thing to do.

But he knew he wouldn't do it. He couldn't. He still wanted her too bad.

A soft thud sounded outside, followed by another and another. Hoofbeats. More than one horse. Harcourt's breath hissed between his teeth as he jerked the Colt from its holster and bolted out of bed.

"Somebody's out there!" He kept his voice pitched low, so whoever was outside wouldn't hear him.

"It can't be Fowler!" Lucy said as she struggled out of bed, wrapping the sheet around her nudity. "It just can't be!"

Harcourt darted to the window and moved the flour-sack curtain aside just enough to peek out. He expected to see riders, since he had heard the hoofbeats of several horses.

But instead, what he saw were large, glowing balls of light surrounding the house.

The sight startled a shocked cry out of him. Lucy came to his side and grabbed his arm, digging her fingers into his flesh. Harcourt didn't even notice the pain of her grip.

"Come out!" a voice boomed. *"Come out, ye sinners and fornicators! Come out and face the judgment of the Lord! I am the Hand of God on Earth, and I shall deliver His vengeance!"*

"Matt, what —"

He pushed her aside, more angry now than frightened. Despite the eeriness of those mysterious lights, those were men out there, and from the sound of what the one who had spoken had said, they were Bible-thumpers like that preacher in town. Matt had always hated being preached at, and he wasn't scared anymore. Hombres like that were all talk. He wasn't afraid of them. As he reached for his pants and pulled them on hurriedly, the voice outside continued its harangue.

"Adulterers! Fornicators! See what your sin has wrought!"

Pistol in hand, too mad to be thinking

straight, Matt stalked out of the bedroom, through the front room, and flung the door open. As he stepped out on the porch, he lifted the gun and said, "Wrought this, you meddlin' son of a —"

The brightest light he had ever seen exploded in his face, throwing him backward and filling his entire being with pain. The last thing he heard was Lucy Vance screaming.

Chapter 11

Carl Gafford thought sometimes that he wasn't cut out to be a farmer. He had failed at it in Arkansas, so he had packed up his wife Nora and come to Texas for a fresh start. They had settled in Comanche County and struggled along for a few years. Carl might not be much good with crops, but he was handy at sowing his seed in other ways, and more often than not Nora's belly was swollen with child. That was why, when the bank finally got the place in Comanche County and Carl had to hitch up the mules, pile all of his and Nora's belongings on the old wagon, and head out in search of greener pastures, they had four young'uns with them too. Four hungry mouths to feed.

He'd heard that there was good land to be had along the Rio Grande, near El Paso. All that stood between him and that land were several hundred miles of hot, rugged country and the possibility of bandits and savages. He and his family would have to live off the land along the way too, but Carl liked to think he was a decent shot with the old rifle he had toted ever since he'd left Arkansas. They'd make do.

And so far they had. They had covered more than half the distance, in fact. The farther west they went, the more inhospitable the terrain became. A man might run cattle in country like this, but he'd be wasting his time if he tried to till that thin, rocky soil and grow anything worth harvesting. Carl sure hoped he hadn't heard wrong about that land along the Rio Grande.

Nora's sunbonneted head rested against his shoulder as he drove the wagon. This early in the day, and she was already dozing off. But Carl supposed he couldn't blame her. The baby had been colicky the night before, and she had been up with him most of the time. Life was hard for a woman, especially here. Carl recalled hearing a man say once that Texas was fine for men and dogs but hell on women and horses. Everything he had seen since leaving Arkansas confirmed that.

The wagon bed was heaped high with the household goods they'd been able to bring along. The three bigger kids rode on top of the pile. Carl was yawning as he and Nora swayed on the seat, when one of the young'uns said, "Pa, what's that?"

"What's what?" Carl asked.

"Up there ahead of us," the boy replied. "Looks like somebody a-layin' on the ground."

Damned if the sprout wasn't right. About fifty yards ahead of the wagon, a man was sprawled facedown on the ground, not moving. Carl's eyes, naturally downcast after the life he'd led, hadn't even noticed him until now. With a muttered "Hell," Carl hauled back on the reins. That fella was probably dead, and Carl didn't want the little ones to see him close up.

Nora roused from her doze as the wagon came to a stop. "What is it?" she asked, anxious but still tired.

"I don't know yet," Carl replied. "Looks like somebody may be hurt." He wrapped the reins around the brake lever and then reached for the rifle on the floorboards at their feet. "I'll go take a look."

Nora's hand closed around his arm for a second. "You be careful."

"I will be."

"I mean it, Carl Gafford," she said. "Anything happens to you so that I'm left alone with these kids, I'll see to it that you never rest in peace."

She wasn't joshing either, he thought wryly as he climbed down from the wagon.

He felt a mite nervous himself as he stalked forward, clutching the rifle tightly. Maybe this was a trick or a trap of some sort. Maybe that fella was a bandit and some of his owlhoot friends were hidden close by. When Carl walked up to him, he might roll over suddenly and point a gun at him and take everything he and his family owned. Lord knows any outlaws who robbed them wouldn't get much, but it was all they had. A man couldn't lose much more than that.

He stopped about a dozen feet away, pointed the rifle at the man on the ground, and said, "Hey. Hey, mister! You alive? If you are, you better say somethin'. I ain't comin' any closer, and I got a rifle pointed right at you."

The man didn't respond. He lay on his belly, with his head turned so that Carl couldn't see his face. He wore denim trousers like a cowboy, but he was barefooted and didn't have a shirt on either. If he stayed there like that much longer, the sun would burn his back to a crisp.

"Damn it, I'm talkin' to you!" Carl squinted at the man, trying to tell whether or not he was breathing. If the man's back was rising and falling, it was so shallowly that Carl couldn't make it out at this distance. With every passing second, Carl was more convinced that the hombre was dead.

Instead of going closer, Carl began to circle around the body, keeping the same distance of about a dozen feet and keeping the rifle trained on the man as well. Something began to seem very, very wrong. The man had black hair, and as Carl moved around so that he could see his face, it looked like that black hair had fallen over the man's features, obscuring them. But the hair was *moving. . . .*

Carl jumped back and let out a horrified yell as he realized that wasn't hair covering the man's face at all. It was a thick layer of flies. His shout startled them enough so that they rose in a buzzing cloud from the man's head, and what was left behind when they flew into the air was even worse. Carl tore his eyes away from the sight, but not before he saw the red of blood and the white of bone shining through it. The man's face was gone from about the nose up.

With sickness boiling up inside him, Carl stumbled a couple of steps to the side and then fell to his knees. As he bent forward, he lost the meager breakfast he had eaten that morning before they pulled out for another day on the trail.

"Carl!" Nora called to him. "Carl, what's wrong?"

He looked up and saw that she had started walking toward him. Resting the rifle butt on the ground so that he could lean against the weapon, he waved her back with his other hand. "Stay there, Nora!" he told her. "Damn it, stay with the wagon, and keep those kids over there! Don't let 'em get anywhere close to this!"

He pushed himself to his feet, thinking that there was nothing he could do for the man. Digging a grave in this rocky ground would be a back-breaking task and would take all morning at least. It made more sense just to drive on, swinging well around the mutilated corpse, of course, so that the rest of his family couldn't get a good look at the gruesome remains.

The only problem with that plan was that the gruesome remains suddenly let out a groan.

Carl stared bug-eyed at the man. How could anybody look like that and still be alive? It just didn't seem possible. Carl backed away. Even though he knew by now this was no trap and that the man was no threat to him, he didn't want anything to do with this atrocity. He wanted to take his family and leave. Anyway, with such a hideous injury, the man couldn't hang on for very long. He would be dead soon, and there was nothing Carl could do to help him.

The man groaned again, and the fingers of one hand clawed at the dirt, as if he were trying to drag himself forward.

Carl muttered a heartfelt "Shit!" and advanced slowly. He was just too damned softhearted for his own good, he told himself. But he knew that no matter how badly he wanted to, he couldn't turn his back and leave this man here.

"Take it easy, mister," he said as he approached the injured man. When he came closer he saw that the face had been destroyed somehow. He had heard about men who had tangled with grizzly bears and had their faces torn off by a sweep of a giant paw. That didn't really look like what had happened here. Indians maybe, he thought. Redskins were notorious for torturing folks. Carl glanced around nervously. If savages had done this, they might still be around.

He stepped past the man on the ground and broke into a run toward the wagon. "Carl, what are you doing?" Nora asked him as he came panting up to the vehicle.

"Give me a blanket," he told her. "And when I give you the signal, drive on over there next to that fella."

"Is he dead, Pa?" one of the kids asked.

"No, he ain't, and we're gonna help him if we can." Carl looked at his children. "That's what you do. You help folks if you can. Understand?"

They nodded solemnly.

He took the threadbare blanket that Nora handed him and turned to hurry back to the injured man. As gently as possible, he rolled the man onto the blanket. The man moaned, but didn't seem to know what was going on. Carl arranged a flap of the blanket so that it covered the ruined face, then stood up and waved for Nora to bring the wagon over.

He motioned for her to pull on past him and then said, "Stop there." He lowered the tailgate. There wasn't room for the man inside the wagon bed, so Carl would have to lash him onto the tailgate. As he bent to pick up the shrouded shape, he saw that blood was already soaking through the blanket where it lay over the man's face. "You kids stay up there in the front of the wagon," he said, his tone of voice making it clear that he wouldn't put up with any sass or disobedience.

With a grunt of effort, he lifted the injured man and placed him on the tailgate. He found some rope and tied the man so that he couldn't roll around or fall off. The man's chest rose and fell raggedly, and Carl felt a little sick to his stomach again when he heard the breath whistling through the nose holes in the poor bastard's skull.

The eye sockets were empty, he noticed, nothing left at all.

"Are you sure he's alive, Carl?" Nora asked.

"I'm sure."

"What are we going to do with him?"

Carl rubbed at his lean, beard-stubbled jaw. "He needs a sawbones. Nothin' *we* can do for him, that's for sure. So I guess we got to find a town. Back yonder in Fort Stockton, didn't somebody mention a settlement called Death Head Crossing?"

Nora nodded. "I think so. But I don't know how far it is. Maybe we should turn around and go back to the fort."

They had already left Fort Stockton two days behind them, and Carl knew the man wouldn't last that long. He might not last another hour. He should have been dead already.

"No, we'll keep goin'," Carl decided. "That's the best thing. Maybe we'll get to that town before it's too late."

"What if we don't?"

"Then we'll have done our best," Carl said. "Just like we've always done. You handle the mules, and I'll sit back here with him for now."

Nora sighed, but she untied the reins, flapped them against the backs of the team, and yelled at the mules until the balky creatures started moving again.

He had said that they would do their best, Carl reflected as the wagon rolled slowly westward, hopefully toward Death Head Crossing.

The only thing wrong with that was a whole life's worth of evidence that his best was seldom good enough.

CHAPTER 12

Jackson and Everett were in the Big Bend Saloon around the middle of the day after Luther Berryhill's funeral. Jasper Whitten, the owner of the place, provided a halfway decent free lunch, and as Jackson put it, "There are things in this world you want to turn down even if they're free. Lunch isn't one of them."

A commotion in the street outside drew their interest. Everett craned his neck to look out over the batwings, but Jackson just glanced in that direction. He seemed half asleep as he lounged back in his chair, but all his senses were alert whether he appeared to be or not. The life he'd led had long since taught him that trick.

"Somebody just drove past in a wagon," Everett reported. "The way folks were trotting along beside it and yelling questions, there must have been something pretty interesting in it."

"We should go have a look for ourselves, I reckon," Jackson said as he uncoiled from his chair and stretched like a big cat. He walked to the batwings and pushed through them with Everett following closely behind him.

They had talked some more about Luther Berryhill's death and their visit to the Winged T the day before, but neither man had reached any conclusions. Berryhill's death was just as much a mystery as ever.

But now, as they walked along the street toward the spot where the wagon had halted in front of a building with a doctor's shingle hung in front of it, Jackson heard Berryhill's name mentioned by one of the excited townspeople. He strode up to the man, gripped his arm, and said, "What's that? What about Berryhill?"

The townie glanced over and suddenly looked worried. Just about everybody in Death Head Crossing knew who Jackson was, and while they might enjoy the notoriety that having a famous gunslinger around brought to their town, at the same time they were a little afraid of him. The man swallowed and said, "That fella those pilgrims just brought in, his face looked like poor Lute Berryhill's."

Another man said, "I got a good look at

him when the blanket he was wrapped up in slipped while they were carryin' him into Doc Musgrave's." A shudder went through him. "I'm liable to have nightmares about that and wake up screamin' for a week."

Jackson and Everett exchanged glances. Two men who'd been shot might not have any connection with each other, but a couple of fellas who died in such a mysterious fashion had to be tied in together somehow.

"Did anyone know who he was?" Everett asked.

The citizens around them all shook their heads. "The way that poor bastard looked, there just wasn't no tellin'," one of them said.

A new voice rumbled, "Let me through. Step aside, blast it."

The crowd parted for Sheriff Ward Brennan. The burly, white-haired lawman headed for the door of the doctor's office. Jackson and Everett were right behind him. No one made a move to stop them until they reached the door, but then Brennan paused and glared over his shoulder at them.

"This is none of your business," he snapped.

"I'm a member of the press, Sheriff," Everett said. "The people have a right to know what's going on."

"Yeah, well, he ain't a member of the press," Brennan said with a nod toward Jackson, "and if you ask me, the people sometimes know too damned much for their own good. But I ain't got time to argue about it."

"That man who was brought in can't be in much of a hurry," Jackson said. "Not if he's in the same shape Luther Berryhill was."

"That's just it," Brennan said. "The fella who came runnin' down to my office to tell me about it said he was still alive."

Even Jackson's normally impassive face showed a little surprise at that news.

"Stay out of the way and keep your mouth shut," Brennan went on, then turned to go into the building. He didn't try to stop Jackson and Everett from following him.

Dr. William Musgrave practiced medicine in the front rooms and lived in the back. He was a stocky man with a neatly trimmed mustache and a crisp accent that betrayed his Massachusetts origins. He was a lunger and had come west for his own health, in search of a higher and drier climate. West Texas, harsh though it might be in many ways, had been good for him.

Now he was bent over a man who had

been stretched out on an examining table. The patient was wearing only a pair of denim trousers, and when Sheriff Brennan got a look at the man's face, he choked out, "Good Lord," and turned his head away for a second.

Everett did the same. Jackson thought the young reporter looked a little green around the gills. Like Dr. Musgrave, Jackson studied the injured man stoically, but that didn't mean he felt nothing. Whatever he felt, though, was his own business.

Another man stood by, looking as queasy as Everett and Brennan. He was tall and gaunt from hardship and hunger. His bib-front overalls and homespun shirt were patched, and the hat that he turned around aimlessly in knobby, work-roughened fingers was stained and shapeless. Even his run-down shoes practically screamed "farmer."

Jackson recalled the equally drab and worn woman and the passel of kids who had been waiting in the wagon outside, and he remembered how the man he had asked what was going on had said something about pilgrims. The farmer and his family must have found the injured man. The pile of goods in their wagon was evidence that they were moving, and they had come across this grotesquely mutilated hombre in their travels.

But just as Brennan had said, the man was still alive, even though he had no business drawing breath as badly hurt as he was. His chest fluttered rather than rising and falling. He couldn't have much time left.

Musgrave straightened from his examination and said, "I can't do anything for him. His injuries are beyond the scope of anything I've ever seen."

"Except for Luther Berryhill," Sheriff Brennan rumbled.

"Yes, the cases are similar," Musgrave agreed. "Not precisely the same, but similar. I examined Mr. Berryhill's body before Cecil Greenwood prepared it for burial, and I was as mystified by its condition as I am by this case."

Jackson narrowed his eyes and moved a step closer to the man on the table. All of Berryhill's face had been gone, destroyed by some unknown means. But about a third of this man's face remained, the lower third.

"He's still got a mouth," Jackson said. "Maybe he can talk."

The other four men in the room stared at him. Finally, Brennan said, "Have you gone loco, Jackson? He ain't conscious, and never will be again!"

Jackson ignored the sheriff and looked at

138

the medico instead. "What if you gave him a powerful stimulant, Doctor?"

"With the punishment he's already endured, it would probably kill him immediately," Musgrave answered.

"But he's going to die anyway, isn't he?"

"Certainly. With that much trauma and blood loss, no other outcome is possible."

"Then you wouldn't be risking anything," Jackson pointed out, "and he might come around enough to tell us what happened to him."

Musgrave frowned dubiously, but Brennan said, "What about it, Doc? Is what he's sayin' possible?"

"Perhaps," Musgrave said, obviously reluctant. "But I'd still advise against it."

"Do it," Brennan said with a curt nod. "We gotta get to the bottom of this any way we can."

Still muttering protests, the doctor prepared a hypodermic injection. In a quiet voice, Everett started to explain Musgrave's actions, but the gunslinger silenced him with a look.

"I know what he's doing," Jackson said. "I was the one who suggested it, remember?"

Musgrave lifted the injured man's arm and injected the stimulant directly into a vein. By the time he lowered the arm to the examining table, the man groaned and tried to stir. Musgrave put a hand on his shoulder to hold him down.

"If you want to ask questions, I'd advise you to do it quickly," he snapped at Brennan.

The sheriff stepped closer, although it obviously bothered him to do so. He leaned down and said in a hoarse voice, "Who did this to you, mister?"

The injured man moved his head. His ears were largely intact, and he must have heard Brennan. Under the hideous wound, his mouth moved. Jackson and Everett leaned closer too, anxious to hear whatever the man said.

"L-light . . . b-balls of . . . light . . ."

Brennan glanced up. "That don't make no sense."

"Who are you?" Jackson asked, ignoring the sheriff's warning look and the earlier admonition to keep his mouth shut. "What's your name?"

"M-Matt . . . Harcourt."

"Damn it!" Brennan burst out. "I know Harcourt. He's another Winged T rider!"

"H-hand . . ."

Brennan looked down at Matt Harcourt's hand, then awkwardly clasped it, figuring that was what Harcourt was asking him to do.

Harcourt didn't seem to feel it. He said again, "H-hand . . . hand of God . . . said he was . . . hand of God . . . on earth." Suddenly his back arched off the examining table, and Brennan grunted as the cowboy's hand squeezed his with bone-crushing force. "Lucy! Lucy! He said . . . we was s-sinners . . . said he was gonna punish us . . . for God . . . hand of God . . . hand of —"

Harcourt fell back on the table. The breath that gusted from his mouth carried with it the stench of carrion.

"I told you," Musgrave said. "His heart gave out under the strain. I told you he couldn't survive such a stimulant."

"He was going to die anyway," Jackson said. "You told us that too. And now we know who he was and who killed him."

Brennan swung to face him. "What the hell are you talkin' about? We know who he was, but we still don't know who did that to him."

"Sure we do. It was a ball of light calling itself the Hand of God." Jackson shrugged and smiled faintly. "Find that and you've got your killer."

CHAPTER 13

The farmer who had found Matt Harcourt and brought him into town was named Carl Gafford. He was on his way to El Paso, he explained, hoping to make a fresh start there after his farm in Comanche County had failed.

He sat in Sheriff Brennan's office a short time after Harcourt's death and twisted his hat in his hands. "I don't know what else to tell you, Sheriff," he said. "I found that poor fella out there, about ten miles northwest of town, just like you seen him. I thought he was dead at first and was fixin' to bury him, but then he moaned and I knowed he was alive. I got him here just as fast as I could, but I didn't figure it'd do any good. Not the way he looked." Gafford gazed around at Brennan, Jackson, and Everett. "What in God's name could *do* a thing like that to a man?"

Brennan grunted. "That's what I've been

tryin' to find out." He sat behind his old, scarred desk with his shoulders slumped and a frown on his weather-beaten face. "It don't make sense, none of it. I'm givin' some serious thought to callin' in the Texas Rangers."

"Before you do that," Jackson said, "tell me what you know about Matt Harcourt."

Brennan glared at him. "Why in blazes should I do that? You ain't a lawman, Jackson. You're just a fiddle-footed gun-thrower!" The sheriff pointed at Everett. "And you can just keep your mouth shut, youngster. I've heard enough about the press."

Everett held up his hands, palms out. "I'm only here as an observer, Sheriff."

"And I've had some experience tracking down killers," Jackson said.

"You mean you've done some bounty huntin'," Brennan snapped.

Jackson shrugged and didn't say anything.

"Oh, hell." Brennan got up and went over to the black cast-iron stove in the corner, where a coffeepot simmered. He poured himself a cup, but didn't offer any to the other men. As he turned to face them again, he went on. "Harcourt rode for the Winged T, like I said. I don't know much about him other than that. He was just another cowpoke. Never got into any trouble around here except for when he got likkered up a time or two and went on a snort. He slept it off back there in one of the cells, paid his fine the next mornin', and went back to the ranch, hangover and all. And he hasn't even done that in the past six months or so. Seems to have settled down a mite."

"Sheriff?" Gafford spoke up. "Can I go now? You don't need me for anything else, do you?"

Brennan shook his head. "No, I reckon not." He reached in his pocket, pulled out a five-dollar gold piece, and slapped it in Gafford's hand. The farmer looked surprised, but took the coin. "Buy some supplies before you pull out for El Paso," the lawman went on in a gruff voice. "Your wife and those young'uns looked a mite hungry."

"Yes, sir, Sheriff, I'll sure do that," Gafford said as he got to his feet and clapped the battered hat on his head. "And I thank you kindly."

After the farmer was gone, Brennan took a noisy slurp of his coffee and then said to Jackson and Everett, "Ain't no reason the two of you should say anything about that. Damned if I want the county commissioners to hear that I was feelin' charitable toward that sodbuster. They're liable to decide that they're payin' me too much and cut my salary."

"About Harcourt," Jackson prodded.

"Oh, yeah. I reckon I'll take a ride out to the Winged T this afternoon and ask Mr. Tillman and Ned Dawson about him. One of them might know where he was and what he was doin' last night."

"Dawson might," Jackson said, "but Tillman won't. I'm not sure he really knows much of anything about what goes on out there."

"I suppose you two are gonna invite yourselves to go along with me."

"We're just trying to help, Sheriff," Everett said.

"Tryin' to get a story to write up for your newspaper is more like it." Brennan reached for his hat. "Well, come on if you're goin' with me."

However, as they stepped out of the sheriff's office onto the boardwalk, they saw that they weren't going to have to go very far. A buggy was rolling down the street toward them, with Benjamin Tillman at the reins. Ned Dawson rode alongside the buggy on horseback.

Brennan lifted a hand to hail them, but that wasn't necessary. Tillman and Dawson were already heading straight for the lawman's office. Tillman pulled back on the reins and brought the pair of buggy horses to a halt. Dawson stopped beside him.

"Good afternoon, Sheriff," Tillman said. He glanced curiously at Jackson and Everett, who stood to one side of Brennan, and then went on. "I need your help. One of my men is missing."

"Let me guess," Brennan said. "You're talkin' about Matt Harcourt."

Both of the visitors from the Winged T looked surprised. "How in blazes did you know that?" Ned Dawson asked as his bushy eyebrows rose.

Brennan jerked a thumb along the street. "Because his body is down at Greenwood's undertaking parlor right now."

"He's dead?" Tillman said. "Good Lord!"

Dawson chewed at his mustache for a couple of seconds, then asked, "What happened to him? He get in a gunfight here in town or somethin' like that?"

The sheriff shook his head and said, "He didn't die here in Death Head Crossing. A family of pilgrims passin' through these parts found his body outside of town this mornin' and brought it in."

"You know that for a fact?" snapped Dawson. "Maybe the folks who brought him in just pretended to find him. Maybe they

146

ambushed Matt, killed him, and robbed him."

"You didn't see that sodbuster and his wife and kids," Brennan said. "They wouldn't hurt nobody."

"How do you know he died violently?" Jackson asked, his voice quiet but penetrating. "Maybe Harcourt dropped dead of natural causes."

Dawson glared at him. "What the hell are you gettin' at? I just figured somebody must've killed him. Matt was a young fella, hale and hearty. It don't make sense he would've dropped dead."

"He didn't," Brennan said. "The same thing happened to him that happened to Luther Berryhill."

"My God!" Tillman cried in a ragged voice. "Will these horrors never end?"

"Only two men have died," Jackson pointed out.

"Only?" Tillman repeated. "Only? Isn't that a rather callous attitude to take, Mr. Jackson? And they were *my* men, men who rode for my brand."

Brennan jerked his head toward the office door. "Come on inside," he ordered. "We got to talk about this."

Tillman complied, stepping down from the buggy and handing the reins to Dawson so that the foreman could deal with them. Brennan added, "You too, Ned."

"Be there in a second," Dawson said as he swung down from the saddle. He began tying his horse and the buggy team to the hitch rack.

A moment later, the five men were inside Brennan's office. Tillman sat down gingerly on the old sofa with its busted springs. Dawson stood beside him. Brennan went behind the desk but kept his hat on as he said, "Tell me about Harcourt disappearin' from the ranch."

"He rode off last night after supper," Dawson said. "He didn't say where he was goin', and I don't reckon anybody asked him."

"I'll bet you have a pretty good idea, though," Jackson put in.

Brennan glared at him. "I'm askin' the questions here."

"Then ask them who Lucy is," Jackson said.

Although Tillman just looked blank at the mention of the woman's name, Jackson could tell from the reaction on the face of Dawson that the Winged T foreman recognized it. So did Brennan, for that matter. "Damn it," the lawman ground out. "Don't tell me Harcourt was sneakin' over to the Vance place and sniffin' around that

148

woman."

Dawson grimaced and then shrugged in resignation. "Reckon he was. Me and some o' the boys knew about it, but we figured it was none of our business."

"What's this?" Tillman demanded. "Was Matt involved in some sort of . . . illicit affair with a married woman?"

"He was seein' Lucy Vance, all right," Dawson said with a sigh. "I would've had a talk with him sooner or later, told him he ought to think twice about doin' such a thing. Hell, if Fowler Vance had ever caught 'em together, he likely would've shot 'em both. . . ."

Dawson's voice trailed off as he realized what he was saying.

"Harcourt wasn't shot," Brennan reminded them. "And I don't reckon Vance would've had any reason to kill Luther Berryhill either. I don't think we can blame him for these killin's, but I'm sure gonna find out where he was last night anyway."

"This is terrible, just terrible," Tillman muttered. "One of my men engaging in adultery."

Jackson's mouth tightened. He didn't understand how anybody could think that fooling around with a married woman was worse than having your face blown off by some mysterious means, but he remembered that Tillman had been a seminary student back East. Obviously, Tillman took such things very seriously.

Jackson had something else on his mind too. "Maybe somebody ought to ride out and check on this Mrs. Vance," he suggested.

"You're right," Brennan said. "If Harcourt went over to the Vance place last night and wound up like he did, something might've happened to the woman too." He started toward the door.

Tillman shot up off the sofa. "We're going with you."

Brennan looked like he wanted to argue, but then he just shrugged. "Suit yourself. I got to warn you, though, what we find out there may not be pretty."

"I want to know the truth, whether it's pretty or not," Tillman said.

For just about the first time, Jackson agreed with the rancher about something. He wanted to know the truth too.

As they followed Brennan, Tillman, and Dawson out of the sheriff's office, Jackson glanced over at his young companion and asked, "You ready to do some more riding, Everett?"

"I don't seem to have any choice in the

matter," Everett replied. "If something happened to Mrs. Vance, I want to know about it." He sighed. "Oh, well. At least the swelling has gone down a little from before."

CHAPTER 14

They got the same horse Everett had used before from the livery stable and started out of town after Brennan, Tillman, and Dawson, who had set out a few minutes before them. As they rode past the church, Everett said, "What do you think that Hand of God business was about?"

"Just what it sounds like," Jackson replied. "Somebody who thinks he's doing the Lord's work is going around killing folks he considers sinners. Look at who's wound up dead so far. Berryhill guzzled who-hit-John, played cards, and went upstairs with the calico cats at the Big Bend. That fella Harcourt was messing around with a married woman."

"Luther Berryhill was hardly the only person around here doing the things you mentioned," Everett pointed out. "If behaving like that was a death sentence, there wouldn't be very many men left in Texas,

I'd wager!"

Jackson chuckled. "You might be right about that. But maybe this Hand of God hombre is just getting started on his chores."

Everett took off his derby and sleeved sweat from his forehead. "That's an unsettling thought. Who could be so deranged as to think that committing cold-blooded murder is doing the Lord's work?"

Jackson used a thumb to point over his shoulder at the whitewashed building they had just passed. "Reverend Driscoll back there seems to take a pretty dim view of folks who break the Commandments."

"But he's a preacher," Everett protested. "He's *supposed* to disapprove of sinners."

Jackson saw the buggy a couple of hundred yards ahead of them, flanked by two riders he knew to be Sheriff Brennan and Ned Dawson. "Then you've got Tillman," he mused. "He said he used to be a seminary student. Maybe he left school because he was too pious even for the seminary."

Everett looked like he wanted to argue, but then he frowned in thought for a moment and finally said, "He *did* seem more bothered by Harcourt's romance with Mrs. Vance than he was by the fact that the man was dead."

Jackson nodded. "Somebody who's bound

and determined that he's doing what El Señor Dios wants him to can talk himself into just about anything, I expect."

"But Mr. Tillman seemed completely surprised when the sheriff said that Harcourt was dead. And he acted like he didn't know anything about what was going on between Harcourt and Mrs. Vance."

"Yeah. He *acted* like it."

Everett rode along in silence for several seconds, then shook his head. "I don't believe it, about either Reverend Driscoll or Mr. Tillman. They just don't seem like killers to me. Besides, there are things that still haven't been explained. What are those balls of light Harcourt mentioned, and what caused those horrible injuries?"

"I'm still chewing on that," Jackson admitted.

They pushed their horses to a slightly faster pace in order to catch up to the other three men. They did so shortly, and the five of them were all together when they reached the ranch owned by Fowler Vance. Brennan and Dawson had led the way, since they knew where the spread was. Jackson studied the terrain and estimated that Vance's place was several miles east of the Winged T. The two ranges probably bordered on each other.

As they drew closer to the house, Brennan suddenly reined in and motioned for the others to stop too. As they did so, the sheriff exclaimed, "What the hell is *that?*"

Jackson had already heard it too. Now all of them could plainly hear the high-pitched wailing that came from inside the ranch house.

A couple of men came hurrying around the house from the direction of the barn. Their swarthy faces and broad-brimmed sombreros marked them as Mexicans, probably vaqueros who rode for Fowler Vance. The fact that Brennan seemed to know them confirmed that guess on Jackson's part.

"Señor Brennan!" one of the men said over the wailing. "It is terrible, terrible!"

"Muy malo," the other vaquero agreed.

"What's happened here?" Brennan asked. Jackson suspected that they all knew the answer to that already.

"Señor Vance, he was on the porch with Señora Vance when we rode up." The man made the sign of the cross. "He was crying like an animal in a trap. You can hear him."

"She's dead?" a grim-faced Brennan asked.

Both of the Mexicans looked down at the ground as if ashamed and nodded.

"Where was Vance last night? Where were the two of you?"

"Señor Vance rode up to Fort Stockton yesterday, to talk to the commandant at the fort about buying some beef cattle for the soldiers. Paco and I . . . we rode to the cantina in Death Head Crossing. There are señoritas there, *muy bonita.* . . ."

"Yeah, yeah, I know," Brennan said. "You were gone all night?"

Both men bobbed their heads. "*Sí,* we just returned a short time ago and found . . . and found Señor Vance and the señora . . . like that."

"She had no clothes on," the other man added in a hushed voice. "And her face . . . *Aiee, Dios mio!*"

"What are they doing inside?" Brennan asked.

"Señor Vance, he took his jacket off and placed it over her. Then he picked her up and carried her into the house. He has not stopped mourning since then."

Jackson said, "Do you know what time Vance was supposed to get back today?"

The vaqueros looked at him, then looked at Brennan. The sheriff nodded for them to answer the question.

"He was not supposed to leave Fort Stockton until this morning. He could not possibly have reached here long before we did."

"We planned to be back here on the rancho before he arrived," the other man added. "But the beds in the back rooms of the cantina were so comfortable and the señoritas were so soft . . ."

Brennan made a curt gesture. "Never mind about that." With a creak of saddle leather, he swung down from his mount and handed the reins to one of the vaqueros. "Better get this over with," he muttered.

Jackson, Everett, and Dawson dismounted too. Dawson looked at Tillman and asked, "You comin', Boss?"

Tillman's face was pale. He swallowed and said, "No, I . . . I'll wait here in the buggy."

"Suit yourself," Dawson said. He stepped up onto the porch with the other three men.

Brennan stopped in the open doorway and said, "You fellas wait here. We got to show a little respect for Vance and not go crowdin' in on him all at once."

Jackson would have preferred to go into the house with the sheriff, but he didn't think it was important enough to press Brennan about it. He hooked his thumbs in his gun belt and leaned a shoulder against one of the posts that held up the porch roof. Everett and Dawson stood nearby, shifting their feet awkwardly.

"Fowler?" they heard the sheriff say as he crossed the front room and paused in another doorway. "Fowler, it's Ward Brennan. I'm mighty sorry about what — Damn it, put down that gun!"

At Brennan's startled outcry, Jackson lunged through the door and was across the front room in a couple of long, fast strides. He reached the other door in time to see a middle-aged man pull the trigger of the revolver he had pressed to his head. The gun roared, and the recoil flung it out of Fowler Vance's suddenly nerveless fingers. Vance went down hard, leaving a spray of blood and gray matter on the wall beside the place where he'd been standing. The bullet had bored through his brain and exploded out the other side of his head, taking a sizable chunk of skull with it.

Sheriff Brennan stood just inside the bedroom, one hand outstretched helplessly toward the man who had just killed himself. Slowly, the lawman lowered his arm. Fresh lines had been etched into his face around his mouth.

"Damn it," Brennan said. "If we'd got here a few minutes earlier —"

"You might have stopped him this time," Jackson said in a flat voice. "But you probably wouldn't have been around to stop him the next time he tried to blow his brains out. And chances are there would have been a next time."

The body of Lucy Vance had been placed on the bed. Jackson could only imagine the care and gentleness with which Vance must have lowered his wife onto the mattress. She lay on her back, with Vance's jacket over her face and her breasts. The rest of her body was nude. Jackson reached down, pulled up the bottom of the bedspread, and draped it over her.

"I don't want to do this," Brennan muttered as he reached for Vance's jacket, "but I reckon I got to."

Everett and Dawson had reached the doorway of the bedroom by now. Outside in the buggy, Tillman called, "Ned! What was that shot? What happened in there? Ned!"

Brennan lifted the jacket. Everett made a sound in his throat and turned his head away. Dawson muttered a curse. Jackson was expressionless as he studied the raw, bloody, empty expanse where Lucy Vance's face had once been. The red-smeared skull that was left leered up at them.

"Just like Berryhill," Brennan said as he replaced the jacket.

"Harcourt rode over here last night to be

with her," Jackson said. He wanted to think about what had happened, rather than what was under that jacket. "Somebody came up outside the house while they were together. Harcourt pulled his trousers on and went out to see what was going on. Mrs. Vance must have followed him. Then, whoever it was . . . did that." He gestured toward the bed. "Only, Harcourt didn't die right away. He survived somehow, but I'll bet the killer, or killers, thought he was dead. They rode off and left both of them on the porch to be found later. Sometime after that, Harcourt came to and crawled off. He couldn't see anymore and was probably in such pain that he didn't know where he was or what he was doing. I reckon it was just pure instinct that kept him going until that sodbuster found him."

"How in blazes do you know all that?" Brennan demanded.

"Vance and those two vaqueros left quite a few hoofprints out front when they rode up," Jackson said, "but they didn't wipe out all the marks Harcourt left in the dirt when he crawled away. I noticed there were two big bloodstains on the porch too, so that has to be where it happened."

Brennan rubbed his jaw. "Yeah, that makes sense, I suppose."

"Ned!" Tillman called again from outside.

Brennan jerked his head toward the door and told Dawson, "Go tell him what's goin' on."

"Fine," Dawson said. "I'll be glad to get outta here, to tell you the truth. It stinks like hell."

He was right about that. The coppery smell of blood filled the air, along with the stench from Vance's voided bowels. As if death wasn't bad enough already, it was also damned undignified sometimes.

Still rubbing his jaw wearily, Brennan looked down at what was left of Fowler Vance and said, "I reckon when he rode up and found her like that, he couldn't stand the idea of livin' without her. He was quite a bit older than her, but he doted on her. Probably left her alone too much, but that don't mean he didn't love her."

"Only good thing about it," Jackson said, "is that he likely died without knowing for sure that she was carrying on with Harcourt."

Brennan snorted. "That's pretty cold comfort."

"In this world, you'd better take what comfort you can get, wherever you can get it," Jackson said.

CHAPTER 15

There was a wagon in the barn. The two vaqueros hitched a team of draft horses to it and brought it around to the front of the house. Benjamin Tillman and Ned Dawson had already started back to the Winged T. Jackson and Brennan carried out Lucy Vance's body, which by now was securely wrapped in the bedspread, and placed it in the back of the wagon. The Mexicans brought out Fowler Vance and lowered his body to the wagon bed beside that of his wife, then spread a blanket over him.

Everett stood to one side, trying to watch everything with a newspaperman's objectivity . . . and trying at the same time not to be sick to his stomach.

He wasn't sure how Jackson could look at all these terrible things and not be affected. Maybe he was just good at holding in his feelings. Or maybe the years he had spent as a gunslinger had hardened him to human suffering. Jackson must have seen a lot of violent death in his life.

"Cecil Greenwood's gonna be a rich man if this keeps up," Brennan commented when both bodies were loaded in the wagon. "Four deaths in a matter of a few days." The sheriff shook his head. "All of 'em buried with closed coffins too."

The vaqueros climbed onto the wagon seat. They would take the vehicle into town. Jackson, Everett, and Brennan mounted up and fell in alongside.

The trip to Death Head Crossing passed mostly in silence. Everett thought about everything Jackson had said. While it certainly seemed like Jackson might be right about the killer being motivated by a belief that he was doing God's work, Everett still couldn't bring himself to believe that Reverend Martin Driscoll or Benjamin Tillman were responsible for the grisly murders.

But he couldn't be completely sure one of the men wasn't guilty either. *Somebody* had killed Berryhill, Harcourt, and Mrs. Vance, and Fowler Vance's death could also be laid at the feet of the mysterious Hand of God, even though Vance had actually taken his own life.

When they reached the settlement, the wagon with its grim cargo naturally attracted a lot of attention. Brennan told the vaqueros to head straight for Greenwood's undertaking parlor, and he rode along to see that no one interfered. Jackson turned his horse toward the Big Bend, saying, "I need a drink."

So maybe he was human after all, Everett thought. Before he could announce his intention to join Jackson at the saloon, he heard his name being called.

He looked around to see Malcolm Graham hurrying toward him on foot. The balding newspaperman lifted a hand in greeting and said, "I heard there was some trouble out at Fowler Vance's ranch. Judging by the looks of what that wagon is carrying, I'd say the rumors must be right."

Everett reined in and nodded. Suddenly he wanted to talk to a fellow journalist, so he called to Jackson, "You go ahead. I'll see you later."

Jackson nodded and rode on toward the saloon.

Gratefully, Everett dismounted. He said, "You've heard about the man who was brought in this morning?"

Graham nodded. "Yes, I talked to Dr. Musgrave about him and also went down to Cecil's to take a look at the body." A shudder went through him. "It was almost as bad as Luther Berryhill's."

"Mrs. Vance's was worse," Everett said in a low voice.

"So she really is dead? But . . . there were *two* bodies in the wagon."

"Her husband killed himself. I suppose the poor man thought that he just couldn't live without her."

Graham said, "Why don't you come over to the office with me? I'd like to hear the whole story."

Everett forced a smile. "That would mean cooperating with a rival newspaperman."

"I don't see what rivalry we could possibly have," Graham said with a laugh. "I put out a little cattle town weekly. You work for one of the largest and most respected newspapers in the country."

"Well . . . I don't suppose it would hurt anything to talk about it." To tell the truth, Everett thought, he was anxious for a little conversation with someone who wasn't quite so taciturn as Hell Jackson.

The two men walked down the street to the office of the Death Head Crossing *Weekly Journal.* It was located in a small storefront with the newspaper's name painted on one of the windows. As they approached, Graham gestured toward the window and said, "Some of us here in town would like to change the name of the place. Death Head Crossing really just isn't a suitable name for a settlement."

"What would you call it?" Everett asked.

"Oh, I don't know. There's a place called Horsehead Crossing over on the Pecos River. People seem to like the word *crossing.* There are some cottonwoods along the creek. We could call the town Cottonwood Crossing."

Everett nodded. "It's certainly not as grim. But it's not as unusual and striking either."

"That's what we want if the town is going to continue to grow and become more civilized."

It was none of Everett's business what the citizens of the settlement called it. He assumed that he wouldn't be staying here too long. Once Jackson moved on, so would he.

Graham opened the door and led the way into the office. Everett instantly smelled the familiar tang of printer's ink. A railing divided the room. One desk sat in front of it while two more were behind it. Beyond those desks were the composing trays, the large racks of type, and the bulky printing press itself.

To Everett's surprise, a woman stood next to the printing press, wielding a wrench and trying to work a balky bolt loose on the machine. She wore a heavy canvas apron that was stained with ink over her dress. When Everett and Graham came in, she turned to look at them and exasperatedly blew a strand of blond hair out of her face. It had fallen over her eyes as she strained at the bolt.

"I can't get this loose, Malcolm," she said. "Can you give me a hand?"

Everett suppressed the impulse to volunteer to help her. She was probably Graham's wife, and Everett didn't want to offend anyone.

Graham chuckled and said, "Of course, my dear." He opened a gate in the railing and stepped through. "This will just take me a minute, Everett. My sister is a genius at keeping that old press running, but sometimes she lacks the brute strength required for the task."

"Your sister?" Everett repeated. He had already noticed that the blonde wore no wedding ring on her finger.

"That's right," Graham said. "Rosalie, this is Mr. Everett Sidney Howard of the New York *Universe.* Mr. Howard, my sister, Miss Rosalie Graham."

She smiled distractedly at him and said, "The New York *Universe.* That's a real paper. Malcolm and I have dreamed of having something like that someday. Nothing as big as the *Universe,* of course, but something better than a weekly with a broken-down press."

Graham took the wrench from her. "Be careful, Rosalie, you're going to have Mr. Howard thinking that we're not proud of the work we do here."

"Pride is one thing. Being able to afford a better press is another." She wiped her hand on her apron, looked at it skeptically, and went on. "No, still not clean enough to shake hands. Let's just say I'm pleased to meet you, Mr. Howard."

"The pleasure is all mine," Everett said.

She was somewhat older than him, probably in her late twenties, and she was certainly attractive. Enough so, in fact, that he found it odd she had never married. That was none of his business, of course, so he tried to put it out of his mind.

Graham gripped the wrench firmly, threw his strength against it, and the stubborn bolt slowly came loose with a faint screeching sound. "There," Graham said when he had it loose enough so that it could be turned by hand.

"Good," Rosalie said. "I can replace that rotor now. What was all the commotion outside?"

Graham's tone grew more serious as he answered, "There's been another killing."

Rosalie looked surprised. "You mean besides that poor man who was brought in earlier today?"

"That's right. Mr. Howard knows all the details."

She turned to Everett, the press momentarily forgotten. "Can you tell us about it?"

Everett couldn't refuse that request. The story was going to be all over the settlement in a short time anyway, he thought, knowing how things were in small towns like this. He might as well make sure that the local paper got the facts, rather than any garbled version that might make the rounds later.

Graham and Rosalie sat down at the two desks behind the railing while Everett leaned on the railing itself. After riding out to Fowler Vance's ranch and back, he wasn't going to be interested in sitting down for a while. He spent the next half hour telling them almost everything he knew about the mysterious deaths plaguing the area. The only thing he held back was Jackson's speculation that the killer calling himself the Hand of God might be Reverend Driscoll or Benjamin Tillman. That still seemed preposterous to him, and anyway, there was no proof one way or the other.

"What an incredible story," Graham murmured when Everett was finished. He had been taking notes while Everett was talking, but now he pushed the pad of paper away from him. "I wouldn't feel right writing about it, though."

"Why not?" Everett asked. "I knew when I agreed to talk to you that you'd probably run the story in the *Journal*."

"This is your story," Graham insisted. "Why don't you write it for us?"

"We could even put out an extra edition," Rosalie suggested.

Everett's eyes widened a little. His byline on an extra? Even in a little newspaper like this one? It was tempting, but he had to shake his head.

"I'm sorry, I can't. I have a contract with the *Universe.* I have to honor it."

Graham sighed. "Yes, of course. I didn't even think of that. In that case . . ." He reached for his notes. "You're sure you don't mind?"

"Go ahead," Everett told him. "The eastbound stage comes through tomorrow, so I'll be writing up my own dispatch tonight and getting it in the mail to New York. You won't beat me into print by too many days."

Rosalie said, "You can write your dispatch

after you have dinner with us tonight. That's the least we can do for you."

"That's an excellent idea!" Graham said with a smile. "What do you say, Mr. Howard?"

Everett didn't have to think over the offer for very long, not with Rosalie looking at him with an expectant expression on her lovely face. "I say call me Everett," he replied, "and I'll be honored to accept your hospitality."

CHAPTER 16

Everett stopped by the saloon where Jackson was sitting at one of the rear tables, nursing a drink and idly laying out a hand of solitaire. Jackson had found that handling cards sometimes helped him to think, and he had quite a bit to ponder at the moment.

Not only did he have to wonder who was responsible for the gruesome deaths of four people and how those bizarre killings had been accomplished, but he also had to ask himself why the hell he cared. There was no payoff in it for him, and he had always been a man who went where the money took him. As he had told Everett, he wasn't actually a hired killer . . . but the way things had worked out, most of the jobs he'd taken on had involved shoot-outs and violent death sooner or later. He didn't think very often about the men who had gone down before his gun, figuring there was no point in it other than realizing that they were dead and he was still alive.

No one was paying him to solve these mysteries. As far as he could see, no one was *going* to pay him. He ought to just get on his horse and ride out, put Death Head Crossing behind him and forget the whole blamed thing. Satisfying his curiosity wasn't worth the time and effort and potential danger. True, he was providing what might be a heck of a story for Everett to write about, but he didn't like the youngster enough to make it all worthwhile.

He supposed he would have to leave it at the fact that sometimes a man had an itch he just had to scratch, whether it made sense or not.

Everett said he was going to be having supper with Malcolm Graham, the publisher of the local paper, and Graham's sister Rosalie.

"Unmarried sister?" Jackson asked with a faint smile as he moved a red jack onto a black queen.

"That's the impression I got. She doesn't wear a wedding ring, and she didn't mention having a husband. She works with her brother, and probably lives with him too."

"Nice to look at, is she?"

Everett reddened quite a bit, so that his face almost matched the color of his hair. "I suppose she's attractive. She's older than me, though. She must be twenty-seven or twenty-eight."

"Yeah, that's pretty old," Jackson said. "She still got her own teeth?"

"I'm sure I wouldn't know." Everett's voice was stiff with embarrassment.

"Well, you just go right ahead and enjoy your dinner with them."

"What are you going to do?"

"You're looking at it," Jackson said as he moved another card and then reached for his glass of whiskey. He sipped from it and sighed in satisfaction.

Everett pushed his chair back and got to his feet. "I'll see you later then."

Jackson nodded but didn't say anything.

He waited until Everett was gone, finishing his drink and the hand of solitaire while he was at it. Then he stood up and left the saloon as well.

Jackson went to the boardinghouse and got his horse from the stable out back. He saddled up and rode out of Death Head Crossing, avoiding the newspaper office as he did so because he didn't want Everett to see him leaving town. If the young reporter spotted him riding out, he would probably want to come along wherever Jackson was going.

Dusk settled over the landscape. In this part of Texas, night fell quickly once the sun slipped below the horizon. By the time Jackson had put a couple of miles behind him, the sky was dark and the stars were out.

Jackson rode in the general direction of the Winged T, but he didn't follow the main trail between the settlement and the ranch, the trail that Luther Berryhill's horse had taken instinctively when its rider was too drunk to navigate. Jackson stayed half a mile or so east of that route, which put him about halfway between the trail that led to the Winged T and the one to Fowler Vance's spread. Since the trails tended naturally to follow easier paths, the terrain was more rugged where Jackson rode, with quite a few hills and ridges. He let his horse pick its way along in the darkness, trusting to the animal's senses and instincts.

Jackson couldn't have said for sure what he was looking for out here. He was just looking. Twice in the past three nights, mysterious lights had appeared in this vicinity and people had died horrible deaths.

If those lights showed up again, he hoped that he would be on hand to see them. He wasn't particularly scared. In his experience, he had never run into anything that couldn't

175

be dealt with by a fast gun hand and a Colt full of bullets.

As he rode, he recalled hearing stories about some mysterious lights near the settlement of Marfa, farther west. Cowboys had been seeing elusive, dancing balls of illumination over there for several years now, and no matter how much people searched, they'd never been able to discover the truth behind the phenomenon. Jackson hadn't seen the Marfa lights himself, but he had heard about them. As far as he knew, they had never caused any trouble and certainly had never hurt anyone. Folks couldn't even seem to get near them. When anybody went looking, the lights were always somewhere else.

That wasn't the case here. The lights Matt Harcourt had seen had heralded his death. Jackson wondered if the so-called Hand of God had gotten the idea for his lights from the ones over by Marfa. That made as much sense as anything else about this business.

He remembered too Ned Dawson's comments about the Winged T having trouble with rustlers. Wideloopers often operated at night, so Jackson kept his eyes and ears open for any signs of that sort of activity too.

From time to time, he stopped to listen

intently, and it was during one such pause that he heard horses moving in the distance. Somebody besides himself was out and about tonight, and Jackson was willing to bet that whoever it was, they were up to no good.

He estimated that there were several riders off to his left, maybe a hundred yards away. He turned his horse in that direction and started riding toward the hoofbeats, moving slowly so that the sounds of his own horse wouldn't alert the men he was trailing.

After several minutes of following those unknown riders, Jackson heard something new — more hoofbeats, and the lowing of cattle. His mouth tightened. Those horsebackers were moving some stock. They were on Winged T range, he figured, but he would have been willing to bet that those men didn't work for Benjamin Tillman.

He hadn't found the mysterious lights, but he was pretty sure he had stumbled across some cow thieves hard at work.

What would he do about it if that was the case? he asked himself. He wasn't a lawman, and he didn't ride for the Winged T. He owed no allegiance to Benjamin Tillman. He figured there were probably five or six men pushing a jag of cattle through the hills.

If he interfered with them, there would be gunplay, and plenty of it. Jackson had never been one to run from superior odds, but in a corpse-and-cartridge session like that, he'd probably wind up the corpse. And for what? To save some cattle for a man who didn't much like being a rancher and probably shouldn't have come out here to Texas to start with?

On the other hand, Jackson reflected, if he could follow the rustlers and find out where they were holding their stolen stock, maybe discover who they were, the knowledge might come in handy somewhere on down the trail. He smiled faintly to himself as he continued to follow the sounds of men and horses and cattle through the night.

The rustlers were moving north. Jackson didn't know how far in that direction the boundaries of the Winged T extended, but he knew that a range of mountains lay that way. Chances were the rustlers held the cattle in some box canyon in those mountains while they changed the brands. Then they would drive the cows east to Fort Stockton or even San Angelo to dispose of them. Jackson had worked as a range detective on occasion, when the pay was right, and he knew how rustlers operated.

The landscape flattened out a little between the last of the ridges and the mountains in the distance. Jackson reined to a halt on top of the ridge and studied the landscape in front of him. His keen eyes spotted movement on the open, semiarid plains. He took the field glasses from his saddlebags and lifted them to his eyes. Focusing on the dark, moving mass, the glasses enabled him to see that his hunch had been correct. He picked out five riders pushing along a group of forty to fifty cattle, a good night's work for the rustlers. They had probably gathered the cows the night before and left them in some isolated coulee, blocking it off with brush so the animals couldn't get out, then returning tonight to drive them off Winged T range and up to the hideout.

Jackson stowed the field glasses away and lifted the reins, ready to ride down off the ridge and resume following the rustlers. But before he could do so, he heard the sudden crackle of brush off to his right. Somebody was there, and his hand moved instinctively toward his Colt as he twisted in that direction.

Flame stabbed from the muzzle of a gun and lit up the night for an instant. Jackson heard the crack of a rifle, and sensed as much as felt or heard the passage of a bullet close by his ear. He palmed out his revolver and brought it up, triggering twice in the direction of the muzzle flash as he jammed his boot heels into his horse's flanks and sent the animal lunging to the side.

Another shot blasted, and from the way Jackson's mount screamed and leaped, he knew the horse was hit. The horse didn't go down, though. Hauling on the reins, Jackson pulled it around in a tight turn and galloped toward the rifleman, firing again as he leaned forward over the horse's neck to make himself a smaller target.

His hat went flying in the air. He knew that a slug had plucked it from his head, which meant he had come within inches of dying. Instead of frightening him, that just made him more angry. He fired again and then, as the bushwhacker's rifle gouted flame once more, Jackson kicked his feet free of the stirrups and rolled out of the saddle as if he'd been hit by that last shot.

He landed hard on the ground and rolled over a couple of times. That took him behind a scrubby mesquite tree, where the ambusher couldn't see him. If the rifleman wanted to make sure Jackson was dead, he'd have to come out of hiding and approach the spot where the gunslinger had fallen.

Lying on his belly, Jackson gripped the Colt tightly and waited for that to happen.

CHAPTER 17

Malcolm and Rosalie Graham lived in a small house on one of Death Head Crossing's side streets, not far from the office of the *Weekly Journal.* Everett met them at the office and then walked with them to the house, through streets growing shadowy with twilight.

Normally at this time on a summer evening, children would still be out playing, but instead Everett heard their mothers calling them to come in. The women's voices had a nervous quality. The recent deaths had everyone in town on edge, and even though the mysterious Hand of God, whoever or whatever it was, had targeted adults so far, no mother wanted her children to be out after dark tonight.

It was a shame things had come to that, Everett thought as he watched several fireflies dancing merrily through the dusk. There ought to be children chasing happily after those bouncing, darting balls of light, laughing happily as they stretched out their hands to grasp them.

Everett broke stride as a realization hit him. From the way the doomed Matt Harcourt had described what happened at the Vance place, it must have seemed like giant fireflies he had seen in those final moments before his sight was blasted away forever.

Rosalie Graham put a hand on his arm. "Are you all right, Mr. Howard?" she asked.

"Yes, I just, ah, tripped a little," Everett said. "These Western boots, you know. I guess I'm still not completely used to them. You have to wear them, though, if you're going to ride horses."

With a smile, Graham said, "Or even if you don't, if you want to fit in out here."

"You're not from here? Texas, I mean."

"Oh, we're from Texas," Graham said. "We were both born and raised in Dallas. But I promise you, that's about as different from Death Head Crossing as you can imagine. Dallas is an actual city, like St. Louis or Chicago. Of course, I'm sure it's nothing compared to New York, but it's nothing like the rest of Texas either."

"How did you come to be all the way out here running a newspaper?" Everett had heard that it wasn't considered polite to ask a Westerner where he came from or what he had done in the past, but he didn't think there would be any harm in posing that question to a man like Malcolm Graham.

"I was always interested in writing," Graham replied. "I got a job on the Dallas *Herald* and worked there for several years before I decided I wanted to have my own paper. I saw a notice that the man who founded the *Weekly Journal* here in Death Head Crossing wanted to sell it and retire, so I wrote to him, made an offer, and here I am. I knew it would be a lot different from being in Dallas, but so far everything has been fine."

Everett turned to Rosalie and asked, "What about you, Miss Graham?" He hoped he wasn't being too inquisitive.

She didn't seem to mind answering the question. "Our parents had both passed away, so I decided to come with Malcolm and keep house for him."

"I'm sorry about your parents," Everett said.

"Of course, as it turned out, Rosalie does just as much work on the newspaper as I do," Graham went on. "I never dreamed she had such mechanical aptitude until the first time I saw her working on that old printing press."

Rosalie laughed. "I assure you, Malcolm, it took me by surprise too. But really, so much of it is just common sense. You can usually figure out how something works if you look at it long enough."

"You can, my dear, not me."

She laughed again, and since she was walking between Everett and her brother, she linked arms with both of them as they went down the street. The gesture was intimate enough to take Everett's breath away. Even though there were two layers of clothing between them, his and hers, he could feel the warmth of her arm against his side, and it sent tremors of pleasure through him.

When they reached the little house where the Grahams lived, Rosalie went into the kitchen to prepare supper while her brother asked Everett, "Would you care for some brandy? I keep a bottle on hand, even though it's not that easy to get out here."

"Why, yes, thank you."

Everett looked at the numerous books on shelves lining the front room while Graham poured the drinks. Graham handed a crystal snifter to him and said, "To your health, Mr. Howard."

"And to yours," Everett replied. After he had sipped the smooth liquor, he went on.

"But you should really call me Everett."

"Certainly. I'm Malcolm, and my sister is Rosalie, as you know."

Everett drank some more of the brandy. "The two of you seem to be an outpost of culture and civilization here in Death Head Crossing. Otherwise, it's just a dusty little cow town. No offense."

"None taken, I assure you," Graham replied with a smile. "We do our best."

"Do you know Mr. Benjamin Tillman? He's from Philadelphia. But of course, you'd know that."

Graham nodded. "Yes, we've met Mr. Tillman. I'm afraid he's not very happy out here. Adjusting and making the best of the situation seems to be beyond him. He'd be better off going back East where he belongs."

The bluntness of the appraisal surprised Everett a little. "I suppose he feels a responsibility to his family to do the best he can with the Winged T."

"Then he should hire a competent manager and leave the running of the place to him." Graham took a drink of the brandy and then shook his head. "Of course, it's none of my business, and anyway, Tillman's too proud and stubborn to do anything that reasonable. He's not going anywhere."

186

Rosalie appeared in the doorway between the parlor and the tiny dining room. "Supper is ready," she announced. "Pour me some of that brandy, will you, Mal?"

"Of course."

The meal was quite pleasant. Malcolm Graham told several stories about what it was like running a newspaper in a frontier town like Death Head Crossing, but for the most part he and his sister wanted to know everything about New York that Everett could tell them. He hadn't talked so much in a long time, especially not to such an appreciative audience. He had a grand time.

"What about this man Jackson?" Graham asked after he had refilled their brandies. "I've heard about him. He's supposed to be quite notorious."

A little shiver went through Rosalie. "I think I'd be afraid just to be around him."

"Oh, no, he's a fine fellow," Everett insisted. "Rough around the edges, of course, but you'd expect that of someone who's lived the life he has. He's been very friendly and helpful to me."

"Is he helping Sheriff Brennan investigate those mysterious deaths? He seems to always be around when something's going on."

"Well . . ." Everett was a little uneasy now,

187

because he didn't really know what Jackson was doing, or why. Clearly, Jackson wanted to get to the bottom of the killings, but he hadn't explained his motivation for doing so. Everett supposed he was just curious. "He's not actually assisting the sheriff, but he *is* investigating. Unofficially, I suppose you could say."

"Has he found out anything?" Graham smiled. "I hope you'll pardon my inquisitiveness. Journalistic curiosity. You understand."

"Of course," Everett said without hesitation. "No, as far as I know, neither Sheriff Brennan nor Mr. Jackson have been able to figure out who's to blame for those terrible deaths or even how they were accomplished. Mr. Jackson *did* find the tracks that Matt Harcourt left when he crawled away from the Vance place, where he was, uh . . ." He glanced at Rosalie.

She smiled. "Don't worry about offending my delicate sensibilities, Everett. I know that Mr. Harcourt was having an illicit romance with Mrs. Vance. The gossip around town is that that's why they were killed."

"Yes, by that so-called Hand of God," Graham said. "He must be a madman. You can't just go around killing people because they don't conform to your own notion of what's right and wrong."

"Some people do," Everett said. "Evidently, the man calling himself the Hand of God does. He killed Luther Berryhill for drunkenness and Harcourt and Mrs. Vance for their adultery."

Rosalie shook her head. "Terrible," she murmured. "Just terrible."

Everett couldn't argue, or even disagree, with that sentiment.

Rosalie changed the subject somewhat by leaning forward and saying, "Tell me . . . is Mr. Jackson's given name really Hell?"

Everett hesitated, not wanting to betray any sort of confidence, but when he thought about it, he wasn't sure he would be doing so. Jackson's name was well known. Everett nodded and said, "Yes, it really is."

"I thought maybe it was just a nickname," Graham said. "Good Lord, what sort of parent would name a child Hell?"

"From what I understand, Mr. Jackson's mother died giving birth to him," Everett explained. "His father was overcome by grief and turned that into resentment toward his son. He felt that by denying him his wife, the baby had damned him to hell. So that's the name he gave the boy."

"I never heard of such a thing," Rosalie said. "He should have been ashamed."

Everett shrugged. "I suppose Mr. Jackson

189

could have gotten it changed later if he wanted to. It must not bother him too much, or he would have."

"He sounds like a fascinating individual," Graham said. "Do you think he would agree to an interview?"

"For your paper, you mean?"

Graham nodded. "Of course. People always like to read about famous gunmen like Wild Bill Hickok and John Wesley Hardin and Hell Jackson. Their fascination with such flamboyant characters seems to be endless."

Everett didn't think Jackson was all that flamboyant. To look at him, you'd take him for a drifting cowpoke. It was only when you noticed how well cared for his gun and holster were, and how his pale blue eyes were always alert and roving as they searched for trouble, that you realized how much danger truly lay within his compact, well-muscled form.

"I don't know whether he'd be interested in doing an interview or not," Everett said in reply to Graham's question. "You'd have to ask him."

"Perhaps you could intercede on our behalf, since you're his friend."

Was he? Everett wondered. Was he really Hell Jackson's friend? Just because the

190

gunslinger was allowing him to hang around didn't mean that they were friends, as much as Everett might wish that was the case. But he said, "I'll see what I can do."

"Thanks," Graham said with a smile. "I'm sure the *Journal's* readers would be interested in learning more about such a notorious man."

"But don't think that we only invited you to supper tonight so we could ask for your help, Everett," Rosalie put in. She reached over and rested a hand on the back of his hand. "You're very good company, and we certainly enjoyed hearing all about New York, didn't we, Mal?"

"We certainly did," Graham agreed.

Everett felt himself blushing as he sat there, but there wasn't a thing he could do about it. The touch of Rosalie's hand was so warm and nice, and the way she smiled at him made him feel . . . he couldn't even begin to describe it.

"I'll see what I can do," he said again, and Rosalie Graham squeezed his hand.

CHAPTER 18

Jackson's horse kept running after he deliberately toppled out of the saddle. But even though it was night, the stars overhead were bright and Jackson had been out in the open enough so that he felt sure the bushwhacker had seen him fall. As he lay there in utter silence, he heard the metallic sound of a Winchester's lever being cocked, followed by the tinny clatter of the empty cartridge that was ejected falling among some rocks.

He didn't know if any of his shots had hit the hidden rifleman, but the sound of the Winchester being readied for another shot told Jackson the man definitely wasn't out of the fight yet. But to continue it, the bushwhacker was going to have to come out into the open.

Jackson wondered briefly if the rustlers out on the flat had heard the shots. They must have, because such sounds traveled well at night in this thin air. They might believe that some of the Winged T cowboys were after them, in which case they would drive those stolen cows that much faster.

But the rifleman who had ambushed Jackson might be one of them, left behind solely for the purpose of cutting down anybody who tried to follow the rustlers toward the mountains. In that case, the thieves would be more likely to exchange grins in the starlight as they figured that whoever had been unlucky enough or unwise enough to trail them had just been ventilated.

Jackson's hand tightened harder on the butt of the Colt. He had only one round left in the cylinder, but he couldn't reload because even the tiny sounds he would make doing so might give away the fact that he was still alive.

Hoofbeats suddenly rattled not far off. As they faded, Jackson grimaced and breathed a curse. The bushwhacker was lighting a shuck out of there, rather than risking his life by checking to make sure that his quarry was dead.

Or maybe it was a trick. Maybe the rifleman was trying to lure Jackson into making a mistake, just as Jackson had done to him.

Time dragged by as the hoofbeats faded away completely and Jackson continued to lay there silent and motionless for at least a quarter of an hour. Finally, he risked taking fresh cartridges from the loops on his shell belt and thumbing them into the cylinder of his Colt. That didn't draw any reaction from the surrounding darkness. Neither did his movements when he stood up, staying in the shadow of the mesquite tree for a few moments before venturing out in search of his horse.

He found the animal fairly quickly. The horse didn't come when he whistled for it, but it had only gone down the ridge about a hundred yards before stopping to crop at some of the tufts of hardy bunchgrass growing out of the rocky slope. Jackson ran his hands over the horse, and found a shallow gash in its rump where one of the bushwhacker's bullets had clipped it. The horse wasn't hurt badly. Once they got back to town where Jackson could see what he was doing, he had some ointment in his saddlebags that would take care of the injury.

And there was no reason not to turn around and go back to town, he reflected bitterly. By now the rustlers and that stolen stock they had been driving were long gone, and Jackson wouldn't be able to pick up their trail until morning. He wondered if it would be worth taking the time and trouble to do so even then.

He swung up into the saddle and turned the horse toward Death Head Crossing. As he rode through the night he continued to be alert for any more signs of trouble. He watched for mysterious balls of light too, but didn't see a thing out of the ordinary. Whoever or whatever had murdered those folks wasn't abroad in the darkness tonight.

When Jackson got back to the settlement, he put his horse in the stable behind the boardinghouse, then by the light of a lantern he lit, rubbed the animal down good and daubed ointment on the bullet gash. "Sorry I got you shot, old fella," he said as he patted the horse's shoulder.

He wasn't ready to turn in, so he headed for the Big Bend Saloon. As he reached the boardwalk in front of the saloon, he saw Everett coming along the street from the other direction. The young reporter noticed Jackson too, and smiled and raised a hand in greeting.

"I figured you went back to the boardinghouse after you got tired of playing solitaire," Everett commented as they met in front of the batwings.

"I stepped out to get some fresh air," Jackson said. He didn't mention his trip to the Winged T or spotting the rustlers before he was ambushed. He intended to continue making these nocturnal jaunts as he searched for the truth of what was going on around here, and he didn't want Everett insisting on coming along. If Everett had been with him when he was bushwhacked tonight, the results could have been disastrous.

Instead, Jackson leaned his head toward the saloon's entrance and went on. "I was thinking about having another drink. Care to join me?"

"Yes, I'd like that," Everett said. "But I think I'd better stick to beer. I already had several glasses of brandy with Malcolm and Rosalie at dinner, and I don't want to get too muddled."

Jackson shouldered through the batwings. "Sounds like things went well with them."

"They're charming people. Very cultured really. Rather out of place in a town like this."

Jackson looked at Everett and frowned.

"Oh, I don't mean to insult the citizens of Death Head Crossing," Everett went on. "I'm sure they're all fine people. But you can't deny that life here is rather . . . raw."

"I've been to Chicago," Jackson said. "That's a bigger town than I ever want to visit again. Too damned many people everywhere you go. You can't walk down the streets without bumping into folks. And the air is full of smoke from the factories all the time." Jackson shrugged. "The lake's nice, I reckon, but I'd rather look at the Pacific Ocean or the Gulf of Mexico."

"To each his own, as the old saying goes." Jackson grunted. "Yeah."

They stopped at the bar for beers and carried the mugs over to an empty table. Jackson took the chair that put his back toward the wall.

"Malcolm asked me about you," Everett said. "In fact, he and Rosalie both seemed quite interested in you."

Jackson frowned into his beer. He wasn't sure if he liked that. "What did you tell them?"

"Just that we've been working together to try to find out the identity of the Hand of God and the reason behind the killings."

"Reckon we know the reason. That fella, whoever he is, doesn't like the way some folks live their lives. He figures that gives him the right to end those lives."

"That's certainly what it sounds like, from what little we actually know. And we wouldn't know that much if Matt Harcourt hadn't miraculously survived long enough to tell us."

Jackson took a long swallow of the cool

beer. "We would have found out soon enough," he said.

Everett looked puzzled. "What do you mean by that?"

"The Hand of God would have found some way to let everybody know." Jackson had been thinking quite a bit about the situation on his ride back into town. "You see, Everett, it doesn't do any good to kill people as an example if nobody knows that's why you're doing it. My hunch is that if Harcourt had died on the front porch of the Vance place like he was supposed to, in a few days your friend Graham would have gotten a letter from the Hand of God, explaining why Harcourt and Mrs. Vance and that cowboy Berryhill before them all had to die, and warning that if folks didn't straighten up and stop sinning, more of them would have the same thing happen to them. Whoever sent the letter would have demanded that Graham publish it in the paper." Jackson shrugged. "Now that doesn't have to happen, because everybody in town already knows about the Hand of God, and they're scared . . . which is just what the son of a bitch wants."

It was a long speech for Jackson, and he downed the rest of his beer when he was finished. On the other side of the table,

Everett stared at him, eyes widening as he thought about what the gunslinger had said.

"You're right," Everett said after a moment in a hushed voice. "It doesn't make sense any other way. But that still doesn't tell us who the Hand of God is, or how he killed those poor people."

"No," Jackson agreed, "it doesn't."

"Maybe Sheriff Brennan *should* call in the Texas Rangers."

"It may come to that."

"In the meantime, are you going to continue to investigate?"

"I don't see that it can hurt anything," Jackson replied with another shrug. "I thought I might ride out to the Winged T again tomorrow and have another talk with Tillman. Want to come along?"

"Of course!" Everett hesitated, then went on. "There's one other matter I need to discuss with you."

"Spit it out, then."

"Malcolm Graham wants to interview you and write a story about you for his newspaper."

Jackson's face hardened.

"I told them a little about you," Everett said, "but there's a great deal I don't know, of course. I told Mal and Rosalie that I would ask you about it."

"Mal and Rosalie," Jackson mused. "Sounds like you've gotten pretty friendly with them in a hurry."

"As I told you, they're fine people."

"And this Rosalie is a good-looking woman, I'd wager."

Everett flushed, the light scattering of freckles across his face blending in with the pinkness rising in his skin. "I just told them I would ask you about it," he said. "The decision is entirely yours."

"I'll think about it," Jackson said, more to ease Everett's mind than anything else. "I'm not too fond of the idea, though. There's been one or two dime novels written about me, and the varmints who wrote them didn't get much of anything right."

"Well, then, this could be your chance to set the record straight. You could tell people the truth about yourself."

Jackson frowned. He hadn't thought about it that way. Maybe Everett was right. Maybe sitting down and letting Malcolm Graham ask him a bunch of questions would be a good thing, even though the very idea of doing something like that made Jackson a mite uncomfortable. He had always been one to keep his feelings and his thoughts to himself. It wouldn't be easy to change now.

"I'll think about it," he said again as he

scraped his chair back and stood up. "For now, though, I'm ready to get some sleep."

Everett yawned. "Yes, it's been a long day."

Thinking about the rustlers he had given chase to and the ambush attempt that had almost ended his life, Jackson told himself that the day had been even longer than Everett knew.

CHAPTER 19

Benjamin Tillman had never been an early riser. He'd never had to be, since he had never held an actual job in his life. Money had never been one of his worries.

But just because he didn't have to be concerned about making a living didn't mean that he had no problems. He had plenty of problems.

Just as he had plenty of secrets.

The sun was well up when he climbed out of bed, dressed leisurely, and went downstairs. One of the Mexican servants brought him his breakfast in the dining room. He asked the woman, "Has my cousin come down yet this morning?"

She shook her head. "No, Señor, I have not seen her. Would you like me to go upstairs and see if she is awake?"

"No . . . no, that's all right. I'm sure Deborah will be down when she's ready."

He tried to concentrate on the coffee and

the food in front of him, but that was difficult to do because he found himself thinking about Deborah instead. The mental image of her lying in the big, soft bed in one of the guest rooms tormented him. He could picture her long, silky brown hair spread out around her head on the pillow. Her full lips would be parted softly as she breathed. The heat had probably caused her to kick the sheet off during the night as she slept, so that she would be uncovered, her nightdress twisted around her body and hiked up over her bare legs, the soft thighs parted. . . .

Tillman put down his fork and clenched both hands into fists as he rested them on the table. He closed his eyes and shuddered as he fought a literal, physical battle against the thoughts swirling unbidden through his head. It was a constant struggle for him not to think about being with Deborah, not to imagine the feel of her body under his hands or the taste of her lips against his mouth.

When he had received the letter from her stating her intention of coming to Texas to visit him this summer, he had been elated and terrified at the same time. More than anything else since coming out here from Philadelphia, he had missed seeing her, hearing the sound of her voice and her laughter. But he knew that if he was around her again, the same feelings that had bothered him in the past would come back. The feelings that had begun to plague him years earlier, when Deborah had just started to become a woman. Even then, he had wanted her. But she was his cousin, and even though such things were legal and in some cases not even frowned upon that much, he could not allow himself to succumb to such unnatural lust. He already knew that he had the calling to do the Lord's work, which made this burning desire to bed down with his own cousin that much more of a sin.

So he had prayed night and day and stayed away from Deborah as much as he could, even though she looked up to her older cousin Benjamin and considered him a great friend. He knew that it must have hurt her at times, the way he went to such lengths to avoid being around her, especially when they would have been alone. But he had to, for fear he would give in to temptation and take her into his arms and tell her how he really felt about her. He knew she would hate him for all eternity if he ever did that. The struggle to prevent that consumed him so that eventually he had been forced to leave the seminary. He could no longer stand his own hypocrisy.

For all those reasons, he had considered it a boon from God when his cousin Rufus died and left this ranch to the family back in Philadelphia. Tillman had jumped at the chance to travel to Texas and take over the running of the ranch. His other cousins, canny businessmen that they were, had thought it was a bad idea, that the Winged T would be more lucrative with an experienced manager in charge of it, but Benjamin had insisted. Since then, he had refused the suggestions in their carefully worded letters that he return home. The Winged T was his salvation . . . or rather, the thousands of miles between him and Deborah was.

Then she had decided to come out here for a visit, and he couldn't bring himself to refuse her even though he knew he should. Just as he had suspected would happen, she had tormented him unwittingly with her beauty, and the emotions he had denied for so long were back in full force.

He couldn't send her away, but he could do penance for his sin.

A soft footstep made him look up from the table. She entered the dining room, a smile on her lovely face. She wore a silken robe belted tightly around her waist, and he knew that underneath was only her night-dress and her smooth, warm flesh. "Good morning, Benjamin," she said. "How are you today?"

Drunk with lust for you, cousin, as always.

The thought went through his mind, but he didn't say it, of course. Instead he told her, "I'm fine. Sit down and have some breakfast."

"I had the oddest dream last night," she said as she took a seat at the other end of the table.

He felt a chill go through him.

"I dreamed that someone was in my room watching me sleep," she went on. "But it wasn't really frightening, because I could tell that whoever it was meant me no harm. In fact, they loved me, almost like . . . like a guardian angel."

"Did you wake up?" he asked, hoping that his voice didn't sound as choked to her as it did to him.

She shook her head. "No. You don't think anyone was really there, do you?"

Thank the Lord she hadn't waked up and caught him there, staring down at her as she slept. That would have ruined everything. He said, "I'm sure it was just a dream. Nothing to be concerned about."

Tonight he would have to make sure that other things occupied him, so that he wouldn't have a chance to sneak into her room again. So that he wouldn't run the risk of reaching down with a trembling hand to touch her . . .

Yes, Benjamin Tillman had secrets, all right.

Everett supposed that eventually a person got used to riding horseback, so that it didn't make the thighs and the rear end and the family jewels ache quite so much. He wasn't to that point yet, however, so he winced as he settled down in the saddle that morning to accompany Jackson to the Winged T.

Jackson noticed the reaction and chuckled. "Don't worry, it'll get better," he said, as if he had just read Everett's mind. "After you've been out here for a while you'll be bowlegged and iron-butted just like the rest of us."

"Lord help me," Everett muttered. If Jackson heard, he didn't say anything in response.

As they rode past the office of the *Weekly Journal,* Everett said, "Have you given any thought to what I asked you last night?"

"About that interview, you mean?" Jackson shrugged. "I reckon I can do it. I've already got you writing about me. Don't see as how it'll do any harm for Graham to do the same thing."

"As a matter of fact, I wrote up a dispatch last night and left it at the stage station this morning to go out in today's mail. Within a week or so, the readers of the New York *Universe* will know all about Hell Jackson and the mystery of Death Head Crossing."

Jackson frowned at that, but again, he didn't say anything. Everett hoped the gunslinger wasn't having second thoughts about their arrangement. The stories he was sending back would really make his name as a reporter. If he traveled with Jackson long enough and shared enough adventures with him, he might even be able to write a book about it. People might talk about him the same way they talked about Mr. Mark Twain and Mr. Bret Harte.

Everett let himself dwell on those thoughts for a while, enjoying the possible future that played out in his head with all its attendant fame and fortune. He forced himself out of that pleasant reverie as he realized that Jackson was talking to him.

"When we get there, why don't you talk to Tillman?" Jackson suggested. "I don't think he likes me much, and you and him have a lot more in common."

"All right," Everett agreed, "but what are you going to do?"

"Thought I'd talk to some of the hands, if any of them are around. If they've seen anything odd going on out on the range, they might be more likely to say something about it if their boss isn't around."

Everett nodded. "What do you want me to ask Mr. Tillman?"

"Pretty much the same thing I'm after . . . whether or not he's heard any talk about strange goings-on, how he feels about what Harcourt told us about the Hand of God, things like that."

Everett looked over at his companion. "Do you still harbor any suspicions that Tillman himself might be behind all the trouble?"

Jackson smiled. "To tell you the truth, Everett, I'm still suspicious of pretty much everybody except you and me . . . and I'm not too sure about you."

Everett thought for a second about taking offense at that comment, until he realized that Jackson was joking. He forced a chuckle.

They came within sight of the Winged T ranch house and headquarters a short time later. Jackson veered his mount toward the bunkhouse and the barns, while Everett headed for the main house. He saw someone sitting in a rocking chair on the porch, and as he came closer he recognized Deborah

Tillman, Benjamin Tillman's cousin from back East. She wore a pretty blue dress with short, puffy sleeves and a square neckline, the sort of garment that a Western woman might wear, and Everett thought she looked very good in it. He was a lucky man, he thought, having dinner with Rosalie Graham last night and now getting to spend time with Deborah Tillman today.

She was reading, but she put her book aside as he reined in and lifted his hat. "Good morning, Miss Tillman," he said. "How are you today?"

"Why, I'm just fine. It's Mr. Howard, isn't it?"

He was pleased that she remembered him from his visit a few days earlier. "That's right," he said. "Is your cousin here?"

"Oh, Benjamin's around somewhere." She stood up. "I'll find him for you. In the meantime, though, why don't you get down off that horse and come up here in the shade? I've never known anything as hot as this Texas sun."

It *was* turning into a very warm day, as usual. Gratefully, Everett dismounted, wrapped his horse's reins around the hitching post, and went up the steps into the shade of the porch. He felt cooler right away.

"I appreciate the hospitality," he said as

he took his derby off again and used his handkerchief to mop sweat off his forehead. "I'm not sure I'm cut out for living on the frontier."

Deborah laughed. "I know I'm not." She was standing fairly close to him, and she moved closer to lay a hand on his arm. Smiling, she said, "Aren't you glad that sooner or later we'll get to go back to civilization?"

Everett would have answered her, would have enjoyed chatting with her for a few minutes before she went to find her cousin, in fact, but at that moment the front door opened and Benjamin Tillman stepped out onto the porch. He halted abruptly and stared at them standing close together, Deborah's hand on Everett's arm and a smile on her face.

Then he shouted, "Get away from her, you bastard!" and launched himself toward Everett, swinging a fist at the startled young reporter's head.

CHAPTER 20

Jackson heard men's voices through the open double doors of the barn, so he reined in there and waited for them to come out. He thought he had recognized Ned Dawson's voice, and sure enough, the foreman was the first one to emerge. The cowboy with him turned around quickly and went back into the barn like he had forgotten something.

Dawson stopped in his tracks and glared up at Jackson. "What're you doin' on the Winged T, gunslinger?"

"Just wanted to know if you've had any more trouble out here lately," Jackson drawled. "Like losing some stock to rustlers maybe?"

Dawson's already unfriendly face became downright hostile at that question. "What the hell do you know about that?" he demanded.

"I don't know anything," Jackson said.

"That's why I'm asking you."

"The hell you don't! Rustlers hit us again last night, and now you show up today askin' about it. I'm supposed to believe that's a coincidence?"

"So you *did* lose some stock."

"Between forty and fifty head, as if you didn't already know that."

Jackson's eyes narrowed and his voice was as hard as flint as he said, "You're not accusing me of being one of those cow thieves, are you, Dawson?"

The foreman didn't back down or look away, but he admitted, "I never heard tell of you bein' mixed up with anything that crooked, Jackson. But it's mighty strange, you showin' up and askin' about such, out of the blue like that."

Jackson shrugged. "Nothing strange about it. A couple of days ago you mentioned that the ranch has had trouble with wideloopers. I just wondered if they had hit you again."

Dawson chewed on his mustache for a moment, then gave a curt nod. "I ain't sure I believe you or not, mister, but I reckon I can give you the benefit of the doubt. Step down from that horse and say whatever else you've got to say."

Jackson dismounted and would have tried to get more information from Dawson about the rustling problem on the Winged T, but at that moment an angry shout came from the direction of the ranch house. When Jackson looked around, he was surprised to see Benjamin Tillman taking a furious punch at young Everett Sidney Howard.

Dawson was shocked too. He exclaimed, "What the blue blazes!"

Both men broke into a run toward the house. Deborah Tillman, who had been standing on the porch with her cousin and Everett, backed away with one hand pressed to her mouth, muffling a scream.

Everett reacted at the last second, ducking and dodging aside so that Tillman's fist thudded into his left shoulder instead of his face. The blow staggered him anyway. He stumbled against the railing at the edge of the porch.

"I'll kill you!" Tillman howled as he tackled Everett. Everett went over backward. Tillman hung onto him, and both men tipped up and over the railing to tumble into several rosebushes that were planted in front of the porch.

Everett yelled in pain from the fall and the thorns, but Tillman didn't even seem to notice them. He was too busy flailing away at the reporter, swinging punch after wild punch. Everett tried to block them, but several slipped through and thudded against the side of his head.

Dawson pounded to a halt in front of the rosebushes. Beside him, Jackson said, "Damn it, we need to break that up!" But Dawson hesitated, clearly reluctant to interfere with his boss.

Jackson grated another curse and lunged forward, getting a few scratches on his forearms as he reached down to grab hold of Tillman. He straightened, hauling the man away from Everett. Holding Tillman by the collar and the belt, he flung the Easterner bodily across the yard in front of the ranch house. Out of control, Tillman hit the ground and rolled over several times before coming to a stop. He lay there on his belly, lifting his head and shaking it dazedly.

"Everett, take my hand," Jackson said as he reached down to help the reporter. Groggily, his face streaked with blood from the scratches left behind by the thorns, Everett complied and grasped Jackson's hand. Jackson lifted him out of the rosebushes, each of them getting a few more scratches in the process.

"What in blazes happened?" Dawson demanded of Everett. "I never saw the boss go loco like that before. What'd you do to him, mister?"

"I . . . I didn't do anything!" Everett panted. "I was just standing there talking to Miss Tillman, and he came out of the house and went mad!" Everett looked at the porch, where Deborah still stood with her back pressed against the wall of the house, her eyes wide with shock and horror. Anxiously he asked, "Miss Tillman, are you all right?"

She managed to nod. "What . . . what have you done to poor Benjamin?"

"Poor Benjamin" was the one who had gone loco, as Dawson had phrased it, and attacked Everett. Jackson put himself between Tillman and Everett, just in case the would-be rancher tried anything else, and asked, "What's this all about?"

Still breathing heavily, Tillman pushed himself to his hands and knees and then staggered to his feet. His face was washed out of color except for two bright red spots of anger on his cheeks. He pointed a shaking finger at Everett and said, "He . . . he was molesting my cousin!"

"I was doing no such thing!" Everett practically yelped. "I was just standing there talking to her. She was about to come looking for you."

"He was touching her!" Tillman accused. "I saw it!"

"You're insane. I swear I didn't —"

Tillman didn't let him go on. "Sinner!" he screamed. "Vile, filthy fornicator!" Sputtering with rage, he went on. "Th-that's all men like you think of! T-touching innocent young women and giving in to all your carnal desires and corrupting everything that's good and pure and holy! You should be punished! Sinner! Sinner!"

Jackson, Everett, Dawson, and Deborah could only stand there and stare at Tillman as he continued his harangue. His raving became more and more incoherent, until finally he covered his face with his hands and began to sob. The wretched sounds continued as he fell to his knees. His back shook uncontrollably.

A limping, bald-headed man in a cook's apron had emerged from the house to stare in confusion at the scene. Dawson snapped, "Hiram, help me get the boss inside." The cook came down the steps, and together he and Dawson helped Tillman to his feet again and led him into the house. Tillman was still crying. His sobs were audible even after the door was closed behind them.

Jackson reached carefully into the rose-bushes, retrieved Everett's derby, and handed it to him. Everett said, "Ow," as he put it on. Several of Tillman's wild blows had connected with his head, leaving painful swollen lumps.

"I . . . I don't know what to say," Deborah said from the porch. "I'm so sorry, Mr. Howard. I don't know what got into Benjamin. I've never seen him like that before. Never!"

"If I did anything to offend you, Miss Tillman, I sincerely apologize," Everett said in a voice stiff with anger. "I thought we were just having a nice conversation —"

"Oh, we were!"

Everett shook his head. "Evidently we weren't. Not in your cousin's eyes anyway. At any rate, I'm sorry, and I won't trouble you again."

"Don't you think you're being a mite hard on the young lady?" Jackson asked. "It's not her fault that her cousin acted like an insane man."

"Benjamin's not insane," Deborah said. "Obviously, he's more . . . troubled . . . than I realized, but I'm sure he's not insane."

Jackson shrugged. He knew loco when he saw it, and for a few moments there, Benjamin Tillman had been stark raving mad. Whether the condition was permanent or not was another question.

Dawson came out onto the porch again and said, "I gave him a slug o' whiskey, and that seemed to settle him down a mite. I think it'd be a good idea if you and your young friend lit a shuck outta here, though, Jackson."

Jackson thought about it for a second and then gave a curt nod. He hadn't found out everything he wanted to know, but there wouldn't be any point in Everett trying to talk to Tillman today — or maybe ever again.

"We'll go," he said. "But if you want to talk any more about what we were discussing, Dawson, you can find me in the Big Bend most nights. I might be able to give you a hand with that problem."

"We'll see," Dawson said, equally curtly. "Now you two vamoose."

Jackson untied the reins of Everett's horse from the hitching post and pressed them into the young Easterner's hands. Trying not to moan in pain, Everett swung up into the saddle, while Jackson walked over to the bunkhouse and retrieved his own mount.

They rode out slowly, side by side. Everett glanced back, and Jackson turned his head to see what he was looking at. Not surprisingly, he saw that Everett was looking at Deborah Tillman, who still stood on the porch, obviously shaken. She didn't lift a hand to wave good-bye to them or acknowledge their departure in any other way.

"All right," Jackson said when they had ridden a couple of hundred yards, "now that we're away from there, you can tell me what the hell happened."

"I already told you," Everett said. "I rode up, said good morning to Miss Tillman, and asked if her cousin was there. She said that he was and offered to fetch him. By that time I had dismounted and stepped up on the porch. We exchanged a bit of small talk, and then Tillman burst out of the house and attacked me."

"You weren't touching the girl?"

"Absolutely not. In fact, *she* was touching *me*. She placed her hand on my arm as we talked, and then she laughed, and then . . . and then Tillman came out . . ." Everett's voice trailed off as he looked over at Jackson. "Good Lord! He acted just like a jealous lover!"

Jackson nodded slowly and said, "Yep. Same thought occurred to me."

"And . . . and when he started ranting about sinners, it sounded like the things that Matt Harcourt mentioned. The things that the Hand of God said about punishing sinners." Everett looked and sounded stunned as the implications of that soaked in on him.

No, Jackson thought as he replayed in his mind everything that had happened during their visit to the Winged T, they hadn't found out everything he had intended when he and Everett rode out here.

But maybe they had found out enough.

CHAPTER 21

There wasn't much else to say about the matter, but during the ride back to Death Head Crossing Jackson and Everett both thought a great deal about what had happened. As they approached the settlement, Everett asked, "What are we going to do now?"

"We don't have any proof against Tillman," Jackson pointed out, "or anybody else either, for that matter. One thing I reckon we can be sure of, though, if he *is* the one calling himself the Hand of God, he's not doing those things alone. He had to have help with those killings."

"So we go after whoever has been helping him?" Everett guessed.

"I plan to keep stirring things up," Jackson said. "Poke a hornet's nest often enough, and sooner or later all the little varmints will come pouring out."

Everett looked like he didn't quite understand what Jackson was getting at, but he said, "So what do you want me to do?"

"For the time being, not a blasted thing. Leave it to me for now."

"Wait a minute," Everett said. "I thought we were partners."

"What gave you that idea?" Jackson asked, deliberately cool.

"But . . . but you said —"

"I said you could tag along with me for a while. You've done that, Everett. Maybe now it's time to move along."

Everett stared at him as if he couldn't believe what he was hearing. Finally, he said, "That's not fair. I've helped you. I've done everything you asked."

"And I appreciate that," Jackson said with a dismissive shrug.

Everett glared for a moment longer, then shook his head and blew his breath out angrily. He kicked his horse in the sides and sent the animal trotting forward, ahead of Jackson and his mount. Jackson let the young man go.

He felt a mite bad about what he had just done. It was necessary, though. The next couple of days were liable to be dangerous, and Jackson didn't want Everett around, wearing the same sort of target he intended to plaster on his own back. Later, when it was all over, Everett would understand why Jackson had been so harsh with him. It had been for Everett's own good.

At least, Jackson hoped he would understand that.

They had reached Main Street. Everett jerked his horse's head toward the boarding-house. Jackson continued on down the street and came to a stop in front of the sheriff's office. He dismounted, tied his horse to the hitch rail, and went inside.

Sheriff Brennan was at his desk, pawing through some papers and looking distracted. He barely glanced up at Jackson and grunted, "What do you want?"

Jackson picked up a ladder-back chair, turned it around, and straddled it. "I was just wondering if you'd found out anything more about those killings."

"Not a damned thing," Brennan said. "Are you still pokin' around in that business, Jackson?" His tone indicated that he wasn't sure what answer he wanted to hear to that question.

"I might be on the trail of something. Ought to know more in a day or two." Jackson kept his own tone deliberately cryptic.

Brennan frowned at him. "What the hell does that mean? Either you know something or you don't."

"If I do, you'll be one of the first ones I tell, Sheriff. You have my word on that."

"I'd damned well better be. I'm still the law around here, you know."

Jackson nodded and stood up. "I'll be seeing you, Sheriff."

"I'm still thinkin' about callin' in the Texas Rangers!" Brennan said to Jackson's back as the gunslinger went out the door.

Calling in the Rangers might be the best thing to do, Jackson thought as he moved along the boardwalk, but it might also do more harm than good. If a troop of Rangers rode into Death Head Crossing, chances were the man behind all the killings would just lie low for a while and wait for the Rangers to leave before he resumed slaughtering people.

Jackson went into the Big Bend and indulged himself in the free lunch, talking to Jasper Whitten as he did so. The saloon owner was justifiably anxious.

"If this keeps up, folks will start leaving town," Whitten said. "Death Head Crossing is liable to dry up and blow away."

"I don't think that'll happen," Jackson told him. "Sooner or later, whoever is responsible for the trouble will be forced into the open."

"Maybe, but when?"

"Might happen sooner than you think," Jackson said.

When he left the saloon, he reclaimed his horse from the hitch rack and walked down the street toward the boardinghouse. He made a couple of stops along the way, at the general store to buy a box of cartridges for his Colt and at the blacksmith shop to see about getting one of his horse's shoes checked. At each place he talked about the killings and made comments that made it sound like he knew more about them than he really did.

He was passing the church as Reverend Driscoll stepped out of the whitewashed building. Driscoll stopped short, the usual dislike evident on his face as Jackson nodded pleasantly to him. "So you're still in town," the minister said.

"That's right," Jackson said. "I've decided to stick around until this whole Hand of God business is straightened out and the killings are stopped."

"Don't use that name!" Driscoll snapped.

"You mean the Hand of God?" Jackson asked, knowing that it would annoy the preacher but not particularly caring if it did.

"The monster who's calling himself that has nothing to do with God," Driscoll said.

"That's a product of his own diseased mind."

"There's nothing unusual about folks doing bad things in the name of God," Jackson pointed out. "Just read the history books."

Driscoll shook his head. "I don't have to read the history books to know that God has nothing to do with the evil that men carry out on each other. The Scriptures say for us to love one another, not kill each other."

"Vengeance is mine, sayeth the Lord," Jackson murmured. "Maybe the Hand of God just thinks he's carrying out that divine vengeance."

"Then he's even more of a sinner than those he condemns."

"Finally we agree on something, preacher," Jackson said. "I don't reckon you'll have to worry about the Hand of God much longer, though. It won't be long until he's put out of the punishment business."

Driscoll looked surprised. "You honestly think so?"

"I know so," Jackson said. He lifted a hand in farewell and led his horse on down the street toward the boardinghouse.

Everett's horse was already put up in the stable behind the house. Jackson took care of his own mount, checking the bullet graze on the animal's rump to make sure it was healing properly. As he went in the back door into the kitchen, he saw Philomena at the sink, washing some of the dishes from lunch. Even with her sleeves rolled up and her arms plunged into soapy water to the elbows, she was mighty pretty, Jackson thought.

She turned away from the sink and grabbed a cloth to dry her hands. "Señor Jackson, what happened to Everett?" she asked as she came over to him, still wiping her arms with the cloth.

"Why, was he upset?"

She nodded. "Very much. He refused to eat, even though the food from lunch was still on the table, and went straight up to his room. He looked like he had been in a fight. And when I asked him where you were, he said that he did not know and did not care."

"Everett's a mite put out with me right now," Jackson admitted. "And he *was* in a fight . . . with Benjamin Tillman."

Mrs. Morton, the proprietor of the place, came into the kitchen in time to hear that. She said, "Good Lord, Mr. Tillman's a fine man. Why would Mr. Howard pick a fight with him?"

"It was a personal matter," Jackson said, not wanting to go into the details with the woman. He couldn't resist adding, "I'm not sure how fine a man Tillman really is, though."

"He's not some gunslinger," Mrs. Morton said, her lips tightening with the same sort of censure that Jackson always got from Reverend Driscoll. She went on. "He's from the East, you know," as if that automatically conferred some sort of special status on someone. "And he's very wealthy."

Jackson nodded. Money really *did* confer special status on folks, whether things ought to be that way or not.

"I don't know what the world is coming to," Mrs. Morton continued. "All this commotion all the time, people brawling with each other and getting killed and . . . and . . . it's just uncivilized, that's what it is!"

"If you're talking about what happened to Berryhill and Harcourt and Mrs. Vance, I don't think you'll have to worry about that for too much longer," Jackson said. "That whole business will be cleared up before you know it."

"Do you really think so?"

He nodded. "I'm sure of it."

"Land's sakes, I hope so! If it keeps up, people will be afraid to come to Death Head

229

Crossing, and then where will we all be?"

Jackson didn't have an answer for that.

Mrs. Morton bustled out, still shaking her head in dismay over the state of the world. Jackson turned toward the rear stairs, but Philomena stopped him by reaching out to lay a hand on his arm. Her fingers were still slightly damp from the dishwater, but they felt good against his bare forearm.

"You are scratched up too, like Everett was," she said.

"We both tangled with some rosebushes."

"Did you mean what you said about the trouble being over soon?"

Jackson nodded. "That's what I'm hoping."

"I pray you are right, Señor, but I fear that the evil in this town will never go away. My grandfather's death made me realize that men will go to any lengths to get what they want. Nothing can change that."

"Maybe not," Jackson admitted, "but you can deal with one varmint, or one bunch of varmints, at a time. You can't just give up."

Philomena smiled. The expression held a trace of sadness. "A man such as yourself cannot give up. You tell people that you are a hired gun, that you care for nothing but money. But I know this is not true. There is much good in you. You simply choose not to reveal it."

Jackson put a hand on her shoulder, leaned forward, and brushed his lips across hers in a kiss. "I'm not saying you're right," he said, "but if you are, let's just keep it between us."

"As you wish." She sighed and turned toward the sink. "Now I must get back to work."

"Me too," Jackson said, although for the moment his work would consist of waiting.

He had planted some seeds today.

Now he had to see what, if anything, was going to sprout from them.

CHAPTER 22

Feeling betrayed, Everett went up to his room and shut the door behind him. Right now he didn't want to see or talk to anyone. He had honestly believed that he and Jackson were partners. He hadn't expected the gunslinger to turn on him like that.

And yet he shouldn't have been surprised, he told himself. After all, he was a naïve young Easterner . . . a dude, a tenderfoot, a greenhorn. No matter what you called it, he knew that Jackson would never have any real respect for anyone like him.

Still fuming, Everett used a cloth and water from the basin on the table next to the bed to clean the dried blood from the scratches on his arms and face. He used his shaving mirror to see how bad the injuries were, and applied sticking plaster to several of them.

Then, after sternly telling himself that he couldn't just hide out in his room for the rest of the day, he went downstairs. Thinking that he heard Jackson's voice in the rear of the house somewhere, he turned the other way and went out the front door.

He wasn't sure where he was going, but he wasn't surprised that his steps led him to the office of the *Weekly Journal.* Since he'd arrived in Death Head Crossing, the only people who had really seemed to understand him were Malcolm and Rosalie Graham. Malcolm was a fellow journalist, and they were both cultured and intelligent. They didn't look down on him because he was from New York. In fact, they seemed to admire him for that.

When he went inside, he found Rosalie alone in the office. She looked at him in surprise and said, "My goodness, Everett, you appear to have been on the losing end of an argument with a wildcat!"

He touched one of the pieces of sticking plaster covering his cuts and said, "Some rosebushes actually. I ran into trouble out at the Winged T."

She came through the gate in the railing and approached him with a sympathetic expression on her face now. "What sort of trouble?" she asked.

Everett hadn't meant to talk about it, but the words came tumbling out of his mouth anyway. "Benjamin Tillman attacked me!"

Rosalie's eyebrows rose even more. "Mr. Tillman did that? No offense, Everett, but I have trouble believing that such a fine gentleman from Philadelphia would act in such an uncivilized manner."

"He's not a fine gentleman. He's a madman. I was simply standing on the porch of his house, talking to his cousin, when he went into a rage. I never expected him to act like that. If Mr. Jackson hadn't been there to break it up, I don't know what might have happened."

Rosalie still didn't seem convinced. "But why would he do such a thing?" she asked. "He must have had a good reason. Maybe he misunderstood what was going on."

"He misunderstood, all right . . . because I think he's in love with his cousin!"

Everett hadn't meant for that to come out either, but it was too late to hold it back now, he realized as Rosalie gasped in shock. But at least he could keep the speculation about Tillman being the Hand of God to himself, he warned himself sternly. As long as he and Jackson were investigating, it was just a theory for them to look into. If it spread further than that, it became malicious gossip.

Shaking her head, Rosalie said, "I find this

all very difficult to believe."

"I'm not making it up," Everett said.

"No, no, I didn't mean that. I believe you, Everett. I just never would have thought such things could be going on around here."

"Can I trust you not to say anything about this to your brother?" he asked. "At this point, Tillman's motives are purely speculation on my part. I'd hate to see such a thing printed in the paper."

She frowned at him. "Give me credit for having some sense of discretion, Everett. I don't automatically repeat everything I hear to Malcolm so he can put it in the paper."

Abashed, he said, "I'm sorry. I meant no offense, Rosalie. This whole business has me so shaken that I hardly know what I'm saying right now." He looked around the office. "Malcolm isn't here?"

"No, he's running some errands."

At that moment, the sound of angry voices came from somewhere in the rear of the building. Despite what Rosalie had just said, Everett felt sure one of them belonged to Malcolm Graham. There was something familiar about the other voice too, but he couldn't place it.

Rosalie turned to look toward the rear of the building and laughed. "Wouldn't you know it?" she said. "That's just like that brother of mine, to make a liar out of me." She raised her voice and called, "Malcolm, is that you? Everett Howard is here."

Graham came bustling through a doorway, a smile of greeting on his face. "Everett!" he said. "Good to see you again. How are —" He stopped short and looked surprised. "I can see how you are. What happened? You don't strike me as the brawling type."

"I'm not," Everett admitted with a rueful expression. "The fight certainly wasn't my idea."

"But who did that?" Graham persisted. "Whoever it was, the scoundrel should be thrown in jail! Have you talked to the sheriff about it?"

Everett glanced at Rosalie, and could tell by her expression that she was going to keep his confidence. "It's nothing," he said. "I'd prefer just to forget that it ever happened."

"Well, that's your decision to make, I suppose. But you really can't let these frontiersmen take advantage of you. You have to stand up for yourself. Rosalie and I learned that as soon as we came out here, didn't we, dear?"

"Of course," Rosalie agreed.

To change the subject, Everett said, "You sounded like you were just having some trouble of your own."

Graham frowned in apparent confusion. "What?"

"That argument you were having back there." Everett gestured toward the rear of the building.

For a second, Graham still looked confused, but then he laughed and said, "Oh, that. It was nothing, just a disagreement with the man who takes our papers around town every Friday, the day we publish." Graham lowered his voice and added, "He's a bit of a drinker, you know. I don't pay him much, but it's enough to buy a bottle of rotgut. Unfortunately, when you're dealing with people like that, they have a tendency to be unreliable."

"Were you able to take care of the problem, Mal?" Rosalie asked.

He waved a hand negligently. "Oh, yes, it's all settled. Nothing to worry about." He turned back to Everett and went on. "Was there some reason you stopped by? Not that we mind the visit."

The real reason Everett had come here was because he was upset over what Jackson had done, but he didn't want to tell them that. Instead, he thought fast and said, "I thought perhaps the two of you would let me take you to dinner tonight. You know, to repay you for having me over to your house."

"That's not necessary —" Graham began.

"But we'd love to," Rosalie broke in. "That's very nice of you, Everett."

"Really?" Graham sounded surprised by his sister's decision, but he shrugged in agreement. "Of course, dear, whatever you say."

"All right," Everett said with a nod, pleased by the way this was turning out. He looked forward to spending more time with Rosalie. To tell the truth, she was even prettier than Deborah Tillman because hers was a more mature beauty, and he thought it was unlikely that her brother would go mad and attack him the way Deborah's cousin had. "I'll leave the choice of restaurant to you, since you're more familiar with the establishments here."

"You're not going to have that much of a choice in Death Head Crossing," Graham pointed out. "There's a fairly nice café, though. Why don't you meet us here about seven o'clock? We'll be through with the day's work by then."

"That's fine." Everett lifted his hat politely as he nodded to Rosalie. "I'll see you both later then."

He had a newfound spring in his step as

he left the newspaper office. His so-called partnership with Jackson might have fallen apart, but the evening promised to be a pleasant one.

If he got to know the Grahams better, he reflected, he might even be able to trust them with the suspicion that Benjamin Tillman was the Hand of God. Malcolm was a newspaperman and was experienced at ferreting out the truth. Maybe he would just exchange one partner for two new ones, Everett thought.

And anyway, Rosalie Graham was much prettier than any old gunslinger!

Jackson took advantage of the opportunity to get some sleep that afternoon, since he planned to be busy once night had fallen again. He didn't see Everett around when he left his room and went to saddle his horse, and he wondered if the young reporter was holed up in his own room, sulking.

That would probably be the safest place for him tonight.

As night was falling, Jackson left Death Head Crossing by the back alleys so there would be less chance of anyone spotting him. He circled around the settlement and headed north toward the Winged T.

Even though his suspicions now centered on Benjamin Tillman, his instincts told him there had to be more to this than one unbalanced hombre driven loco by his feelings for his cousin. There was no chance in hell that Tillman had pulled off those murders by himself. He'd had help from somebody, and it was doubtful that whoever was helping him was doing it because they were crazy too.

There was also the rustling to consider. Tillman wasn't stealing cows from his own ranch. Try as he might, Jackson couldn't figure out any way for that to make sense.

And, he reminded himself, he had no proof yet that Tillman was responsible for the Hand of God slayings, only the fact that the man had attacked Everett and yelled a lot of crazy things. Being loco was no crime by itself.

Jackson didn't really expect the rustlers to strike again this soon, but he wanted to be close by if they did. And if the Hand of God and his mysterious balls of light that killed people put in another appearance, Jackson wanted to be there for that too. He planned to spend as many nights as it took poking around the Winged T.

And there was a chance that the varmint he was looking for would come to him, rather than the other way around. That was why he had gone around the settlement earlier in the day, hinting to everyone he could find that he had found out something important. It was his hope that would draw the enemy to him.

Just one more way of poking at that hornet's nest . . .

Within an hour of leaving the settlement, he was on Winged T range, once again riding through the rugged terrain where he had encountered the rustlers — and an unknown bushwhacker — the night before. He had just passed between a couple of boulders when he heard the ominous sound of Winchesters being levered. Reining in sharply and twisting in the saddle, Jackson reached for his gun.

"Hold it!" came the shouted command. "Touch that Colt and we'll blow you out of the saddle, Jackson!"

A grim smile crossed Jackson's face as he looked up at the pair of riflemen covering him from the top of the boulders. He had used himself for bait — and the trap had just slammed shut.

CHAPTER 23

Jackson thought at first there was something wrong with the heads of the two gunmen who had the drop on him. They were misshapen and didn't look fully human. But then he realized that they were wearing hoods of some sort instead of Stetsons. That accounted for the odd shape.

Keeping his hand away from his gun, he called up to them, "Take it easy, boys. I'm not looking for trouble."

"I think that's exactly what you're lookin' for, mister," one of the men replied.

Jackson had heard both of them speak now, and the voices of both men were familiar. He couldn't place them, but he knew he had heard them sometime in the fairly recent past.

"If this is a holdup, you won't get much," he drawled. "My stay in Death Head Crossing hasn't been very profitable."

"It's not a holdup," the man on the left

said. "We're not after your money. I think you know why we're doin' this."

"You been pokin' your nose into things that're none of your business," the other man said. "And I'm gonna enjoy shootin' it off."

"In that case, what you should have done," Jackson said, "was shoot me without taking the time to gloat about it."

"You son of a bitch! Ventilate him!"

Jackson had already slipped his boots out of the stirrups without the gunmen noticing. Now he went out of the saddle in a fast dive to his left. That kept his gun arm on the high side.

One of the men yelled in alarm. Both of them fired. Jackson didn't know how close the shots came to him, but neither hit him and that was what mattered. His gun was in his hand by the time he hit the ground. He fired while the men were levering fresh rounds into their rifles. The bullet punched into the belly of the man on the right, doubling him over. He dropped his Winchester. It skittered down the front side of the boulder, followed a second later by the man's body.

The shot was luck as much as anything, Jackson knew. He was damned good with a gun, no point in denying it, but at night, firing upward at a steep angle like that . . . well, everybody needed a little luck sometimes. He swung the Colt to the left and triggered again, at the same instant as the second man's rifle cracked and flame gouted from the muzzle.

The Winchester's bullet smacked into the ground close enough to Jackson to fling grit in his face and make him wince and blink. Pawing at his eyes, he scrambled to his feet and lunged behind his horse, hating to use the animal for cover but knowing he had no choice. Another shot blasted from the rifle, telling Jackson that the man was still in the fight. Chances were, Jackson's shot hadn't even touched him.

But Jackson wasn't hit either. He grabbed the horse's reins and dragged the animal with him as he ran at an angle toward the boulders. He snapped another shot at the man on top of the boulder, who was kneeling now. The high-pitched whine told Jackson his bullet had ricocheted off the rock.

With the hoofbeats sounding like thunder close beside him, Jackson rounded the right-hand boulder. The remaining gunman couldn't see him now. He let the horse go and gave it a slap on the rump to keep it moving. The hoofbeats receded into the darkness.

The rifleman wouldn't know if Jackson had gone with the horse, or if he was still close by, waiting.

Jackson pressed his back against the rock, which was almost uncomfortably warm because it retained quite a bit of the heat from the day. He listening intently, thinking that for the second night in a row he had found himself being shot at and then playing a cat-and-mouse game with his would-be killer. It wasn't a pleasant feeling, but it wasn't all that unusual, either.

The bushwhacker had himself in a predicament too. Being on top of that boulder had given him the advantage of the high ground, but now he couldn't get down from it without Jackson hearing him. Jackson waited patiently, and after a few minutes, he heard the scrape of boot leather on rock. The man was trying to climb down as quietly as he could, but he couldn't manage it in complete silence.

A soft thud told Jackson that the man had slid the rest of the way and hit the ground. Instantly, while the man would still be off balance, Jackson whipped around the boulder where he waited and opened fire, squeezing off two fast shots toward the moving patch of darkness he saw beside the other boulder. Colt flame bloomed redly in the shadows as the man returned the fire, this time with a handgun, aiming at Jackson's muzzle flashes.

Jackson was already belly-down on the ground, though, having thrown himself forward as soon as he squeezed off the shots. The slugs whistled harmlessly over his head. With a better target now, he fired again, a single shot. He heard the man grunt in pain.

With his Colt empty for the moment, Jackson rolled up against the slight overhang of the boulder, hoping that no snakes had curled up there. He shook out the empties and started thumbing in fresh cartridges from his shell belt. He didn't know how badly the man was hurt, but he was pretty sure his last shot had scored a hit.

Suddenly he heard the thud of running footsteps, and then a horse nickered. *Son of a bitch,* Jackson thought as he snapped the Colt's cylinder closed and came up on his knees. The bastard had a mount tied up somewhere close by, of course, and now he was trying to get away.

As hoofbeats pounded, Jackson emptied the Colt into the darkness, aiming at the sound of the running horse. The horse kept moving. Jackson bit back a curse as he pushed himself to his feet and quickly started to reload again. He didn't know where his horse was. He whistled, but the animal didn't come.

With his gun still in his hand, Jackson went around to the front of the boulder he had used for cover. Using his other hand, he found a match in his shirt pocket. He couldn't hear the running horse anymore, so he figured it was safe to light the lucifer. He snapped it into life with his thumbnail. The sudden glare of flame showed him the crumpled body of the man he had shot, lying on the ground in front of the boulder, a dark pool of blood underneath him.

Jackson hooked a boot toe under the man's shoulder and rolled him onto his back. The man wore a duster, the front of which was sodden with blood. Nobody could lose that much blood and remain conscious. Jackson holstered his gun and reached down to grasp the flour-sack hood that still concealed the man's face. He pulled it off.

The match flame burned down to the point that Jackson had to shake it out before it singed his fingers. But he had gotten a good enough look under that hood to see that the man's eyes were glazed over in death. He recognized the face as well, and now he knew why the voices of the two men had been familiar. They were the hardcases who had confronted him in the saloon right after he met Everett for the first time. The men who had been friends with the three hombres he had killed for torturing old Julio. The ones he had handled with such humiliating ease.

Had they been waiting to settle that score with him ever since? Biding their time until they were ready to bushwhack him?

Jackson might have believed that was all it amounted to if it had not been for two things. One was the fact that they had been wearing hoods. If this had been an attempt at a simple revenge killing, there would have been no need for that. The other thing was the way one of the man had said that Jackson was sticking his nose into things that were none of his business.

They had been acting on orders from someone else, Jackson realized. Sure, they had probably been glad to take on the job of killing him, but it hadn't been entirely their idea. Somebody had given them that task.

The Hand of God.

A small, grim smile tugged at the corners of Jackson's mouth. His efforts had borne fruit. The killer calling himself the Hand of God was scared of him. Maybe Jackson was even closer than he had thought.

He turned as he heard a horse approaching. The gun in his hand came up. It was only his own mount, though, he saw as the animal came closer. He holstered his gun as the horse bumped its nose against his shoulder.

"Took your own sweet time about answering that whistle," he said as he swung up into the saddle. The horse tossed its head as if in apology. "Don't reckon I can blame you, though," Jackson went on. "You keep getting shot at."

Leaving the dead man where he lay, Jackson rode in the direction the other bushwhacker had fled. Actually tracking somebody at night was next thing to impossible, but sometimes if you started in the right direction you got lucky.

Not only that, but Jackson was aware that the headquarters of the Winged T lay in the direction he was going. The bushwhacker was wounded, and a hurt animal tended to head for its den. That was one more thing pointing to Benjamin Tillman as the twisted mind behind the killings.

After he had ridden along for a while, Jackson spotted something on a stretch of open, sandy ground. He reined in and looked down at the dark blotch on the earth, then dismounted and touched a finger to it. Sticky. He picked up some of the dirt and rubbed it between his fingers. That was a splash of blood on the ground. The man he had wounded must have fallen off his horse here before mounting up again and riding on. Jackson was convinced he was still going in the right direction.

He urged his horse to a faster pace, heading straight for the Winged T now and moving as quickly as he could. He thought it was unlikely that he would catch up to the bushwhacker before the man reached the ranch, but it wouldn't hurt anything to try.

A short time later, lights appeared in the distance. Not mysterious floating balls of witchfire, but rather yellow rectangles of illumination. Those would be lights in the windows of the buildings at the Winged T headquarters, he knew. And as he closed in on them, he saw movement between him and the lights. The wounded bushwhacker approaching the ranch? It was certainly possible. Like a wolf on the scent of prey, Jackson arrowed toward the spot.

But if he had actually been a wolf, he might have sensed the other predators around him. As it was, he had no warning before the lasso settled over his shoulders and jerked tight, pinning his arms to his side. Jackson lurched in the saddle and tried to get his hand on his gun anyway, but before he could do that another rope caught him. The loops were so taut around his chest that he couldn't even draw a deep breath to yell a curse. He barely managed to pull his feet free of the stirrups so they wouldn't catch as he was hauled out of the saddle. If they had, he might have suffered a broken ankle or leg.

Not that it was likely to matter, he thought as he slammed to the ground with the ropes still pinning him. Another loop snagged his neck, cutting off his air even more. The only question now was what the manner of his death would be.

He didn't have time to ponder it. Bulky, shadowy figures loomed around him, and a gun butt smashed against his head, driving the last vestiges of consciousness from his brain.

CHAPTER 24

Rosalie Graham was alone in the newspaper office when Everett opened the door and stepped inside a couple of minutes before seven o'clock that evening. She greeted him with a smile, and he thought again how pretty she was with that blond hair and those cornflower-blue eyes.

"Hello, Everett. I hope you're hungry."

"Famished," he said. "Where's Malcolm?"

"Something came up, and Malcolm won't be able to join us," she said.

Everett didn't know whether to be disappointed or elated. He had looked forward to talking more with his fellow newspaperman, but on the other hand, the prospect of having dinner alone with Rosalie . . . having her all to himself for an hour or two . . . was certainly intriguing.

"Nothing major, I hope?"

"What? Oh, you mean the problem requiring Mal's attention." Still smiling, she shook her head. "Nothing major at all. He got word that there'd been a fire at one of the ranches south of town, so he rode out to talk to the rancher and find out how bad it was. That's news, you know."

Everett nodded. "Yes, of course. All the local tragedies, as well as the triumphs, have to be covered, I would think."

She came through the gate in the railing and offered him her arm. "In the meantime, we'll go down to the café and have a nice dinner. They fry up a fairly good steak there."

Everett slipped his arm through hers and enjoyed the feel of her closeness, just as he had the night before. He smelled the fresh scent of her hair and felt a little giddy from it.

As they strolled along the street toward the café, Rosalie asked, "Did you ever get a chance to ask Mr. Jackson about doing an interview for the paper?"

Everett didn't tell her that he wasn't even sure whether he and Jackson were still on good terms. Instead, he gave an honest answer. "Yes, I talked to him, and he agreed to do the interview."

"Excellent. I'll tell Malcolm. I take it your dispatches for the *Universe* have been well received?"

"I don't really know," Everett admitted. "I've only had a chance to send in a few of them, and I haven't heard anything back from my editor. I'm not sure the first story has even run yet."

"Well, I'm sure that when it does, your readers in New York will be fascinated."

When they reached the café with its tables covered by blue-checked cloths, Everett ordered steak dinners with all the trimmings for both of them. While they sipped coffee and waited for their food, Rosalie asked him more questions about life in New York and his work on the newspaper there. Even though Everett was a little ashamed to be doing it, he embellished his role at the *Universe* a bit, making it sound like he was more important there than he actually was. But surely that exaggeration was forgivable, he told himself, because what man *wouldn't* exaggerate a bit to impress a pretty girl?

When he asked her about her and her brother's life in Death Head Crossing and in Dallas before that, she deflected the questions, insisting that there was nothing remarkable or interesting about their lives. Everett might have pressed the point, but he was enjoying talking about himself too much. He was aware of that, but couldn't seem to stop it. That was how powerful the spell cast by Rosalie's smile was.

The plump, white-aproned waitress brought platters of food from the kitchen and placed them on the table. Everett already knew from his experiences at Mrs. Morton's boardinghouse that Westerners were hearty eaters, but even so the size of the steak surprised him a little, as did the mound of hash brown potatoes. There were biscuits and gravy too, along with corn and greens and then deep-dish apple pie for dessert. He tried to do justice to the meal, washing down the food with gulps of strong black coffee, but he was afraid he failed.

"Don't worry," Rosalie assured him with a soft laugh when he made a comment about there being enough food to provision an army. "You just haven't been out here long enough to develop a true Western appetite yet. If you stay in Texas, you'll learn to eat like a Texan."

Everett started to say that he would stay in Texas or go elsewhere depending on what Jackson wanted to do, but he stopped himself. He didn't know if Jackson would even allow him to come along when he left Death Head Crossing. So he just returned her smile and said, "Yes, I suppose so."

When they were finished with their supper, Everett paid for it and told Rosalie, "I still owe your brother a meal."

"Don't worry about that. You've shown me a fine time this evening, so I'm sure Malcolm will be glad to call everything even."

"The pleasure has been all mine," Everett assured her.

As they walked back to the house where Rosalie and her brother lived, Everett's mind was racing. Would she invite him in when they got there? Was it possible she would allow him to kiss her? His thoughts might have gone beyond even that, but he wouldn't allow them to do so. If he did, his brain would become so inflamed that his head might explode.

What actually happened was that Rosalie paused, turned to him, extended her hand, and said, "Thank you, Everett. It was a perfectly lovely evening."

The implication was obvious. It had been a lovely evening, and he shouldn't try to ruin it by making it into anything else. He smiled, hoping that his expression didn't look too pained, and took her hand.

"Thank you for being such charming company," he told her.

As he walked away from the house, he took some solace from the fact that her handshake had been warm and had lingered a second or two longer than it had to. He resolved then and there to ask her to have dinner with him again while he was in Death Head Crossing.

The pleasant possibilities of such a rendezvous were going through his mind when someone suddenly grabbed him violently from behind.

Jackson couldn't get his breath, couldn't see anything, and for a terrifying moment after his senses returned to him, he thought he had been buried alive. Shut up in a wooden box under the ground. He opened his mouth to scream, but no sound came out.

That was because a gag had been shoved into his mouth and tied in place, he realized. Would his captors have bothered to gag him if he was buried alive? That seemed unlikely, since no one would be able to hear him if that were the case. His madly hammering pulse slowed a bit, and nerves stretched almost to the breaking point eased slightly. He was alive, he told himself. *Alive.*

That meant he still had a chance.

The swaying motion told him he was on horseback. He tried to move his hands and lift his arms, but all he succeeded in doing was hunching his shoulders slightly. His wrists were tied to the saddle horn. He tested his leg muscles, and determined that a rope had been passed under his horse's belly and used to tie his feet together. Whoever had taken him prisoner had done a good job of lashing him onto the horse so that he couldn't fall off.

They might not know yet that he was awake, so he continued to slump forward as if unconscious. He hoped they hadn't noticed that small movement of his shoulders.

He couldn't see anything, but he could still hear, although the sounds were muffled for some reason. Several other horses were moving nearby. He had already known that more than one man was responsible for his capture, since at least three lassos had come sailing out of the darkness to settle around him. From the sounds he heard now, he judged that there were seven or eight riders around him. They had him surrounded so that if he came to, he couldn't try to make a break for freedom.

He didn't want to escape, Jackson realized, at least not just yet. What he wanted was to know who these men were.

One of the riders had to be holding his horse's reins and leading the animal. The man pulled back on them and said, "Whoa," bringing Jackson's mount to a halt. They must have reached their destination. The man's voice was thick, disguised somehow, as he went on. "Get him down from there." Jackson didn't recall ever hearing it before, but it was hard to be sure under the circumstances.

He felt a knife slice through the bonds on his wrists and ankles, parting the ropes with a jerk. Hands grasped him. Keeping his body limp, he let himself be dragged out of the saddle and dropped on the ground.

"Get the hood off of him," the leader ordered.

Jackson had already noticed a faint smell of flour, and figured out that his vision was obscured by one of those flour-sack hoods like the ones worn by the men who'd ambushed him earlier tonight. It was pulled off of his head now. Light hit his eyes.

Something was wrong. His vision was still obscured. He could see lights moving around him, but they were blurry, indistinct. All he could make out was their brightness and circular shape. As he blinked his eyes he felt something against them. A cloth of some sort was bound around his head, covering his eyes. It was thin and gauzy, but it blocked his sight enough so that he couldn't make out details, only the lights and vague shapes moving around him.

"He's awake," the leader said with a sneer in his voice. "Get him on his feet."

Strong hands gripped Jackson again and hauled him upright. If they hadn't killed him so far, what was the likelihood that they would kill him now? He hoped it was small, but unfortunately, he couldn't answer that question for sure. He might be dealing with madmen here . . . or at least one madman, the man in charge.

"Tie him to that tree."

Jackson didn't like the sound of those orders, or the cold, flat voice in which they were issued. His captors hustled him over to what felt like the trunk of a pine tree. Its rough, sticky bark pressed painfully against his face as his arms were pulled around the trunk and he was tied to it as if he were hugging it. What felt like rawhide thongs were pulled painfully tight around his wrists.

"Hell Jackson, do you hear me?"

"I hear you," Jackson grated. He couldn't very well play dumb now.

"Your very name declares you to be a tool of the Devil. And like all of Satan's minions, you have the blood of innocents on your hands."

"I never killed anybody who didn't have it coming."

"Silence! You speak the lies of Lucifer!"

The bastard was spreading it on mighty thick, Jackson thought, but for whose benefit? His? Or were the melodramatic utterances intended more for the other men? Jackson had no idea.

"I am the Hand of God on Earth," intoned the leader of his captors. "I have been sent to do the Lord's work, and that work is the punishment of sinners. Liars, drunkards, fornicators, and thieves! All are sinners, and all will know the wrath of the Hand of God!"

Jackson had been testing his bonds. The son of a buck who'd tied them had been good at it. Jackson figured he could work his way free, but it would take him a while. That was time he might not have. He thought about what happened to Berryhill, Harcourt, and Mrs. Vance, and an image of himself with his face destroyed filled his brain. He had to push it away stubbornly so that he wouldn't panic.

"You will not be killed," the so-called Hand of God went on, "but you *will* be punished. You are being spared so that you can go back to Death Head Crossing and warn all the sinners there to beware of the Lord's vengeance. You will serve as an example, Hell Jackson, an example to all who would dare to defy the Hand of God!"

The next words were almost more chilling than anything that had gone before.

"Bring the whip."

CHAPTER 25

Instinctively, Jackson jerked against the bonds that held him to the tree trunk. He couldn't budge them. An inarticulate shout of rage welled up his throat, but couldn't escape from his mouth because of the gag. All that came out was a muffled groan.

"Bare his back," the Hand of God ordered.

Jackson heard ripping sounds as his shirt was torn away from him. Here in the thin atmosphere of West Texas, the nights were cool despite the heat of the day, and he felt the chill of the air against his skin. He tugged against his bonds again, still to no avail.

"Go ahead," the Hand of God said.

Jackson heard a hissing sound, like a snake might make, but he knew it was no serpent. It was a bullwhip being shaken out and readied for use. His blood congealed in his veins at the thought of what was coming.

263

Even though he tried to prepare himself mentally, the first stroke of the lash across his back was even worse than he expected it to be. The whip struck him with such physical force that he was driven hard against the tree trunk, scraping his face against the bark, and at the same time it burned like fire as it laid open the flesh of his back. The pop of the whip as it was pulled away was added torment.

"Again," the Hand of God said.

Jackson hadn't made a sound when the first stroke landed, and he set his jaw and steeled himself to continue that stubborn silence, denying them the satisfaction of hearing him cry out. Again, the whip slashed blazingly across his back. He squeezed his eyes tightly shut and ground his teeth together.

"Again."

On the third stroke, a grunt of agony escaped from his mouth, despite his efforts to hold it in. His whole body was filled with pain now, and he would have collapsed if his arms hadn't been bound so tightly around the tree that he couldn't. He had been shot and stabbed several times in his life and had suffered other injuries, but he had never been whipped like this before. It was the worst torture he had ever endured.

"Go ahead until I tell you to stop," the Hand of God told the man who wielded the whip.

The fourth stroke fell and then the fifth, and Jackson whimpered, the sound so tiny that maybe none of his captors heard it. But Jackson knew he had made it, and he hated himself for that moment of weakness. He clenched his jaw even tighter, until it seemed that the bones might break.

His entire existence was pain. It had grown so large that there was no room for anything else in his awareness. But as the whip continued to brand him, a blessed numbness started to spread through him. He could still feel the flesh of his back being shredded, but it didn't hurt as much anymore. Then, after a while, it didn't hurt at all. The Hand of God had said that they weren't going to kill him, but it was beginning to look like he was going to be whipped to death after all. In his stunned lassitude, he didn't really care.

But then the fiery agony of his back kindled a different kind of flame deep inside him. Anger began to grow. No one had ever dared to treat him like this. His need for vengeance swelled. If the Hand of God was dumb enough to let him live after this, then sooner or later the bastard would regret that decision. Jackson swore that to himself as he drew strength from the inferno of rage that now blazed within him.

He was only vaguely aware of the voice saying, "That's enough. Cut him down."

His hands and arms had gone numb. He didn't feel the knife cutting his bonds, didn't even realize he was free until he slumped to the ground. The pain of the blood rushing back into his hands took him by surprise, so that he gave a little hissing cry at the pins and needles. He had held it in for the most part during the whipping, only to give in now and shame himself.

One more mark against the Hand of God.

"Put him back on his horse."

Jackson was lifted into the saddle and tied onto the animal's back as he had been before, so he couldn't fall off. The Hand of God continued. "Take him close enough to the settlement that the horse will go on the rest of the way by itself. Be careful not to let anyone see you."

"Sure, Boss," one of the other men said. "I don't know if this fella's gonna live long enough to make it back, though."

"Oh, he'll make it. He's tough. Haven't you ever heard of Hell Jackson, the famous gunslinger?"

The Hand was talking in a more normal

tone now, instead of making ominous pronouncements. But Jackson still couldn't pin down the voice. Did it belong to Benjamin Tillman or not? Jackson suspected that the Hand of God wore a hood like the other men, to hide his face and muffle his voice.

Jackson felt the horse lurch into motion. The animal's every step sent a fresh jolt of agony through him. The ride back to Death Head Crossing was going to be a long, painful one.

He let his mind drift. That was the easiest way to cope with the pain. Just go somewhere else, he told himself. Go somewhere it doesn't hurt so bad. He imagined himself sitting beside a high mountain stream, a fishing pole in his hand and the sun warm on his face.

Time meant nothing. He couldn't have said whether he had been swaying in the saddle for minutes, hours, or days when he heard a voice say mockingly, "So long, Jackson." The horse continued to plod forward.

Sometime later — again, Jackson couldn't have said how long it was — he heard a stifled scream. Then hands were tugging on the bonds around his wrists. As the ropes came free, he felt himself start to slide, and instinctively grabbed at the horn to keep himself from falling out of the saddle. His fingers slipped off, though, and he toppled off the horse.

He didn't know if anyone was there to catch him or not. He didn't feel himself hit the ground, but that could have been because a sea of blackness had already swallowed him whole.

Most nights, Philomena enjoyed her walk home from the boardinghouse, even though her simple little hut was all that awaited her. It was good to be away from Señora Morton. The woman didn't treat Philomena and the other girls who worked for her too badly, but they were always aware that she looked down on them. She made that clear with her glares of disapproval, her little sniffs of disappointment when not everything was done exactly as she wished, her occasional comments about Mexicans and how lazy they were. But in all that, Señora Morton was no different than most people, and Philomena had grown to tolerate her.

The boardinghouse was usually stuffy too, since Mrs. Morton didn't like to have the windows open. So Philomena enjoyed the night air as she walked home. Sometimes, cowboys would ride past and, emboldened by whiskey, would call out crude comments to her. Philomena always ignored them, holding her head high and proud as she did so, and the men usually laughed and rode on. Whenever one was particularly bold and got down from his horse to approach her, she always drew the knife from under her skirt and threatened him in rapid Spanish as she brandished the blade at him. So far, that had been enough to make the men back off and leave her alone. But perhaps some night it would not be. . . .

No one would bother her if Señor Hell Jackson walked at her side, she thought tonight. She imagined how nice it would feel to stroll through the night with him. He was not a handsome man; his face was too rugged and stern for that. But she liked his face anyway, and had thought more than once about how it would feel to stroke his lean cheek with her fingertips as she looked into his eyes. She wished he was waiting for her tonight in her hut.

She noticed a horse plodding along the street toward her. It had just entered the edge of town, so Philomena couldn't see the rider very well in the shadows. But as the horse came closer, she realized that the man wore no hat, which was unusual for this part of Texas. Something was familiar about him too. Perhaps it was the broad spread of his shoulders.

Philomena caught her breath as she realized that the rider looked like Señor Jackson. Something was wrong, though. He always rode with his back straight and his head up, and this man was slumped forward. He usually kept his mount moving at a brisk walk too, but tonight the horse plodded along like there was no hand on the reins. The rider swayed first to one side and then the other, catching himself at the last second before falling.

Telling herself that this could not be Señor Jackson, Philomena broke into a run toward the horse and rider. As she came closer, she recognized the animal as the one Señor Jackson always rode. Man and horse passed through a slanting patch of light that came from a window of a building they passed, and Philomena saw the familiar dark hair and hard-planed face. It *was* him. There was no doubt about it now. But he was hurt, and as Philomena dashed up and grabbed the horse's reins, she saw that his shirt had been stripped off of him and his back was dark with blood. She clapped one hand over her mouth to stifle the scream that tried to escape.

Señor Jackson needed help, not some hysterical woman crying. Philomena saw now that his hands were tied to the saddle horn, and his feet had been lashed together under the belly of the horse. She took out her knife and cut that rope, but she hesitated to saw at the bonds around his wrists for fear of the blade slipping and cutting him. So she put away the knife and began trying to untie the ropes. The knots were stubborn. Her nails broke and began to bleed. She kept at it, every bit as stubborn as those knots.

Finally, one came free, then another and another, and the ropes fell away from Jackson's wrists. He was half conscious at best, but he was still aware enough of his surroundings to make a grab for the saddle horn as his balance deserted him and he started to fall. He missed and toppled from the saddle.

Philomena was there to throw her arms around him and break his fall, but he was considerably larger than her and it was all deadweight now, because he had passed out completely. Either that or he really was dead, she thought, but she forced that idea out of her head. He could not be dead. She would not allow it.

He had knocked her to one knee when she caught him. She struggled upright, using the strength that a lifetime of hard work had given her. Her bare arms pressed against his back, and she shuddered as she felt how raw and sticky with blood it was.

They weren't far from her hut. There was a shortcut down a nearby alley, in fact. Philomena had to drag him. He was out cold and couldn't help her. It seemed to take forever to reach her hut. She backed all the way there, keeping her arms locked around Jackson so that he wouldn't fall and get dirt on his torn flesh. His head rested on her shoulder. She felt his warm breath on her skin, so she knew he was still alive and thanked the Blessed Virgin for that.

She kicked the door open behind her and pulled him inside. The hut was dark, but she didn't need light to get around in it. She knew every inch of it. Panting with the effort, she got him over to the bunk and carefully lowered him onto it, turning him so that he lay facedown. Still fighting against panic, she straightened and thought that she had to go find someone to help him. He needed a doctor, or at the very least more medical care than she could provide. She backed away from the bunk, then turned and plunged through the door, out into the night once again.

She didn't even notice in the moonlight that her arms were stained with blood where she had held him.

She emerged onto the main street and looked around wildly. She was about to turn toward the doctor's house when she spotted a familiar figure walking away from her. *Señor Everett!* He would know what to do. She ran after him, too breathless to even call his name.

When she reached him, she grabbed his arm and jerked him around. The fierce control she had imposed on herself finally snapped. She began to sob, and the only words she could manage to get out were, "Señor Jackson! Help! Help!"

CHAPTER 26

Everett let out a startled yell as he was pulled around to face the person who had grabbed him. He jerked loose and brought his hands up to defend himself, because he was certain he was being attacked.

But instead of fighting back, he was shocked to see Philomena standing there. Tears began to run down her face as she sobbed, "Señor Jackson! Help! Help!"

"Philomena!" Realizing that she was hysterical, Everett took hold of her shoulders and gave her a little shake. "Philomena, snap out of it! I'm not Señor Jackson! I'm Everett!"

She stared at him for a second, then said, "I know that!" She leveled an arm, pointing. "There, in my hut! He needs help!"

It took a moment for her words to soak in on Everett, because he was staring at her arm . . . an arm that was smeared with blood from the hand almost to the shoulder.

Her other arm was the same way, he saw. Even the short sleeves of her low-cut white blouse had crimson smears on them.

"Philomena!" he said, aghast at what he took to be her injuries. "What have you done to yourself?"

"Oh!" she exclaimed in obvious exasperation. "I have done nothing! It is Señor Jackson who is hurt! He is lying in my jacal!"

Everett understood now, and suddenly he was afraid for Jackson. That was the gunslinger's blood on Philomena's arms. Jackson had to be hurt pretty badly to have lost that much blood.

"Take me to him," Everett said, and Philomena grabbed his hand and tugged him toward the mouth of an alley.

"Through here," she said. "It is closer."

Everett couldn't see where he was going in the gloom, but Philomena seemed to know the way, so he trusted her. She had no reason to be leading him into a trap. Anyway, she was too upset to be faking anything. Her agitated state seemed genuine to Everett.

They came out at the rear of her hut. She flung open the back door and pulled Everett inside. As she let go of his hand, she said, "I will light the lamp."

As Everett waited in utter darkness, he

heard the rasp of heavy breathing. Philomena muttered something in Spanish that sounded like a curse, and Everett wondered if she was having trouble with the lamp. But then, with the scrape of a match, light flared up. The glow from the match in her fingers only vaguely illuminated the room.

Everett saw a dark shape huddled on the bunk next to the wall, but he couldn't make out the details. Then Philomena held the flame to the wick of a lamp and lowered the chimney as it caught. Yellow light spread throughout the room, flickering for a couple of seconds before it steadied.

"My God!" Everett said as he stared at Jackson. The gunslinger lay facedown on Philomena's bunk. His back had been torn to shreds. Everett couldn't imagine what could have done such a thing. A grizzly bear maybe. Did they have grizzly bears in this part of Texas?

Everett knelt beside the bunk while Philomena brought the lamp over to give him a better look at the damage. Everett had to turn his face away from the torn flesh for a moment and take a deep breath to calm his nerves. When he had steeled himself, he looked again at Jackson's back and asked Philomena, "Do you have any idea what did this?"

Her face was grim as she nodded. "I have seen such things before, below the border where the *hacendados* rule like kings. He has been whipped."

"Whipped! You mean . . . someone did this to him deliberately?"

"Very deliberately," Philomena said. "It takes much practice and skill — terrible skill — to use a bullwhip in such fashion."

"He needs a doctor. I'll stay with him while you run down to Dr. Musgrave's office and fetch him —"

"N-no."

Everett stared. He hadn't realized that Jackson had regained consciousness. The gunslinger turned his head slightly so that he peered up at Everett through one narrowly slitted eye.

"No," Jackson grated again. "N-no doctor . . ."

"But . . . but you're badly hurt!"

"Ph-Philomena . . ."

She leaned closer. "I am here, Señor Jackson. You must have the *curandero* —"

"You can . . . take care of me," he broke in. "I don't want anybody to . . . know about this."

Understanding dawned in Everett's mind. "With your reputation, you're afraid that if word gets around about you being incapacitated, your enemies will show up and try to kill you."

Jackson didn't confirm or deny that theory. He just said again, "No . . . doctor."

Everett looked over at Philomena and asked, "Can you care for him?"

"I . . . I can clean the blood off his back and keep wet cloths on the wounds," she said. "I can squeeze the juice from a plant that grows here and spread it on his back. It helps injuries to heal."

Everett thought it over for a moment and then nodded. "That's probably just about as much as Dr. Musgrave could do. We'll give it a try. We can always seek the doctor's help later if we need to."

"You are sure about this, Señor Everett?" She didn't sound like she thought it was a very good idea.

Everett nodded again. "We might be putting Jackson in more danger by exposing what happened to him. Right now, you should heat some water, and we'll start cleaning him up."

Jackson lifted his head slightly and husked, "Mescal."

"I don't know if a drink would be a good idea —" Everett began.

"He needs something for the pain," Philomena said as she straightened. She fetched

and the rest of his men . . . lassoed me . . . tied me to a tree . . . then one of 'em went to work on me . . . with a bullwhip."

"The bastards," Everett said as Philomena pressed a hand to her mouth.

"The Hand said he was . . . punishing me . . . but not killing me . . . because he wanted me to come back here . . . tell folks in town all about him . . . tell them that he was going to punish all the sinners . . ."

"But instead you don't want me to say anything to anyone about this?"

"No. Let him do . . . his own dirty work. Gonna lie low . . . let him wonder . . . what happened to me."

"Then what?"

A savage smile pulled at Jackson's mouth. "Soon as I'm up to it . . . I plan to meet up with the Hand again . . . and do a little punishing of my own."

CHAPTER 27

The next few days were miserable ones for Jackson. By the morning after the whipping, he was so sore and in so much pain that he could barely move. Philomena kept spreading the juice from the plants on his back, and that helped some. But he got awfully tired of lying on his stomach on her bunk, and it bothered him when he realized she was sleeping on a pallet on the floor. He offered to move down there, but she wouldn't hear of it.

Despite the pain he was in from his back, his brain still worked all right. He wanted to keep his presence at Philomena's a secret, so that the Hand of God would wonder what had happened to him and why the message he had given Jackson to take back to Death Head Crossing had not been delivered. The first night, he had Everett take his horse and hide it in a shed that belonged to one of Philomena's friends, another of the women who worked at the boardinghouse. Philomena also sent word to Mrs. Morton the next day that she was ill and wouldn't be able to work for several days.

"That won't cost you your job, will it?" Jackson wanted to know.

Philomena shrugged. "If it does, I do not care. I would rather stay here and take care of you."

"Just like a woman," he said as he summoned up a smile. "You see somebody in as bad a shape as I am, and you just can't resist taking care of him."

"You did what you could to help my grandfather, Señor Jackson. This is a debt I will never be able to repay."

It was more than that, though, and Jackson knew it. He hoped Philomena wouldn't take it too hard when the time came for him to leave Death Head Crossing, as it inevitably would.

But not until he had settled the score with a certain hood-wearing madman . . .

Everett served as Jackson's eyes and ears, dropping in at Philomena's several times a day to report what was going on in the settlement. When Jackson first asked him to do that, Everett said, "Are you sure you trust me to take care of something so important?"

"Everett," Jackson said in a chiding voice, "you're not mad at me because I told you to let me handle things for a while, are you?"

"Well . . . it seemed like you didn't trust me anymore!" Everett burst out. "I thought we were partners, but then everything changed."

Jackson wasn't the sort of man who made a habit of explaining himself, but in this case he said, "I knew I might be running into some trouble — hell, I *hoped* I'd be running into some trouble — and I didn't want to put you in danger. I didn't want what happened to me to happen to you. A beating like this probably would have killed you."

"I suppose that's true," Everett admitted. "But I don't mind running a few risks. A journalist has to do that sometimes."

Jackson nodded. "I'll keep that in mind."

By the time several days had gone by, Jackson was able to sit up and move around a little. The cuts on his back were beginning to heal, thanks to Philomena's care. She wrapped bandages around his torso to hold the torn flesh together and to protect him from further injury. It would be a good while before Jackson was back to normal, but at least he could feel the progress he was making, and that was encouraging.

In the meantime, the Hand of God had evidently been lying low too. Sheriff Brennan told Everett that there hadn't been any more trouble, and Everett reported that fact to Jackson.

The three of them sat together around the table in Philomena's hut that evening. Jackson felt good about being up and around again, although Philomena warned him about not trying to do too much too soon.

"Don't worry," he told her. "I know I'm not ready to strap on my six-gun and go looking for the Hand of God just yet. That showdown will have to wait a while longer."

"I was thinking about riding out to the Winged T again," Everett said.

Jackson frowned. "I'm not sure that'd be a good idea."

"Tillman has to be puzzled about your disappearance," Everett argued. "He might let something slip that would prove he's behind all the trouble."

"Anything he said to you wouldn't prove anything unless other witnesses were around to hear it too," Jackson pointed out. "And he might decide to just kill you and not take a chance on you telling anybody else."

"Well, there is that possibility," Everett

admitted.

"Maybe you'd better wait a while. Let Tillman stew in his own juices for now."

Philomena said, "You are certain that Señor Tillman is the one who calls himself the Hand of God?" She added under her breath, "It is blasphemy."

Everett began, "Of course he's —" The young reporter stopped when he saw the frown on Jackson's face. "You *are* convinced of Tillman's guilt, aren't you?"

"Everything seems to revolve around the Winged T," Jackson said, "and Tillman's loco enough that I wouldn't put anything past him. The way he jumped you that day is proof of that."

Everett lifted a hand to his face and touched one of the scratches from the rosebushes that could still be seen faintly. Most of them already had healed up.

"But something bothers me about this whole thing," Jackson went on. "Something's not right about it."

"He is insane," Philomena said. "Of course it is not right."

"We'll see," Jackson said. "We'll see."

The next day, in fact, they saw.

Everett was in the newspaper office, talking to Malcolm Graham. Rosalie wasn't there, which had come as a disappointment to Everett when he walked in and found Graham working at the composing trays, setting type for the next issue of the *Journal.*

After a few minutes of small talk, which elicited the information that Rosalie would be in later, Graham asked, "Where's that friend of yours these days, Everett? I'm still waiting to do that interview with him."

"You mean Mr. Jackson? I don't really know. I haven't seen him for several days myself." Everett shrugged. "We're not really friends. He goes his own way. He may have even left this part of the country."

"But I thought you were going to travel with him and write about him," Graham said with a puzzled frown.

"That didn't work out as well as I had hoped."

Graham seemed to accept that answer. "Well, if you happen to run into him, tell him I'd still like to talk to him and maybe take his picture."

"You're a photographer too?"

"I dabble in it," Graham said with a smile. "I've given some thought to opening a photographic studio here in Death Head Crossing, if the town ever grows big enough to support one."

Everett was interested in that, and would

have asked Graham more questions about the subject, but at that moment they heard the sudden clatter of hoofbeats from the street. Someone was in a hurry, and that meant news.

Both men hurried to the door to look out. They saw Ned Dawson, the foreman of the Winged T, gallop past the newspaper office. Everett caught a glimpse of Dawson's face, and was surprised to see how pale and shocked the man seemed to be. Dawson fogged it on down the street, pulling his lathered horse to a stop in front of Sheriff Ward Brennan's office.

Everett and Graham exchanged a look, and without saying a word, they started toward the sheriff's office. Dawson dismounted and hurried inside without looking around, obviously intent on the mission that had brought him to Death Head Crossing.

As Everett and Graham entered the sheriff's office, Brennan was saying, "Slow down, slow down, Ned. What's all this uproar about?"

Dawson said, "I'm tellin' you, there's bad trouble out at the ranch." He glanced at the two newcomers. "Damn it, do these newspaper fellas have to be here?"

"I'm sure you've heard of freedom of the

press, Mr. Dawson," Graham said. "Mr. Howard and I certainly have a right to be here."

Brennan rumbled, "This is still my office, and I'll decide who stays and who goes." He glared at Dawson. "But I can't figure that out until I know what the hell's goin' on. Just spit it out, Ned."

Dawson rubbed at his grizzled jaw for a moment, then shook his head. "I can't. I don't even know where to start. You'd better just come out there and have a look for yourself, Sheriff. I sure don't know what in blazes to make of it."

Brennan sighed in exasperation. "You can't even tell me what happened?"

"That's the hell of it," Dawson said. "I ain't rightly sure. I just know it's bad."

Brennan nodded curtly and reached for his hat. "All right, I'll ride back out there with you. But this better not be a waste o' my time, that's all I'm sayin'."

"I'm coming too," Graham declared. "I'll saddle my horse."

Acting on a hunch, Everett followed his instincts and said, "I'll accompany you."

"Dad-gum it!" Dawson burst out. "Pretty soon we'll have the whole blamed town traipsin' out there!"

"No, just these two fellas," Brennan said,

"and I reckon they've got a right to be there, bein' journalists and all. Or do you think I need to take some deputies too?"

The foreman's face was bleak as he shook his head. "No, you won't need a posse. Whatever happened, it's all over now."

Everett didn't much like the sound of that. The finality of Dawson's statement was obvious.

Brennan looked at the two newspapermen and said, "I can't stop you from comin' along, but that don't mean I have to wait for you. You'd better hurry up if you're ridin' with us."

Everett and Graham hustled out of the sheriff's office. Since their horses were kept in different places, they agreed to meet back in front of Brennan's office as quickly as possible. "Don't waste any time," Graham warned. "Sheriff Brennan means what he says."

Everett hurried to the stable behind the boardinghouse and slapped the saddle on his horse. He wished there was time to stop by Philomena's and let Jackson know that something important was going on, but he couldn't afford the delay. Everett's movements as he saddled up were still awkward, but he was getting better at it with practice.

Graham was waiting on horseback when

Everett rode up a few minutes later. "The sheriff and Mr. Dawson just left," Graham said. "We can probably catch them if we hurry."

"By all means," Everett agreed.

The two men rode hard out of Death Head Crossing, following the lawman and the foreman of the Winged T. Everett couldn't help but wonder what they would find when they got to the ranch. The way Dawson had acted, it couldn't be anything good.

CHAPTER 28

The Hand of God must have struck again, Everett thought as he rode. Tillman had gotten tired of waiting for Jackson to deliver his "message," so he had taken the initiative and dealt out more death and horror.

Everett spotted Dawson and Sheriff Brennan ahead of them. The two men were fairly easy to follow because of the dust cloud that rose from the hooves of their horses. That was how Everett and Graham knew when Dawson and Brennan veered off the main trail between Death Head Crossing and the ranch headquarters. Everett was pretty sure they were already on Winged T range, but he didn't know the countryside as well as Jackson did. He wished the gunslinger was with them now, instead of recuperating back in the settlement.

Several minutes after leaving the main trail, Dawson and Brennan came to a stop. Everett saw them sitting on their horses next to a line of trees that he assumed marked the course of a stream. Brennan swung down from his saddle as Everett and Graham hurried to reach the scene.

Everett's horse slowed from its gallop as the young reporter hauled back on the reins. Everett was almost thrown forward over the horse's head as it came to a skidding halt. Graham brought his mount to a stop much more gracefully. On the way out here, Everett had noticed how well Graham rode. Graham had lived on the frontier long enough to pick up that skill.

Dawson cast a sour look in their direction as they dismounted. They followed Brennan into the trees and found the lawman standing on the bank of the creek Everett had assumed was there. Benjamin Tillman's buggy was parked beside the stream, too. The shade under the trees was thick enough so that at first Everett could make out only a couple of vague shapes sitting in the vehicle.

Then as his eyes adjusted to the dimness he felt sick horror course through him. Beside him, Malcolm Graham muttered a shocked "Oh, my God."

Benjamin Tillman and his cousin Deborah both sat motionless on the buggy seat. Tillman's left arm was draped around Deborah's shoulders as she leaned against his side. Her head rested on his shoulder. Her eyes bulged grotesquely from their sockets, and the tip of her tongue protruded a couple of inches from her mouth. The skin of her face was an unnatural blue.

She was dead. A glance was enough for anyone to see that. As Everett struggled to control the sickness inside him, he told himself that she had been strangled. The cruel marks of a madman's fingers could be seen on her throat, above the high neck of her dress.

Tillman's head was tipped far back. Brennan moved to one side of the buggy and leaned over to get a better look. "Son of a bitch," he muttered. "He must've put the gun barrel halfway down his throat before he pulled the trigger."

For the first time Everett noticed the revolver lying next to the buggy. Tillman's right arm was flung out to the side, and as Everett studied the scene he had no trouble reconstructing what had happened. Tillman had put the gun in his mouth and fired the fatal shot, and the recoil had jerked his arm to the side. The gun lay where it had fallen when it slipped from Tillman's nerveless fingers.

Graham started to step forward, but Brennan lifted a hand to stop him. "You don't want to look too close at this," the sheriff warned. "The back of his head is blown clean off."

Graham was pale and shaken, but he said, "Sheriff, I . . . I have a responsibility. When the richest man in the county commits suicide after murdering his own cousin —"

"How do you know he did that?" Brennan asked.

"Well . . . you can see for yourself! Poor Miss Tillman has been strangled, and there's no one else out here —"

"Someone else *could* have done it," Everett broke in. "Maybe Tillman found Deborah's body after someone else killed her." His own voice sounded strange to him. How could he be discussing something so tragic in such a calm tone? "Mr. Tillman was quite fond of his cousin," he went on. "Maybe he felt that he couldn't live without her and decided to end his own life?"

Brennan chewed on his mustache and nodded slowly. "Yeah, I reckon it could've happened that way . . . but I think Graham's a lot more likely to be right in this case." He turned his head and called Dawson's name.

The foreman entered the grove of trees on the creek bank with obvious reluctance. "What do you want, Sheriff?"

"Who found the buggy?" Brennan asked.

"One of the hands, a fella name of York. He saw the buggy parked over here and thought the horses looked like they was spooked, so he rode over to take a look. He was on his way to ride the boundary line not far from here."

"Was that his idea?"

"Hell, no. I told him to do it. It was just a routine chore."

"You didn't have any idea Mr. Tillman and his cousin were out here?"

"How the hell would I have known that?" Dawson demanded. "I hadn't even seen the boss this mornin'. Nobody had except Hiram. He said Mr. Tillman was up early, but he didn't see either of 'em leave the house."

"What did this fella York do when he saw what was in the buggy?"

"What do you think? He lit a shuck back to the bunkhouse and told me he'd found the boss and the gal out here dead. I stopped long enough to ask Hiram if he knew what was goin' on; then I rode out here as fast as I could. When I'd taken a look, I headed for town to fetch you. I'd already told York to keep everybody else away from here."

Brennan nodded. "Yeah, I reckon you handled it about right. How come you wouldn't tell me what happened?"

"I wanted you to see it fresh, so I could tell if it looked the same to you as it does to me."

"How else could it look? But why in blazes would Tillman do such a terrible thing?"

Everett thought he had a pretty good idea, but he didn't want to speak up just yet.

Graham suddenly pointed into the buggy and asked, "What's that?"

Brennan frowned. "What's what?"

"That paper sticking up from Mr. Tillman's vest pocket."

Gingerly, Brennan reached up to the motionless body and slid a folded piece of paper out of Tillman's pocket. Everett, Graham, and Dawson crowded closer as the sheriff unfolded the paper, revealing lines of cramped handwriting that filled almost the whole page.

"Good Lord," Brennan muttered as he began to read. "He killed her, all right. This here's the proof of it."

Everett craned his neck in an attempt to read the lines Benjamin Tillman had written. He could only make out some of them, but those were enough.

. . . driven mad by lust for my poor, innocent cousin . . . knew I could never have her . . . seized by a frenzy of desire . . . Deborah

fought back, called me awful names . . . not even sure what happened, but I found myself with my fingers locked around her sweet neck . . . no hope, no forgiveness . . . cannot live without her . . .

"Son of a bitch!" Brennan said. "He goes on to say that he was the one callin' himself the Hand of God!"

. . . thought if I dedicated myself to the Lord's work . . . punished the sinners . . . would give me strength to resist temptation . . . avenger of the Lord . . . kill all the evildoers . . . but the worst evil was in me . . .

. . . must be with Deborah . . . only way to see her again . . . forgive me for this terrible thing and all the other things I've done . . . end it all . . .

"Incredible," Graham muttered. "So Benjamin Tillman was the Hand of God all along. He was responsible for what happened to Luther Berryhill and Harcourt and poor Mrs. Vance."

"Yeah, this letter doesn't leave any doubt about that," Brennan said. "But he didn't carry out all those killin's by himself. Not a damn tenderfoot like him. He had to have help." The sheriff looked pointedly at Ned Dawson.

"Damn it!" Dawson yelped. "You don't think *I* had anything to do with this, do you?

This is the first I've heard about it, I swear!"

"What about some of the other members of the Winged T crew?" Graham asked. "Could Tillman have paid them to help him?"

Dawson grimaced. "Well, I reckon that's possible. They're a pretty salty bunch, and some of 'em ain't been ridin' for the Winged T all that long, so I don't know 'em too well. If the money was right, some of the boys might've been willin' to go along with the boss and help him with his mischief."

Everett thought that the bloody depredations of the Hand of God amounted to a lot more than mischief, but he knew what Dawson meant.

"I'll be wantin' to talk to every damn cowboy on the place," Brennan said. "If any of 'em take off for the tall and uncut when word of Tillman's death gets around, I reckon we'll know which ones were helpin' him."

"You'd better be careful, Sheriff," Graham warned. "Anyone who was mixed up in this probably won't want his part in it to get out."

Brennan nodded grimly. "I know. I don't intend to give any of 'em the chance to get the drop on me."

Dawson waved a gnarled and calloused

301

hand toward the buggy and its passengers. "What are you gonna do about this?"

"Tie your horse to the back of the buggy and climb in," Brennan said. "You can drive it into town, to Cecil Greenwood's undertakin' parlor."

Dawson shook his head. "You can go ahead and draw your Colt if you want to, Sheriff, but I warn you, you'll have to use it. I ain't gettin' up there with them, even at gunpoint."

Brennan looked over at Everett and Graham, both of whom made a point of gazing elsewhere. Everett didn't think his stomach could stand being crowded onto that seat with the two corpses.

"Oh, hell, all right," Brennan said to Dawson. "I don't want to do it neither. Go get that spring wagon ol' Hiram uses to fetch supplies from town. We'll put the bodies in the back of it and cover 'em up. I'll stay here with the buggy while you're fetchin' the wagon."

The foreman nodded. "I reckon that'd be all right."

"What about us, Sheriff?" Graham asked. "Do you need us anymore?"

"I don't recollect sayin' I needed you to start with," Brennan snapped. "I reckon you want to get back to town and start writin' your stories. Well, you can have at it as far as I'm concerned."

"Thank you, Sheriff." Still looking upset, Graham walked back to his horse. Everett followed, but he glanced back at the buggy with the grim-faced lawman standing beside it. From there, Everett couldn't see what was inside the buggy, but that didn't matter. He was afraid the memory of what he had witnessed today would be burned into his brain for a long time, if not forever. He was anxious to get back to Death Head Crossing.

Not to write about it, though. He wanted to tell Jackson about the tragic, unexpected turn this affair had taken. The gunslinger might even be disappointed.

Because he wouldn't get to settle his score with the so-called Hand of God after all.

CHAPTER 29

One of Philomena's friends did her shopping for her, since she was still supposed to be sick. The woman had just left after dropping off some supplies when a horse came to a fast stop outside the hut.

Jackson was seated at the table while Philomena put away the provisions. At the sound of the hoofbeats, he put his hand on the butt of the Colt lying on the table. The gun he had carried when he came to Death Head Crossing was gone, taken from him when he was captured by the Hand of God. Everett had replaced it with a new Peacemaker bought at the local mercantile, and Jackson kept the revolver close at hand at all times.

He picked it up as the door burst open, then relaxed as he saw that the visitor was just Everett. The young reporter seemed mighty upset about something, though, so Jackson hung onto the gun, just in case trouble was following hot on Everett's heels.

"Dios mio!" Philomena said. "Señor Everett, what is wrong? You look as though you have seen *el espectro.* A ghost."

"Not a ghost," Everett said with a vehement shake of his head. "But a couple of corpses, though."

"Who's dead?" Jackson asked in a flat voice.

"Benjamin Tillman and his cousin."

Jackson's eyes narrowed, but that was his only visible reaction to the shocking news. Philomena gasped and put a hand to her mouth.

"What happened to them?"

Everett took off his derby and set it on the table. He sat down across from Jackson and distractedly raked the fingers of one hand through his red hair. "It was awful," he said. "Truly awful. I've never seen anything like it."

"The Hand of God killed them?"

"You could say that. Tillman really *was* the Hand of God, just as we suspected, and he murdered Deborah and then killed himself because he was driven insane by lust and guilt."

"Tell me everything you know about it," Jackson said.

For the next few minutes, Everett filled

him in on the situation, starting with Ned Dawson's hurried ride into town. The young man had a reporter's eye for details and flair for description, so he was able to paint a vivid picture of what had happened. Too vivid for Philomena, who sat down at the table too and wiped at the tears that welled up in her eyes.

"The poor señorita," she said when Everett was finished. "Ah, *Dios mio,* the poor señorita."

"You saw Tillman's letter with your own eyes?" Jackson asked.

Everett nodded. "The sheriff was holding it, but I saw him take it out of Tillman's pocket and I was able to read part of it. There's no doubt in my mind about what happened. Tillman confessed to everything." Everett sat back in his chair and rested his hands on the table. "That means it's over. Really over."

"Sounds like it," Jackson agreed.

"It's just a shame we couldn't have put a stop to Tillman's lunacy before Deborah had to die."

"We're not the law. Nobody appointed us to right the wrongs of the world."

"No, of course not," Everett said, "but she was blameless in this. It wasn't her fault that she inflamed her cousin's mind to the point of madness."

Jackson grunted. "That the way he put it in his letter?"

"Pretty much." Everett sighed. "What are we going to do now?"

"I don't know about you," Jackson said, "but I plan to keep on getting over that beating I took and enjoying Philomena's company."

"Yes, of course, but where will we be going from here, once you're able to travel again?"

"How do you know we'll be going anywhere?"

"Why, our agreement still holds, doesn't it? You're going to let me travel with you so that I can write about your adventures?"

"Maybe I plan to settle down right here in Death Head Crossing and not have any more adventures," Jackson said with a faint smile. "How would you feel about that?"

Everett looked surprised. "But . . . but how could a man such as yourself do that? You've always been a drifter. Fiddle-footed, you called it. How could you trade a life of excitement for settling down in one place?"

"Most men stay in one place," Jackson pointed out. "They might move around some, but sooner or later they put down roots. And they manage to live just fine without being shot at on a regular basis or bullwhipped by insane fanatics."

"I just can't accept that! Your whole history tells me —"

"Señor Everett," Philomena broke in. "Señor Jackson is, how do you say, joshing you." She looked at Jackson with more than a hint of sadness in her dark eyes. "He will not stay in Death Head Crossing. He is a man who could never settle down."

"Oh," Everett said. "Oh, I see."

"Don't worry about it, Everett," Jackson drawled. "When I get ready to ride, I'll let you know. That'll still be a while, though, until this back of mine heals up better."

"Yes, of course. I understand now."

He didn't understand everything, though, Jackson thought. Everett hadn't seen the look in Philomena's eyes or heard the unspoken words.

Señor Jackson is a man who could never settle down.

As much as I might wish that he could . . .

With Tillman dead and the Hand of God mystery cleared up, there was no reason for Jackson to lie low anymore. He was able to be out and about as long as he took it easy, so the next day he put in his first public appearance since the beating he had endured, walking with Everett down to Sheriff Brennan's office. The lawman's bushy white eyebrows rose in surprise when Jackson walked in.

"I thought you'd left town, Jackson," he said. "Haven't seen you around in almost a week."

"I've been laid up for a spell," Jackson explained as he sat down carefully in front of the sheriff's desk. "I ran into the Hand of God and his men up in the hills on the Winged T."

Brennan's eyebrows climbed even higher. Then he glared at Everett and asked, "How come I didn't know about this?"

Jackson took the young reporter off the hook by explaining, "I asked Everett not to say anything to anybody. Tillman had me lashed to a tree and then had one of his men work me over with a bullwhip. Whipped me just about to within an inch of my life. I'd show you, but my back is still bandaged up."

Brennan lifted a hand and shook his head. "I'll take your word for it. Go on."

"Before he had me whipped, the Hand of God talked about how he was the avenger of the Lord and how he was doing God's work by punishing sinners and evildoers."

Brennan nodded and tapped a blunt finger on a piece of paper on his desk.

"Yeah, it's all right here in the letter Tillman wrote after he strangled that cousin o' his, before he blew his own brains out. The man was plumb loco."

Jackson leaned forward. "So that's the letter I've heard about?"

"Yeah."

"Can I take a look at it?"

"I don't see why not." Brennan pushed the paper across the desk to him.

This was the first chance Everett had gotten to take a good look at the letter. He leaned over Jackson's shoulder to study it as the gunslinger read Tillman's cramped writing. The note left no doubt about the Easterner's guilt.

"Loco, all right," Jackson said with a nod as he sat back. "What's going to happen to the bodies?"

"Cecil Greenwood's embalmed them. He's going to take the coffins over to San Angelo and put them on the train so they can be shipped back East. Tillman and the gal will be buried in Philadelphia."

"He never should have come out here," Jackson said, "and Miss Tillman never should have come to visit."

"Folks do things all the time they never should have," Brennan said. "Problem is, they don't know it until after it's too late."

That pretty much summed it up, Jackson thought.

The sheriff looked over at Everett. "I reckon you wrote up this whole thing for your paper back in New York?"

"That's right," Everett said with a nod, "including the part Mr. Jackson played in it. I spent most of the night writing, in fact, and I sent the dispatch off in this morning's mail. In a week or two, the readers in New York will learn all about the Hand of God and his reign of terror."

Brennan grunted. "Reign of terror," he repeated. "Yeah, folks were pretty spooked, all right."

"They can go back to their usual sinning now and not have to worry about the Hand of God," Jackson said. "All they'll have to worry about is the real Señor Dios."

As they left the sheriff's office, Everett said, "You know, word will get around town quickly about what happened to you. You'll be famous as the only man to encounter the Hand of God and survive."

Jackson frowned. "I never set out to be famous for that or anything else."

"Well, I'm afraid you're not going to have much choice in the matter." Everett nodded down the street. "Here comes Malcolm Graham."

"And I'm still too stiff and sore to run and hide," Jackson said dryly.

The local newspaperman bustled up to them on the boardwalk and said, "Mr. Jackson! I was afraid you'd left town without sitting down for that interview you promised me for the *Journal.*"

"No, I'll be around here for a while yet," Jackson said.

"Excellent! I have a lot of questions to ask you, and if it's all right with you, I'd like to take some photographs of you. I can't print them in the paper, of course, but if I had a portrait of the famous Hell Jackson, I'm sure I could sell copies of it. You might even want one for yourself."

"I know what I look like," Jackson said. "You take pictures, do you?"

"Yes, I do. Have you ever had a photographic portrait made?"

Jackson nodded. "Once, over in Fort Worth. I didn't expect to find a picture-taker all the way out here, in a little town like Death Head Crossing."

"Oh, photography is the coming thing. Soon everyone will have portraits made."

Jackson nodded. "That sounds fine. It'll have to wait for a few days, though, and so will that interview. I've been laid up, and I need to get more of my strength back."

"You've been injured?" Graham was surprised. "How?"

Jackson pointed a thumb at Everett. "Ask this young fella. He can tell you all about it."

"Are you sure?" Everett asked.

"It doesn't matter now," Jackson said. "It's all over, remember?"

CHAPTER 30

A lot of the townspeople turned out later that day to watch as Cecil Greenwood and one of his boys drove the hearse out of town. Inside were the coffins containing the bodies of Benjamin Tillman and his cousin Deborah, and everybody knew it. The trip to San Angelo and back would take several days, so folks hoped that nobody would need burying before Cecil got back.

Jackson, Everett, and Philomena were among those who turned out to watch the solemn leave-taking. "There he goes," Everett said as they stood in front of the boardinghouse. "A man who caused a great deal of fear and misery, all because of his own twisted desires."

"Everybody's desires are twisted to somebody," Jackson said. "I need a drink."

As Everett had predicted, Jackson's already formidable reputation had grown even more because of his encounter with the Hand of God. He couldn't go into the Big Bend or any of the other saloons in town without people flocking around him and wanting to hear all about it. Jackson was a reticent man by nature, and all the attention bothered him. He just wanted to be left alone.

Jackson stopped going to the saloons and spent the next several days staying close to his room in the boardinghouse. Philomena had gone back to work there. She was upset that Jackson was no longer staying with her, but since there wasn't any reason for him to lie low, he didn't want to compromise her reputation any more than it already was.

Jackson and Everett visited Sheriff Brennan's office again to find out if he had discovered anything about the men who had helped the Hand of God in his crimes. "Nearly a dozen of the Winged T hands have disappeared," Brennan told them. "I reckon they were the ones Tillman paid to give him a hand with his dirty work. They might still be lurkin' around here somewhere, but chances are they all split up and headed for parts unknown. I don't have the time or the manpower to hunt 'em down, so I reckon we'll have to settle for the mastermind behind the whole thing bein' dead."

One day, when Jackson was strong enough to ride again, he was gone all day and Everett had no idea where he had gotten off to. The possibility that Jackson might have run out on him, despite Jackson's earlier statement that Everett could continue to travel with him, worried the young reporter.

But late that afternoon, the gunslinger rode in from wherever he had gone and was at the boardinghouse for supper as usual. He dodged Everett's questions about where he had been during the day. Everett was frustrated, but he knew that trying to get Jackson to talk when he didn't want to was a waste of time.

The next day, Jackson and Everett finally walked over to the office of the *Weekly Journal.* "Come in, come in," Malcolm Graham greeted them effusively. "Make yourself comfortable, Mr. Jackson. I can't tell you how much I've been looking forward to conducting this interview."

"I'm not saying I'll answer every question you've got," Jackson warned as he sat down and put his hat on the desk beside him. "But you ask 'em and we'll see what happens."

"That's fine. Rosalie, fetch Mr. Jackson a cup of coffee. Everett, how about you?"

Everett nodded. "Coffee would be fine,

thank you." He watched Rosalie with appreciation as she went to the stove in the corner, filled cups from the battered old pot, and brought them over.

Graham sat down on the other side of the desk and pulled out a pad of paper and a pencil. "First of all, Mr. Jackson, tell me where you were born."

"In Missouri, where the Ozarks run across the southern part of the state," Jackson replied. "Some would call me a hillbilly, I reckon, but I left there at a fairly young age, right after the war, and haven't been back since."

Graham glanced up at him. "Is it all right if I ask which side you fought for? I know that's a sore subject with some people."

"I fought for the Confederacy, but I wasn't in the army. I was a guerrilla, until it got to be too much for me to stomach. As long as we were making war on Yankee soldiers, it was fine, but it got to where the folks who lived around there were as scared of us as they were of the Yankees. I figured that wasn't right, so I left to head west." Jackson shrugged. "Turned out it didn't matter much. Lee surrendered at Appomattox less than a week later."

Graham wrote quickly on his pad, the pencil moving with a swift dexterity. "What

317

did you do after that?"

Everett made some notes of his own to add to future stories for the *Universe* as Jackson continued to talk, spinning yarns of two decades spent as a scout, lawman, bounty hunter, and hired gun. It seemed almost impossible that one man could have done so many different things, but Everett was coming to understand that some Westerners were a different breed of men, with a huge capacity for action, adventure, and danger. Hell Jackson belonged to that breed.

"This is wonderful," Graham said as he continued to scribble notes. "It'll make a fine story, Mr. Jackson. I can't thank you enough for consenting to the interview."

"Well, I reckon it wasn't as bad as I thought it might be," Jackson said with a shrug. "Anything else you want?"

"That photographic portrait, if you don't mind."

Jackson looked down at his clothes, which were typical range garb. He had bought a new hat to replace the one lost when he was lassoed and pulled out of the saddle by the hardcases working for the Hand of God.

"I don't have anything fancy to wear," he said.

"I don't want you dressed up," Graham said. "I want you to look just like you

318

normally do. In fact, do you have a rifle?"

"A Winchester."

"If you could get it and hold it while you're posing . . ."

"I'll fetch it from your room," Everett volunteered.

"That's a good idea," Graham said. "I'll get started setting everything up."

"Why don't I walk over to the boarding-house and back with you?" Rosalie suggested to Everett.

The young man's heart leaped, but he tried to sound nonchalant as he said, "That would be fine."

As they left the newspaper office, Graham was telling Jackson to stand in front of a blank wall. "I don't have any photographic backdrops yet, but I hope to someday," he explained.

As Everett and Rosalie walked along the street toward the boardinghouse, she said, "Mr. Jackson has certainly lived an exciting life, hasn't he?"

"He has indeed. If I continue to write about him, he may wind up as well known as Wild Bill Hickok and all the other famous gunmen."

"I'm not sure he'd want that," Rosalie pointed out.

"Sometimes people don't have a choice.

Fame is thrust upon them."

"Or infamy . . . like Benjamin Tillman."

"Yes, it's a shame that had to turn out like it did. Six people died for no good reason."

Rosalie linked her arm with Everett's. "I suppose Mr. Tillman thought he had a good reason for everything he did."

"I suppose."

"Well, let's not talk about that now," Rosalie went on, her voice growing brighter. "It's over, and we should look to the future. To that end . . . why don't you have dinner with us again tonight?"

Everett smiled over at her. "I'd like that very much."

When they reached the boardinghouse, he went upstairs and got Jackson's rifle. The Winchester was heavy in his hands as he brought it back down. Philomena was walking through the house with a load of clean sheets in her arms as Everett reached the bottom of the stairs, and she stopped to look at him with a puzzled frown.

"You are going hunting, Señor Everett?" she asked.

"No, no, this is Jackson's rifle. He's posing for a photographic portrait by Mr. Graham, and Malcolm wanted him to be holding the Winchester."

Philomena nodded in understanding. "Be

careful. Guns are dangerous."

"Oh, I think I know that." But Everett took care to keep his finger away from the trigger anyway.

When he and Rosalie got back to the newspaper office, Graham had his camera set up. It was a large, bulky apparatus on a tripod, with a black cloth attached to it that the photographer would drape over himself as he bent to look through the lens. The cloth would keep any stray beams of light from striking the photographic plate and damaging the portrait.

"Give the rifle to Mr. Jackson, please," Graham said distractedly to Everett as he poured powder from a can into a tray attached to a long handle. Everett handed the Winchester to Jackson, who was starting to look a little impatient and uncomfortable.

"This is taking a while," Jackson commented.

"Anything worthwhile does," Graham said. "I think you'll be very pleased with how this turns out, Mr. Jackson. At least I hope so."

Finally, Graham had everything ready. Jackson stood against the wall, the Winchester in his left hand held down at his side, slanting across in front of his thighs, his right thumb hooked in his gun belt so that his hand was close to the butt of his Colt. His left leg was slightly in front of the right. He looked casual but still alert. His Stetson was thumbed back slightly so that the hard planes and angles of his face were clearly visible. He wore a stern expression.

"That's perfect," Graham said. He had draped the black cloth over his head and shoulders as he leaned forward to study Jackson's pose through the camera's lens. As he raised the tray of flash powder, he added, "Now stay very still. . . ."

A few more seconds ticked by slowly while Graham made sure everything was ready. Jackson stood absolutely still, and Everett wondered if that was starting to be painful for him. The gunslinger's back still wasn't completely healed.

When the flash powder went off with a *whoosh!* it took Everett by surprise, both the sound and the brightness of it. He jumped a little. Jackson squinted his eyes, but that was his only reaction. Otherwise, he remained as stone-faced as he was most of the time.

"I think I got it," Graham said as he emerged from under the black drape. "But would you mind if I exposed another plate, Mr. Jackson, just in case?"

"All right," Jackson said. "Don't take too

long about it, though."

"Thank you. We'll get this done as quickly as possible. Rosalie, would you prepare another tray of flash powder while I load another plate into the camera?"

"Of course," she said as she picked up the can of powder Graham had been using earlier.

The procedure went a little faster this time, and it took only a few more minutes to make the second portrait of Jackson. As Graham removed that plate from the camera, he said, "I can't thank you enough for your cooperation. Are you sure you wouldn't like to have one of the portraits when I get them ready?"

"I would," Everett spoke up.

"Of course," Graham said with a smile. "You've been a great help too, Everett."

Jackson said, "I reckon I'll take one, if it's not too much trouble."

"No trouble at all," Graham assured him. He put out his hand and said again, "Thank you."

Jackson shook with him, then left the office. Everett followed, and as he went out the door, Rosalie called after him, "Don't forget about tonight."

"Oh, I won't," he answered with a smile.

"What happens tonight?" Jackson asked

as he and Everett walked toward the boardinghouse.

"I'm having dinner again with Rosalie and her brother."

"She's a mighty pretty lady," Jackson drawled. "A mite taken with her, are you, Everett?"

Everett felt his face growing warm. "We're just friends. Anyway, she's older than me."

"Just by a few years," Jackson said. "You might want to be careful, though. Remember, we'll be leaving Death Head Crossing before too much longer. Wouldn't want to break any hearts when you go."

"I know." Everett was glad that Jackson was still going to let him come along.

But when he thought about riding away and never seeing Rosalie Graham again, he couldn't help but feel a twinge of regret.

CHAPTER 31

Since it was possible that tonight would be the last time he would see Rosalie Graham, Everett had a bouquet of flowers in his hand that evening when he arrived at the Graham house. They were colorful wildflowers. Philomena had showed him where to find them, but he'd done all the gathering and arranging of the bouquet. He'd even gone to the general store and purchased a yellow ribbon that he tied around the bouquet.

Malcolm Graham opened the door in response to Everett's knock. His eyebrows went up and a smile appeared on his face when he saw the flowers Everett clutched in a sweating hand. "Oh, ho," he said. "Young Lochinvar come to call, eh?"

Everett had been hoping that Rosalie would answer the door. He suppressed his disappointment and thrust out the hand with the flowers in it. "Here," he said. "These are for your sister."

"Well, don't give 'em to me," Graham said with a chuckle. "You can give them to Rosalie yourself. I'll tell her that you're here."

He stepped back to let Everett into the house. As Everett entered, Graham turned and called, "Mr. Howard is here, Rosalie. And he has something for you."

With soft footsteps, she came into the room and paused just inside the doorway. Everett thought she was beautiful in a dark green gown that left her shoulders mostly bare. She became even more lovely when a smile lit up her face at the sight of the flowers.

"For me? Oh, Everett, they're beautiful." She came forward to take them from him and leaned forward to kiss him on the cheek. It was just a peck, but it made his face flame. "I'll put them in a vase."

While Rosalie went to do that, Graham clapped a hand on Everett's back and said, "Well, come in, come in. Care for a drink? I still have some of that brandy."

"That would be fine," Everett managed to say, hoping that he didn't sound too tongue-tied with embarrassment. He wasn't sure why Rosalie should affect him that way. He had known beautiful women back in New York, he told himself. At least, he had been acquainted with beautiful women, he amended. He hadn't actually *known* them. But he had passed many of them on the street.

Graham poured the drinks and brought Everett's glass of brandy over to him. Rosalie came back into the room carrying a pottery vase that looked like it had been made by Indians. The flowers were even prettier in it. She put the vase on the table and said, "Supper is almost ready," then disappeared back into the kitchen.

"What are your plans now?" Graham asked as he and Everett sipped the brandy. "Will you and Mr. Jackson be moving on?"

"I haven't really discussed it with him," Everett said, "but I assume we will be. A man like him never stays in one place for very long."

"He's already been here in Death Head Crossing for quite a while, hasn't he? I mean, compared to how long he usually stays."

Everett nodded. "He didn't want to leave until those killings were cleared up. I got the feeling that he was very intrigued by them."

"But now there's no reason for him to stay, eh?"

"Well," Everett frowned, "I've been thinking about it, and we still have no idea how the murders were actually accomplished, or what those mysterious floating balls of light were that accompanied the killers."

Graham shrugged. "Surely that doesn't matter now, what with Benjamin Tillman dead."

"No, I suppose not, but little things like that nag at a person's mind."

"Don't let them," Graham advised. "It would be better to put the whole thing behind you." He smiled. "Just don't leave town until I have those portraits ready for you. They should be done tomorrow."

"I'm sure we'll still be here for a day or two longer. Maybe more than that. Like I said, I haven't really talked about it with Mr. Jackson."

Rosalie came in with a platter that held a juicy ham. She set it on the table and returned to the kitchen for the rest of the food, then said, "Sit down, gentlemen."

They sat and ate, and once again Everett was impressed by how good the food was and how much of it there was. While Rosalie's meals weren't as gargantuan as the ones at the café, Everett was still pleasantly stuffed by the time he was finished. He would have let his belt out a notch if he hadn't been in the presence of a lady.

"Why don't you gentlemen step out onto

the porch and enjoy the evening air while I clean up a bit?" Rosalie suggested when the meal was done.

"I could help with the dishes," Everett suggested.

"Nonsense, you're our guest. Go along with Malcolm now."

Everett allowed her to shoo him out of the house along with her brother. Grinning, Graham stood on the front porch and rocked back and forth on the balls of his feet. "Cigar?" he asked.

"Don't mind if I do," Everett replied. The good meal and Rosalie's beautiful presence had him feeling expansive. He took the cigar Graham offered him. The newspaperman lit it, then held the match to the tip of another cigar and puffed it into life.

"Nothing better than a good cigar after a meal," Graham said as he blew out a cloud of smoke. "Well, I suppose I can think of a few things. . . ." He nudged Everett with an elbow and laughed.

Everett was a little embarrassed, but tried not to act like it. Graham had accepted him as a fellow man of the world, and that was a welcome change from being regarded as a babe in the woods, which was much more common in Everett's experience.

Graham grew more serious and went on.

"It's probably a good thing you're leaving town."

"Oh? Why do you say that?"

"Because Rosalie likes you. I can tell. If you were here longer, she'd be mighty sad to see you leave."

"Mr. Jackson said sort of the same thing."

"Did he? Well, Jackson's a smart man, anybody could tell that. But I don't want to see my sister hurt."

Everett began, "I would never —"

Graham held up a hand to stop him. "Not intentionally, no. I know that. But if Rosalie got attached to you . . ." He shrugged. "Well, as I said, it's a good thing you'll be leaving soon. You might even suggest to Mr. Jackson that you pull out as soon as possible."

"I'll do that," Everett said, even though it saddened him to think that he might not see Rosalie again after tonight. He was glad he had brought those flowers for her while he had the chance.

"Anyway," Graham added with a laugh, "I can't take a chance on you staying around here. Rosalie might decide to marry you, and then I'd lose her services as cook and housekeeper and printer's devil."

Everett was about to say that he was sure she meant a lot more to Graham than that, when a soft footstep behind them announced her presence.

"Malcolm," she said, and Everett thought he heard a note of strain in her voice, "there's something out in the kitchen you need to deal with."

Graham turned to her, a look of surprise on his face. "Really? All right. You stay here and entertain our guest." He clenched his cigar between his teeth and strode into the house.

Rosalie joined Everett at the porch railing. The night was cool and pleasant, and the fresh scent of her hair came to him on the gentle evening breeze. He felt his heart begin to pound. One kiss, he thought. He had to have one kiss from her before he left Death Head Crossing. Surely she wouldn't begrudge him that much.

But instead of asking for that, he said, "Would you like for me to put this cigar out?"

"What?" She still seemed distracted. "Oh, no, that's fine. They don't bother me. I'm used to Malcolm smoking them. They're one of his vices."

"He's a fine man. I'm sure he doesn't have many vices."

She laughed, but didn't sound particularly happy. "You might be surprised."

He wondered what she meant by that, but he didn't think it would be proper to ask. All family members got on each other's nerves from time to time, he supposed, and they *were* brother and sister after all.

Before he could say anything, the sound of a crash came from inside the house. Rosalie gasped and turned sharply toward the front door. Everett swung around as well and took a step toward the door.

"We'd better see if your brother is all right."

She caught hold of his arm, stopping him. "No! I mean . . . I'm sure Mal is fine —"

Another crash sounded inside the house, and a man's angry voice said, "You double-crossin' son of a bitch!"

The voice didn't belong to Malcolm Graham.

Everett pulled free from Rosalie's grip. "There must be a thief in the house!" he said. "Get out of here, Rosalie! Run to the sheriff's office! I'll help Malcolm!"

She grabbed at his coat again, but missed. Everett threw the door open and plunged inside. He was aware that Rosalie had ignored his advice and was following him, but he didn't stop to argue with her. The sounds of the fight were intensifying. Graham had to be in danger, somewhere in the rear of the house.

Everett's fists were clenched and ready to throw a punch as he ran into the kitchen. By the dim light of a small lamp, he saw two figures locked in a desperate struggle across the room. They lurched back and forth, crashing against the table and the counter. Dishes slid over and shattered. The man wrestling with Malcolm Graham wore dusty range clothes and was trying to get his hands around Graham's neck. Graham was holding him off as best he could.

"You bastard!" the man grated. "You promised me a thousand dollars!"

Everett gaped, openmouthed with astonishment. He recognized the man fighting with Graham as one of the hardcases who had confronted Jackson in the saloon on Everett's first day in Death Head Crossing. That encounter had been Everett's introduction to the violence so common in the West, and he would never forget any of the details, including the faces of the two gunmen.

And as he stared, he remembered that Jackson had met those men again, on the Winged T. He had shot it out with them, in fact, and killed one of them. The man who had survived, the man who was now trying to choke Graham, had been wounded but had headed for the Winged T bunkhouse. He was one of the killers working for . . .

Working for the Hand of God.

The struggling men turned, and Graham saw Everett over his opponent's shoulder. "Damn it!" he rasped. "Stop it, York! We've got bigger problems now."

York . . . That was the name of the Winged T hand who had found the bodies of Benjamin and Deborah Tillman. Everett's brain was whirling crazily now. Nothing he was seeing and hearing here in the Graham kitchen made any sense.

One of Graham's flailing hands fell on a water pitcher on the counter and grasped the handle. He swung the pitcher up and crashed it against the side of York's head, shattering the vessel. York let go of Graham and staggered, catching himself against the counter. Graham reached over and plucked the gun from the holster on the hardcase's hip.

But instead of covering York with the weapon, he swung the pistol around and pointed it at Everett. "Don't move," he said, panting a little from his exertions.

"M-Malcolm," Everett said, forcing the name out through a suddenly dry mouth and throat. "What are you doing? If this man broke in here, we should fetch the sheriff —"

"I said don't move, and you might as well shut up too! You've seen too much."

"Oh, Malcolm," Rosalie said from behind the young reporter. "Now we're going to have to kill Everett too."

Chapter 32

Everett didn't know whether to feel sick, scared, or astonished. All those emotions and more warred within him. Fear and confusion won out. Every trace of affability had vanished from Malcolm Graham's face. His gaze was icy and merciless as he looked over the barrel of the revolver at Everett.

The hardcase who owned the gun slumped against the counter, bleeding from a gash on his head that had been opened up when Graham crashed the pitcher against his skull. "Damn it, Graham," he said as he wiped away the gore that dripped in his left eye, "you didn't have to wallop me like that. We could've worked things out."

"You were trying to strangle me, remember?" Graham reminded him without taking his eyes off Everett.

"Aw, hell, I was just mad because you didn't pay me and the boys all the money we had comin' to us. You know we have to light a shuck outta these parts. We just need some travelin' money."

"You would have gotten the rest of your money if you'd been patient," Graham said in a cold, angry voice. "You'll still get it. First, you're going to give me a hand with this problem, though. But I'm not going to pay you any extra for helping me get rid of this meddling bastard. We wouldn't have to kill him if it wasn't for you."

Everett's pulse hammered like a drum in his head, a drum being played by a madman. He started to turn toward Rosalie, hoping that she could explain things, hoping that once he saw her beautiful face everything would make sense again.

She lifted a little pistol she had taken from somewhere under her dress and pressed the barrel into his throat just under the jawline. "Don't," she said.

Everett felt like crying, but he didn't allow the fear to overcome him. He sensed that he had to keep them talking. As long as they were talking, they wouldn't kill him.

"What . . . what's going on here?" he forced out. "I don't understand any of this."

"Oh, I think you do." Graham gave the gun back to York and went on. "Keep him covered." Then he moved closer to Everett and smiled again, but it wasn't a friendly expression anymore. "I happen to know that you're a smart young man, Everett. You've seen and heard more than enough to figure out what's going on."

Everett shook his head. "I haven't, I really haven't. I don't have any idea. If you just let me go, Malcolm, I'll —"

"You'd run straight to Hell Jackson, that's what you'd do. You know that Benjamin Tillman wasn't the Hand of God at all." Graham laughed. "I was."

"But why . . . why did you want to . . . kill sinners?"

"Sinners? Sin had nothing to do with it! This was about money, Everett. Like everything else in this world, it was all about money."

York said, "We better not risk a shot. Want me to take him out and cut his throat or stove in his head?"

"And announce to the entire world that he was murdered? You see, York, this is why *I* do the thinking, not you." Graham shook his head. "No, we have to make sure that young Mr. Howard's death appears to be an accident."

"How we gonna do that?"

"The printing press," Rosalie said with the air of someone who has just come up with an idea.

Graham nodded. "Excellent. You really do have an inventive bent, my dear. What exactly did you have in mind?"

"We can make it look like Everett was working with the press when he got his hands caught in it. They'll be crushed and mangled, and since he was alone at the time, he'll bleed to death before anyone finds him."

Everett stared at her, unable to believe that such a sweet, beautiful woman could come up with such a thing.

Graham nodded. "I like it," he said. "Everyone knows that Everett's a newspaperman. They might wonder why he was messing around with the press in the middle of the night, but it's not all that far-fetched. We'll make certain that he's injured badly enough to bleed to death, of course, and then we'll be shocked and saddened to discover his body there in the morning."

"You're crazy!" Everett couldn't hold the words in. "You're all insane!"

"Not at all," Graham insisted. "In fact, it's a very clever plan, just like the one to get rid of Benjamin Tillman. He's dead and out of the way, and no one has the slightest suspicion that he didn't die by his own hand. We even have his confession to prove it."

York gave a hard laugh. "Yeah, and it wasn't easy to make him write it out neither. Had to threaten that gal cousin of his before he'd do it. Damn fool greenhorn believed that I'd really let 'em both go if he did what I said. He sure looked surprised when I stuck that gun barrel in his mouth and pulled the trigger."

"You killed Tillman," Everett said, "and . . . Deborah?"

"Well, hell, I couldn't very well let her live after she'd seen me blow her cousin's brains out, now could I?"

A shudder went through Everett. "You killed them both and then made it look like Tillman strangled her and committed suicide?"

"You see?" Graham said. "I told you you were smart enough to figure it out, Everett."

"But . . . but *why?* Tillman never did anything to you. Why kill him? Why make it look like he was the madman calling himself the Hand of God?"

"Oh, all right, if you're going to be so insistent. Tillman took a highly prosperous ranch and was ruining it. He had no concept of how to handle such an operation, and yet he refused to go back East where he came from and allow a competent manager to step in and make the Winged T a lucrative proposition again. So some of his relatives in Philadelphia took matters into their own hands and decided to get rid of him. They left it up to me to decide how to go about doing that."

"How did they even know about you?" Everett asked. The story Graham was telling him was incredible, but he sensed it was true.

"I have . . . connections of my own back East, I suppose you could say," Graham replied. He hooked his thumbs in his vest and went on with pride in his voice. "I'm known as a man who can get things done. This little backwater cow town was a good place for Rosalie and me to hide out for a while after things got too hot for us, but even here opportunity to make a profit came our way."

"Then everything you told me about coming from Dallas was a lie?"

"We actually did live in Dallas for a while," Graham said, "but we weren't raised there. We're originally from your own hometown, Everett. New Yorkers, my friend, New Yorkers."

Everett rested his head in his hand for a moment. How could he have been taken in so completely by them? He had believed everything they told him. Not only that, but he could see now that by befriending him, they had been able to keep track of everything that was going on in the investigation of the murders. They had used him, and now he was going to pay the price for his gullibility.

"We should get on with this, Malcolm," Rosalie prodded.

Graham waved a hand. "In a minute. Everett's no threat to us now, and I'm rather enjoying explaining all this to someone who's intelligent enough to appreciate it."

Everett grunted in self-disgust. "Not very intelligent," he said. "Dumb enough to be taken in by the two of you, in fact." He turned his head to look at Rosalie. "I thought that you . . . I thought . . ."

"You think too much," she said, and there wasn't even a hint of warmth in her voice.

Graham said, "Actually, I believe Rosalie is probably the more ruthless of the two of us. I know she's more brilliant and creative than I am. She's the one who took the information we were given by Tillman's relatives and devised the plan to get rid of him."

"Why did Deborah have to die too?" Everett asked. "And what about Luther Berryhill and Mrs. Vance and that cowboy, Harcourt? What earthly connection did they have with all of this?"

"Window dressing, my young friend, window dressing. You see, before Tillman left Philadelphia, he made the mistake of confessing to one of his relatives that he was in love with his cousin and had been ever since she was a girl. The relative — one of our employers — passed that bit of knowledge on to us, in the event that we might be able to make some use of it. Actually, it became the centerpiece of our plan."

Despite her impatience, Rosalie evidently took pride in the scheme too, because she said, "We wanted to make Tillman look insane enough to murder his cousin and then kill himself, so we turned him into the Hand of God and set him loose on some of the sinners in the area, making it all seem appropriately mysterious. Of course Tillman didn't really know anything about it. Malcolm played the part beautifully."

Graham smiled. "Yes, I made a good crazed vigilante, didn't I?"

"Are we gonna kill this hombre or not?" York asked.

"Of course, of course. In fact, I suppose we should get on with it." Graham gave the hardcase a curt nod.

York took a step toward Everett. Despite the mental turmoil Everett was in, he knew that his life hung in the balance here. If he didn't do something to stop them, he would die, just as sure as anything. Knowing that his life was numbered in minutes made him a lot more willing to take chances. Without giving any warning of what he was about to do, he spun toward Rosalie, who had stepped back but still had the little pistol in her hand.

They had said they didn't want to shoot him, so he risked making a grab for the pistol. She cried out in alarm and anger as he lunged toward her. He got a hand on her wrist and forced the gun aside. As he reached for the pistol with his other hand, he thought that if he could get hold of the weapon and then turn back to deal with York before the hardcase could reach him —

The barrel of York's gun thudded against the back of his head, ending that hope. Everett sagged as his knees tried to fold up under him. He pawed at Rosalie in an attempt to hold himself up. She slashed at him with the pistol, viciously raking its barrel across his face. He grunted in pain and went down.

"Now you've marked him," Graham scolded. "How is the accident with the printing press going to explain that gash on his face?"

"He hit it on the corner of the press when he fell," Rosalie said.

Graham thought about it and nodded. "Yes, that should work. I like it." He stepped closer to her and put his arms around her.

The last thing Everett saw before he passed out on the floor was Graham pulling Rosalie against him and pressing his mouth to hers in a passionate kiss.

CHAPTER 33

Everett wasn't unconscious for long. He regained his senses, but only vaguely at first, as he was being dragged through the night. Strong hands had hold of him from either side. That would be Malcolm Graham and the hardcase called York, he thought as he forced his stunned brain to work again. They were probably taking him through back alleys from the Graham house to the newspaper office, so that no one would see them lugging his semiconscious form.

He let his head loll loosely on his shoulders, deciding it would be better if they continued to think that he was out cold. If they did, they might slip up and give him a chance to make a break for freedom.

That would be his *last* chance. If luck didn't smile on him soon, he would die tonight, in horrible pain from the mangling he would receive from the printing press.

The pen is mightier than the sword. That

was how the old saying went. And people liked to talk about the power of the press.

But Everett would have been willing to bet that no one had ever used an actual printing press as a murder weapon before.

He heard rapid footsteps ahead of them. That would be Rosalie, leading the way. A door opened, probably the back door of the newspaper office. Everett was dragged inside, his feet bumping over the threshold. Graham and York let go of his arms, allowing him to slump to the floor. Everett lay still and waited to see if they would move away. He didn't trust his muscles to function fully just yet.

The door closed, and a moment later Everett heard the rasp of a match being struck. He kept his eyes closed, but even so he was aware of things growing brighter around him as a lamp was lit. He heard the faint clatter of the glass chimney being lowered into place.

"All right, I helped you bring him over here," York said. "How about the rest of that *dinero* you owe me and the other fellas?"

"I told you, I'm waiting for the rest of the money to arrive from Philadelphia," Graham said. He sounded irritated. "I'll get word across the border and let you know when I've got it, and we'll make arrangements then for you to get paid."

"You're askin' us to be mighty trustin', mister."

Rosalie said, "Why shouldn't you trust us? Malcolm and I have a good setup here. We're not going anywhere. No one suspects us of anything. And in addition to what we've already paid you, you and the others have the money you made off that stolen stock. We didn't even ask for a share of that."

"Yeah, I reckon that's true," York admitted. "That was a sweet deal, gettin' paid to get rid of Tillman so the Winged T'd make a profit again, and all the while me and the boys were the ones rustlin' the ranch's cattle."

"Why get paid once when you can get paid twice, I always say," Graham said. "So you see, you don't have anything to complain about."

"I reckon not. We gonna go ahead and kill this dude now?"

"I don't see a point in wasting any more time, do you? Pick him up, and we'll take him in the front room where the press is."

Everett had hoped they would go in the other room and leave him there, if only for a moment, but obviously that wasn't going to happen. He couldn't wait any longer. As York grabbed him under the arms and started to lift him, he suddenly straightened his legs and drove himself upward. The top of his head smashed into York's jaw with blinding force. Unfortunately, Everett was as stunned by the impact as York was. He tore free of the killer's grip, but staggered wildly as he tried to turn toward the rear door and run.

"Grab him, damn it!" Rosalie called in a low, urgent voice.

Everett struck out blindly, flailing around him with his fists. One of them hit Graham in the chest and knocked him back. Everett's head cleared slightly. He lunged toward the door, hoping it wasn't locked.

Before he could reach the knob, York tackled him from behind. Both men went down. Everett's head struck hard against the floor. Even though he didn't pass out this time, his muscles refused to work and he couldn't fight back as York hauled him roughly to his feet.

"Hang onto him this time," Graham said with a scowl. He rubbed the place on his chest where Everett had punched him.

York wrestled Everett toward the door leading into the front room, where the printing press was located. Rosalie picked up the lamp and went first. She opened the door and stepped into the other room. York was right behind her, forcing Everett along. Graham brought up the rear.

York and Everett bumped into Rosalie as she gasped and stopped short. Graham said, "What the hell's wrong now?"

A new voice drawled, "I've got a story for you, Graham, about how the real killers behind all the trouble around here have hang-ropes waiting for them. You won't be able to print it, though, since you'll be one of the varmints dancing on air."

Everett stared in shock over Rosalie's shoulder as the light from the lamp in her hand revealed the man who had spoken. Gun in hand, Hell Jackson leaned casually against the railing that divided the room.

Everett looked like he had been knocked around quite a bit, and Jackson was genuinely sorry about that. If he could have worked things out differently, he would have. He had been keeping an eye on the Grahams, waiting for them to slip up since he didn't have any solid proof against them. What he had learned from the replies to the telegrams he had sent in Fort Stockton a few days earlier was interesting, but not enough to convict anybody of anything.

Then earlier tonight, he had seen York slipping in the back door of the Graham place while Everett was still there, and Jackson had hoped that the youngster would get out before all hell broke loose. That hadn't been the case. The whole bunch had left the house a short time later, with Graham and York dragging Everett like he was unconscious — or dead. Hoping the latter wouldn't turn out to be the case, Jackson had trailed them. When he realized they were heading for the newspaper office, he circled around and got ahead of them, forcing the lock on the front door and slipping inside as the others were coming in the back.

He wasn't sure what they had in mind for Everett, but it couldn't be anything good. The things he had overhead while eavesdropping on the conversation in the back room confirmed that. They planned to kill the young reporter. Not only that, but Jackson had also learned that York and the other Winged T hands who were really working for Graham were responsible for the rustling as well. He'd already had a hunch that was the case, but it was nice to have it confirmed. The whole thing was just about wrapped up now. All he had to do was march the Grahams and York down to Sheriff Brennan's office and tell the lawman to lock them up. Everett's testimony, and the other things Jackson had dug up, would convict them.

Unfortunately, Rosalie Graham didn't cooperate. Instead, she hissed, "You bastard!" and threw the lamp at him.

Jackson ducked as the lamp sailed over him to crash on top of the desk in front of the railing. The glass shattered, and instantly the splashing coal oil was aflame, garishly lighting up the room.

Figuring that York was the most dangerous of the trio, Jackson weaved to the side, trying to get a shot at the hardcase. Instead, cursing bitterly, York pulled Everett in front of him with one hand and clawed at the pistol on his hip with the other. The gun came up and flame gouted from the muzzle as York thrust it under Everett's arm at Jackson.

The bullet screamed past Jackson's ear, but York only got one shot off before Everett twisted desperately in his grip and brought up an elbow, smashing it in York's face. That loosened York's grip enough for Everett to tear free and throw himself to the floor.

That gave Jackson a clear shot. York stumbled, righted himself, and tried to fire again, but before he could pull the trigger, the Colt in Jackson's hand roared twice. Both slugs smashed into York's chest and threw him backward. He hit the printing press and bounced off to pitch forward onto his face, the gun slipping from his hand as he fell. He had dark stains on both the front and back of his shirt — ink from the printing press on the back, blood from the pair of wounds on the front.

With a sharp pop, the gun that had appeared in Rosalie's hand fired toward Jackson. He swung his Colt toward her as the small-caliber slug whined past him. He didn't like the idea of shooting a woman, but he liked even less the thought of being shot by her.

Still lying on the floor, Everett hooked a foot around Rosalie's ankle and jerked it as hard as he could. She yelped as her feet went out from under her. As she fell backward, her head thudded against the wall, stunning her.

Everett had acted without thinking, trying to stop Rosalie from shooting at Jackson again so that the gunslinger wouldn't be forced to kill her. He had been even more successful than he had hoped. Rosalie was out of the fight, at least for the moment.

But that left Malcolm Graham, and the renegade newspaperman had snatched something out of a desk drawer and now lunged at Jackson with it. The weapon was a sawed-off shotgun, Jackson saw as he pivoted back toward Graham. He wasn't sure if he would be able to bring his Colt to bear before Graham could pull the twin triggers.

He didn't have to. Everett lunged up from the floor, grabbed the sawed-off's barrels, and wrenched them upward just as Graham fired. Instead of a double load of buckshot, what seemed like an exploding sun erupted from the barrels, right in Graham's face. Both Everett and Jackson were half-blinded by the flash, but they heard the beginnings of the scream that lasted only an instant before it was cut off.

Graham went over backward with nothing but a smoldering ruin where his face had been.

The fire from the broken lamp was still burning on top of the desk. Jackson glanced at Rosalie, saw that she was still stunned, and holstered his gun. He looked around, spotted a bucket of sand sitting beside the door where it was kept for emergencies like this, and picked it up to dump it on the flames. They sputtered and went out, except for a few big sparks that fell to the floor. Jackson stomped them out with his boots. That left the newspaper office cloaked in gloom.

Not for long, though, because with a

pounding of footsteps, Sheriff Ward Brennan ran along the boardwalk and threw the door open. He had his six-gun in one hand and a bull's-eye lantern in the other. As the light played over the stunned form of Rosalie Graham, the bullet-riddled corpse of the killer called York, and the ruined remains of Malcolm Graham, the lawman thundered, "What the blue-blazin' billy hell is goin' on here?"

Jackson had helped Everett to his feet. Ignoring the sheriff's demand for information, Jackson asked, "Are you all right?"

"Yes, I . . . I think so." Everett swallowed hard. "But I'm still not sure exactly what happened."

"I've got most of it figured out." Jackson looked at Rosalie, who moaned and shook her head as her senses started to return to her. "Luckily, we've got one left alive to fill us in on the rest of it."

Rosalie didn't look at Jackson, Everett, or Brennan. Instead, she gazed around wildly and cried, "Mal? Mal, where are you —"

She screamed as her eyes found what was left of Graham. Cringing back against the wall, she shrieked in horror and then crawled swiftly across the floor to his body. She threw herself on top of him and continued screaming. Her back rose and fell in jerking motions as she dragged in air so she could scream some more.

"Good Lord!" Brennan said as he came farther into the room. "Is that her brother? Can't hardly tell with his face blowed off like that."

"No," Jackson said. "That's not her brother."

CHAPTER 34

"Actually, Malcolm Graham was Rosalie's husband," Jackson said.

About an hour had passed since the carnage in the newspaper office had taken place. Rosalie was locked up in one of the cells down the hall from Brennan's office, and the bodies of Graham and York had been hauled off to Cecil Greenwood's undertaking parlor. There wouldn't be anything Greenwood could do to make Graham presentable.

The weapon that had blasted away his face now lay on Brennan's desk. The lawman nudged it and said, "Hell, it's just a sawed-off shotgun."

Jackson sat in front of the desk, straddling a chair he had turned around. Everett slumped on the battered old sofa against the front wall. He had a cup of coffee cradled in his hands, but he wasn't drinking it. He was just staring into the blackness instead, seeing only God knows what.

Jackson nodded toward the shotgun and said, "What made the blasted thing so hellish was what it was loaded with. Rosalie Graham came up with the idea of loading shells with a concentrated mixture of gunpowder and photographic flash powder instead of buckshot. She and her husband wanted something to spook folks, and they figured that would do it. They probably didn't realize just how effective it would be, though. That flash powder burns so hot it could blast a fella's face right off."

"Husband, you say?" Brennan repeated, still stuck on that part of it.

Jackson nodded. "They just pretended to be brother and sister. Probably started years ago, when they were swindling and blackmailing folks. Rosalie would take some fella to her room and get him in a compromising position, then Graham would bust in and pretend to be her outraged brother. They pulled that trick quite a few times before they went on to more complicated swindles and outright thievery. They were suspected in a few murders too, but they always ducked out and got away before anybody could prove anything against them."

Everett finally spoke up. "How do you know all this?"

"I sent some wires that day I rode up to Fort Stockton."

"Wires to who?"

Jackson smiled. "I know some folks in the U.S. marshal's office, the Justice Department, the Texas Rangers, and various other places."

"I thought you were just a gun-totin' drifter," Brennan said.

"That's a pretty good description," Jackson admitted. "Doesn't mean that's *all* I ever was."

Everett lifted the cup and took a long swallow of the strong black brew. He sat up and said, "Why go to all the trouble of killing those other people and making it look like Tillman was a lunatic?"

"Tillman's relatives back in Philadelphia didn't want anything to ever connect them to his death. Graham figured if everybody thought Tillman was crazy enough, nobody would question the idea that he murdered his cousin and killed himself." Jackson shook his head. "And to tell you the truth, I think Graham and Rosalie got some enjoyment out of throwing a scare into folks. They thought they were so much smarter than everybody else around here."

"That's why he let you go. He wanted you to tell people about the Hand of God and strengthen the frame around Tillman."

Jackson nodded. "I figured that much from the start."

Brennan said, "You knew Tillman wasn't really loco?"

"I didn't say that," Jackson said. "He was a mighty disturbed hombre. Everett can vouch for that, the way Tillman jumped him that day."

"He really loved Deborah," Everett said. "To the point of being obsessed with her, I think."

"Yep. Graham took advantage of that."

"How'd you know?" Brennan persisted. "How'd you know Tillman wasn't responsible for those killin's?"

"I didn't at first. It seemed unlikely to me that he could have planned and carried out such a thing. He just didn't seem smart enough and ruthless enough. But then the bodies of him and his cousin were found, along with that letter York forced him to write, and that looked like the end of it, whether I wanted to believe it or not."

Jackson stood up and went to the stove to pour himself a cup of coffee. When he turned back to the other two men, he went on. "Then Graham interviewed me for the paper and wanted to take a picture of me. When I heard him talking with that camera hood over his head so that his voice was muffled, I realized he sounded a little like the Hand of God had that night when he and his men ambushed me. Then when I saw that flash powder go off, that started me thinking about how those other folks might have been killed." He shrugged. "It sort of just fell together after that. I was watching the Grahams, hoping to get some proof against them that would stand up in court. Of course, where Malcolm and York are concerned, it won't come to that now."

"What about those balls of light?" Everett asked. "You haven't explained those."

"That's something else Rosalie came up with. Check the shed behind the Graham house, Sheriff. You'll find some big smoked glass globes made so you can put a small lamp inside them. The glass amplifies and diffuses the light from the lamp so that it looks even bigger than the globes really are."

Everett stared at him. "Amplifies and diffuses . . . ? Who the hell *are* you?"

"Just a gun-toting drifter," Jackson said with a smile.

"You're a real Westerner now. Got your own horse and saddle and everything."

Everett shifted uncomfortably on the back of the horse. "Yes, but I don't know if I'll ever get used to riding the blasted thing."

"Sure you will," Jackson told him. "Just give it time."

They were riding side by side down the street where Philomena's hut was located. Their saddlebags were full. Jackson planned to head for El Paso, so he had stocked up with provisions. Since Everett was going along, he had followed the gunslinger's example.

"One thing still bothers me," Everett said as he adjusted his derby so that it shaded his eyes a little better. "I know it's unlikely the gunmen who were working for Graham will ever be found and arrested, and I suppose I can accept that, but those men back in Philadelphia, Tillman's relatives, are going to get away with it. They were really as much responsible for what happened as Graham and Rosalie were."

Jackson nodded in agreement. "Yeah, that's true. That's why I plan on sending some more telegrams when we get to El Paso. Reckon those fellas are liable to find some deputy U.S. marshals on their doorsteps one morning, especially when Rosalie gets through testifying. I don't expect a judge would sentence her to hang anyway . . . but she'll get out of prison a lot sooner if she cooperates."

"I suppose so. I'd hate to see them escape the consequences of what they did."

Jackson glanced over at him. "You can always write about it. Make a good story for that paper of yours."

They brought their mounts to a stop in front of Philomena's hut. She must have been waiting for them, because she stepped outside with a solemn look on her face. "I knew this day would come," she said.

"It always does," Jackson told her as he swung down from the saddle. Everett looked the other way as Jackson went to Philomena. Even a reporter could be discreet every now and then.

When Jackson let go of her, she reached into the pocket of her skirt and brought out something small that she pressed into Jackson's hand. "Take it with you," she said, "so that El Señor Dios will smile upon you."

He opened his hand and looked at the crudely shaped Madonna and Child she had given him. "Part of your grandfather's treasure," he said.

"He would want you to have it."

"Even with this, I'm not sure El Señor Dios will ever smile on me. My name *is* Hell, you know."

"We cannot help our names," Philomena said, "only what we are."

Smiling, Jackson bent his head to hers again.

A few minutes later, the two men headed west, leaving Death Head Crossing behind them. Everett squirmed in the saddle, trying to find some way to ease his muscles, but Jackson rode easily, from time to time lifting a hand to touch the pocket where he carried a bit of treasure with him.

ABOUT THE AUTHOR

Spur Award nominee **James Reasoner** is one of the most prolific and in-demand Western writers working today, with more than 200 books to his credit, both under his own name and as L. J. Washburn. He was a contributor to Bantam's *New York Times* bestselling *Wagons West* series. Some of his other titles include *The Wilderness Road, Wind River, Under Outlaw Flags, Dark Trail,* and *Medicine Creek.* He lives in Azle, Texas, outside of Fort Worth, on a real working ranch.

The employees of Thorndike Press hope you have enjoyed this Large Print book. All our Thorndike and Wheeler Large Print titles are designed for easy reading, and all our books are made to last. Other Thorndike Press Large Print books are available at your library, through selected bookstores, or directly from us.

For information about titles, please call:
(800) 223-1244

or visit our Web site at:
http://gale.cengage.com/thorndike

To share your comments, please write:
Publisher
Thorndike Press
295 Kennedy Memorial Drive
Waterville, ME 04901